"Sprinkled with real recipes and hints of magic realism throughout, this tale of homecoming makes for a light bite to satiate yourself with."

—*Vogue* (HK)

"Lim serves up love, loss, heritage, and hints of the supernatural on a silver platter in this magical and mouthwatering debut. . . . This eminently filmable tale of finding one's own path while honoring one's history is delicious and spellbinding."

—*Publishers Weekly* (starred review)

"Vivid and lyrical with a touch of magic. *Natalie Tan's Book of Luck & Fortune* explores culture, community, and the complex love between mothers and daughters, leaving your heart full . . . and your belly hungry. I absolutely loved it."

—Helen Hoang, author of *The Kiss Quotient*

"*Natalie Tan's Book of Luck & Fortune* is for every reader who likes a side of magic with their foodie fiction. You'll want to move into the Chinatown neighborhood for the mouthwatering dumplings and the charming, eclectic neighbors. Exquisitely written, [this book by] Roselle Lim sifts through the complicated relationships between mothers and daughters, the freedom in unraveling family secrets, and the power of resilience."

—Amy E. Reichert, author of *The Coincidence of Coconut Cake* and *The Optimist's Guide to Letting Go*

"Roselle Lim serves up a feast for the senses and the heart with this magical tale of love, loss, and redemption in San Francisco's Chinatown. Filled with luscious, mouthwatering recipes, *Natalie Tan's Book of Luck & Fortune* explores the hidden ties of family, mental illness, and desires lost and found, through the delectably transformative power of food. I had to stop myself from running out to buy juicy roast pork, plump crispy dumplings, and sweet pea sprouts!"

—Yangsze Choo, *New York Times* bestselling author of *The Ghost Bride* and *The Night Tiger*

"*Natalie Tan's Book of Luck & Fortune* is a magical feast for the mind, the heart, and the senses. With mouthwatering prose, crystallized characters, and a healthy dash of magic, Lim has created the perfect recipe for a truly delicious page-turner. I devoured this book. Sign me up for seconds!"

—Samantha Vérant, author of *How to Make a French Family*

"What a treat! Reminiscent of Joanne Harris's bestselling novel *Chocolat*, *Natalie Tan's Book of Luck & Fortune* is heaped with heart and topped with the sweetest sprinkle of magic, creating a literary and culinary feast. Infused with ancient traditions and tantalizing recipes, [this book by] Roselle Lim cooks up a mouthwatering tale that's sure to delight!"

—Lori Nelson Spielman, *New York Times* bestselling author of *The Life List*

"Loss, homecoming, romance, recipes, and magic mingle in this debut novel. . . . The book is distinguished by the love Lim shows the neighborhood, the characters, and the food." —*Kirkus Reviews*

"For those beachgoers who love the magic of summertime and new beginnings, there is a book coming out soon that is simply meant for you—Roselle Lim's *Natalie Tan's Book of Luck & Fortune*."

—Elite Daily

"Summer beckons a reading list that is as light, fun, and feel-good as the season itself. Roselle Lim's *Natalie Tan's Book of Luck & Fortune* definitely fits that need. . . . Lim's magical storytelling, excellent cast of supporting characters, and mouthwatering recipes make this book a must for your summer reading list."

—*BookPage*

"A smashing debut that will leave readers hungry for more."

—Fresh Fiction

"When you read this book, you can feel the love of culture and food within its pages. More importantly, you can see how entangled food, culture, and family can become. It's a book about how food can bring people together, but also drive them apart. Filled with lush, lyrical writing, *Natalie Tan's Book of Luck & Fortune* is the kind of book that'll fill you with warmth, and make you extremely hungry."

—Book Riot

TITLES BY ROSELLE LIM

Natalie Tan's Book of Luck & Fortune
Vanessa Yu's Magical Paris Tea Shop

Vanessa Yu's Magical Paris Tea Shop

Roselle Lim

BERKLEY
New York

BERKLEY
An imprint of Penguin Random House LLC
penguinrandomhouse.com

Library of Congress Cataloging-in-Publication Data

Names: Lim, Roselle, author.
Title: Vanessa Yu's magical Paris tea shop / Roselle Lim.
Description: First Edition. | New York: Berkley, 2020.
Identifiers: LCCN 2019059053 (print) | LCCN 2019059054 (ebook) |
ISBN 9781984803276 (trade paperback) | ISBN 9781984803283 (ebook)
Classification: LCC PR9199.4.L5545 V36 2020 (print) |
LCC PR9199.4.L5545 (ebook) | DDC 813/.6—dc23
LC record available at https://lccn.loc.gov/2019059053
LC ebook record available at https://lccn.loc.gov/2019059054

First Edition: August 2020

Printed in the United States of America
1 3 5 7 9 10 8 6 4 2

Cover art and design by Vikki Chu
Book design by Laura K. Corless

To Robert, *mon cœur et ma vie*,
and to the beautiful city of Paris

One

I predicted the future on my third birthday. My aunts had been drinking their tea, and Ma had left her cup on the small table beside the sofa. As any curious child would, I imitated the habits of the older women: my two small hands cradled the ceramic of the handleless cup, fingertips not quite encompassing its circumference. I took a sip. As I gazed at the tea leaves floating at the bottom, my vision blurred and my mouth filled with the bitter taste of chewing on a grapefruit rind.

"The Hofstras are moving. Jeff doesn't love Rachel anymore."

I fell to the floor in tears, feeling the force of a sadness I could not comprehend. My aunts rushed over to me as Ma held me in her arms. There were whispers in Mandarin and Hokkien, but I heard only the name of my aunt—Evelyn—repeated.

Any possibility of a life of my choosing was extinguished like the candles on my birthday cake.

Every prediction had a taste. The family's new business venture was savory: a bite of roasted pork belly. A family squabble was bitterness: the dregs of a stale, cold cup of tea. A joyous fortune like Auntie Ning's pregnancy and baby girl was sweet: the sticky center of deep-fried sesame balls.

My last happy prediction was four months ago, for my cousin Cynthia's nuptials, which now brought my aunt, uncle, and me to Williams Sonoma to browse through her wedding registry. Three weeks ago, I bought an abstract, mixed-media painting for my cousin at one of my favorite galleries. We had decided it would be perfect in her dining room above the low, minimalistic, bleached birch buffet table she loved. Today, I was tagging along to help my aunt and uncle with their purchases.

Walls of pristine metal cookware gleamed alongside shiny new appliances aligned on golden wooden shelving. None were of any interest to me. I only stepped into this store to buy gifts for others. My preferred merchants peddled paintings, not pots and pans.

Auntie Faye tapped my arm. "I don't understand why she needs so much cookware. The girl doesn't cook."

"Maybe it's aspirational," I suggested. "I mean, you can't fault her for wanting to learn eventually."

Cynthia and I were both inept in the kitchen; we overcompensated with a library of takeout menus to the best restaurants: digital copies for convenience, paper preserved as trophies.

Although I had predicted this wedding, and I loved my cousin, I felt uneasy. With Cynthia married, I would become the oldest unwed cousin. Being single meant the focus of the attention was on you at every gathering and function. There was nowhere to hide from the probing questions. My cousin Chester described it as "being naked and vulnerable, and none of your relatives will give you a fig leaf." The joke was tailored to my tastes, and I appreciated it.

Uncle Michael examined a set of pastel Le Creuset ramekins. They shifted in their box with a slight ceramic clink as he lifted them to eye level. "I think these are mostly for Edwin. He can bake a decent Sacher torte. Cynthia invited me over last week to show off her soon-to-be husband's skills."

In his midfifties, dashing, and sharp, Uncle Michael was always my favorite. Like all my aunts and uncles, he appeared at least a decade younger. I always likened him to a Chinese Gregory Peck circa *Roman Holiday*. A lead user experience designer at a large financial corporation in Fresno, he lived three hours away and I never got to see him enough.

"Vanessa," my aunt began, "now that Cynthia is getting married, you should think about—"

My uncle jabbed my aunt in the ribs.

"Michael!" Auntie Faye held her stomach, feigning injury.

"This is about Cynthia, not about Vanessa."

A diminutive woman with dark hair swept into an elegant updo, my auntie Fay embodied the ideal salon owner: flawless skin, perfect hair, stylish wardrobe, and the subtle scent of Chanel No. 5. She knew she looked good, and wasn't the type to hide her assets behind false modesty. I adored her for it.

I moved away from the polite argument between my aunt and uncle.

A South Asian saleswoman in her midtwenties, close to my age, approached me with a smile. "If your parents can't decide on a registry item, we can definitely explore the gift card option instead."

I laughed.

The effortless rapport I had with my uncles and aunties often led strangers to misidentify them as my parents. We tended to play along instead of explaining the mistake.

"They'll work it out. I'll suggest the gift card idea, though, in case they don't." I thanked the salesperson and returned to my bickering "parents."

"Don't push Vanessa." Uncle Michael tucked the set of ramekins under his arm.

"Not pushing is why she's still single in the first place. Linda isn't aggressive enough in her setups."

Ma's machinations to get me married began the moment I was born, and I had rebelled against them ever since. Dad identified the strain of stubbornness as a classic Yu trait, and this failing of mine was excused, but only to a certain extent.

I cleared my throat.

Auntie Faye paused and smiled. "We're only trying to look out for your best interests."

"I know I am," Michael interjected, "but I'm not sure about Faye." He tipped his head toward the registers. "I'm buying these. You two should figure out where you want to go for lunch."

Auntie Faye grabbed my arm and steered me toward the fine china. Of all the goods in the store, these were the most appealing, with their beautiful patterns of florals mixed with modern designs and colors. A few months ago, I treated myself to a set of milk-white La Porcellana Bianca plates as an impulse purchase. The gorgeous hollowed spiral design had a sculptural quality I could not resist. My dad praised my adult decision and excellent taste while we ate take-out tandoori chicken.

Auntie Faye lowered her voice. "Any new predictions?"

In addition to mahjong, it was a Yu family pastime to hedge bets on my predictions. To them, I was their beloved fortune-teller. My gift was as accepted as the science of Chinese numerology or the zodiac charts my uncles consulted before making business decisions.

"No, Auntie. Thank goodness."

She frowned. "Maybe we can get one during lunch."

My aunt was the family's gossip queen. I often thought she chose a career as a beauty salon owner to facilitate her need to know everyone's business. If gossip were a commodity, she would control the market.

"Auntie, I am not a fortune vending machine."

"I just want to be here if anything comes up."

Uncle Michael, armed with a paper shopping bag, approached us. "Faye, why don't you go check out. I need to talk to Vanessa for a minute."

"Tell me if she says something." Auntie Faye waved and headed for the till. "I'll just buy a gift card and be done with it."

I let out a relaxed sigh. "Thank you for the save."

"You know her. She needs to be the first for any kind of news." He wrinkled his nose, jarring his glasses a little askew. "How are you holding up?"

"I feel the pressure. I already know Ma's planning something, but I don't know what. She is determined that I have a plus-one for the wedding. At least you're good in that department. How are things with Jack?"

"Good! I think I have prepared him for the family. He'll be ready for Cynthia's wedding."

Jack McCrae stepped into Uncle Michael's life six months ago after I invited Michael to Jack's photography exhibit and introduced them. Two months later, I had the formal pleasure of "meeting him" over hotpot. Jack was an energetic and passionate photographer. His photographs left me with an enigma. I wanted to know more about his subjects and the story behind them all. The portraits of my uncle were unabashed love letters: pictures that caught my uncle in his joyful moments. I didn't need to be present to know the photographer contributed to said happiness: I had witnessed it firsthand on numerous occasions.

This man loved Uncle Michael.

"Maybe you can bring a friend instead?" he asked. "That might placate your mother for now."

"I have no friends unless you count the cousins. And one of them betrayed me by getting married."

"The horde" comprised the twenty-seven fourth-generation cousins; not enough for a full football roster, but enough for two teams of softball in the summer. The sports activities were fun, but I preferred the wine and painting nights.

"If you and your aunt haven't decided where to eat, I know just the place." He offered his arm and escorted me to the exit, where Auntie Faye was waiting.

Uncle Michael chose a quiet Indian fusion restaurant ten minutes away, and while we browsed the menu, I ordered mango lassis for all three of us. My uncle and aunt were engrossed in a conversation about the lavish prizes and ongoing bets on who would win the aunties' upcoming annual mahjong tournament. The tension eased from my shoulders as I sipped the delicious drink in peace.

Without intention I spied a pattern in the golden droplets clinging to the glass. My stomach churned as the taste of buttermilk pancakes soaked in maple syrup flooded my mouth. A prophecy coalesced like hard, round candy until it pushed against my teeth and expanded.

"Johnny is planning to propose to Andria next Tuesday and she will accept, but only if the proposal involves an inherited diamond citrine ring."

Auntie Faye leaped from her chair, kissed me on the cheek, and excused herself as she pulled out her phone while heading outside for some privacy—ironic considering she was about to broadcast gossip.

Uncle Michael leaned in and whispered, "Every time that happens, I wonder if it's painful."

"It's uncomfortable. That's about it," I replied. A string of happiness danced within me before vanishing like the notes from a plucked harp. They were replaced by a throbbing in my right temple. I hadn't had a headache in a while. I dismissed it as a sign I was either tired or hungry.

"There's no guarantee when it'll happen," I continued. "Ma and the aunties have tried more than enough times to compel it out of me. Of course, they failed. I'm just happy it's not something horrible this time."

"Have you talked to Evelyn?"

Aunt Evelyn was a member of the San Francisco Yus: the more prosperous branch with the tea import-export empire. My limb of the family tree, the Palo Alto Yus, operated the accounting firm that supported the tea business. A respected clairvoyant, she and I disagreed regarding our "gift." We last spoke after I had invited her to the Andy Warhol exhibit at the San Francisco Museum of Modern Art. We hadn't left the lobby before quarreling. She went home. I walked through the museum alone.

"I don't think she's happy with me. I spent my whole life avoiding her attempts to educate me. Every time I try to talk to her about it, we argue. You'd think, of all the people in the world, we'd be on the same page." I sighed, and traced the rim of the empty glass. "All she cares about is the rules and how we need to follow them."

"I think you two have more in common than you realize. As for this prophecy, it's going to be complicated. If the ring is what I think it is, Johnny will need to grovel."

I stifled a giggle.

Auntie Faye returned and sucked in her lips. "*Aiyah*, this is not going to be easy. What kind of ring again?"

I repeated the description.

She tapped her temple. "We have to find this ring. We know Johnny can't do better. The girl is a catch, and we can't let her get away from the family."

I glanced over to see my favorite uncle attempting to hide his amusement.

"Auntie Faye, maybe you should ask Uncle Michael?"

"Michael, who owns the ring?" she demanded.

"Ning. It was bequeathed to her by Great-Auntie Nancy three years ago."

Auntie Faye's indignation peppered the air along with a litany of Hokkien and Mandarin curses. My fluency with the dialect was pidgin, limited to food and numbers. The previous generation's enrollment in Chinese school cemented their command of Mandarin, while their parents spoke Hokkien at home. The cousins and I were spared language education, but not music lessons. Uncle Michael once joked that if our generation wanted to form a symphony, we could.

"Ning can't stand him. She won't give him the ring," Auntie Faye hissed. "Remember the family picnic at Mitchell Park? She couldn't stop complaining about him, saying that he has more metal on his face than a Honda Civic."

Uncle Michael smiled. "The solution is easy. Have him take her out to dinner. Upscale and French. He needs to shave first and borrow something fashionable from Chester's closet. Also, buy a bottle of pinot grigio in the fifty-dollar range. Ning loves her wines. It'll help sweeten the pot."

"Ah, Michael, you're so smart. This is why I love you." Auntie Faye patted his cheek, then turned to me. The heat from her focused gaze caused a bead of sweat to trickle down my temple. "Now that Johnny is getting married . . ."

My time was running out.

Two

Yu formal family functions are a symphony of chaos, and weddings were no exception. Nuptials ranged from traditional to Western with a scandalous elopement or two. Every Yu injected a quirk of their own, and Cynthia was no different: she rescheduled the tea ceremony with the groom's family to after the ten-course reception dinner. Cynthia would have moved the entire wedding ceremony to the evening if her mother, Auntie Gloria, hadn't threatened to kill her youngest daughter. Only after Cynthia stated that she *would* be late to her own wedding did her mother agree to delay the tea ceremony. Cynthia did rack up the most tardies despite living ten minutes away from her high school.

I relaxed in the safety of the hotel's rooftop garden. The dinner reception in the grand ballroom wouldn't begin for another hour. Uncle Michael and Jack kept me company. Jack, introduced to the family earlier this morning, had been swarmed with affection. The escape twenty floors up was for our mutual benefit.

"Brace yourself," Uncle Michael warned, breaking the silence. "Your mother mentioned to me that she has a prospect in mind."

I winced. My fingers pinched a piece of the embroidered lavender skirt of my cocktail dress. Feeling the fine needlework's bumps and ridges soothed my elevated nerves. "He's probably already here. Ma always comes prepared."

Jack added, "Weddings are always the breeding ground for setups."

"Cynthia betrayed me. She told me she was going to be the lone old maid to take the pressure off the rest of us. Then she met Edwin. Now Johnny . . . Everyone agreed he would never get married."

The cousins and I had formed a union where we used our collective bargaining power to negotiate with our parents. Traditions, and which to follow, became the common talking points, while the most intense debates revolved around marriage. As heated as these discussions became, I was grateful that our parents were more reasonable than my grandparents had been with them. Later generations benefited from the earlier generations in America who fomented the seed of rebellion and the integration of Western values.

"Johnny's prophecy should have stayed hidden," I groused.

Uncle Michael raised a brow. "Really?"

"No," I admitted. "I've never seen Johnny this happy and I can't help but share in his joy. I just wish it didn't involve unpleasant consequences on my end. It's stirring up the aunties into a froth. My mother doesn't need more ammunition. I want to date, but I don't want it to be the precursor to an arranged marriage."

"I thought you're fourth-generation Chinese," Jack said.

"I am, but the whole tiger parenting instinct is hard coded in their genes." I rubbed my temples. "I know they mean well. A relationship is just not possible until I get this prediction thing under control."

"I have to admit, it's an interesting ability, or burden in your case," Jack said.

"It's got its downsides."

He stood beside my uncle in a complementary navy suit. Jack reminded me of a rugged Pierce Brosnan. Uncle Michael wore charcoal gray with a gold tie. They could be on the cover of any men's fashion magazine. Jack brought his camera equipment and worked the wedding, his gift to the couple. This was his rare break, and I suffered a twinge of guilt for having complained so much.

Before I could apologize, Jack glanced over his shoulder to see the elevators opening. "The women are coming."

He and Uncle Michael moved in unison to head off the pack of aunties, herding them back into the elevator and disappearing behind closing doors. It was a reenactment worthy of the battle of Thermopylae. I was touched by their sacrifice.

Closing my eyes, I took a deep breath and attempted to let the tension roll off my shoulders. Prophecies accompanied an assortment of drinks I imbibed or that I saw in the cups of others. I avoided tea because it was the most powerful stimulant. Drinking it resulted in vivid visions that even the aunties cautioned against.

I glanced down at my watch. Ten more minutes until I had to make my appearance downstairs. The sky above was a riotous blaze of pinks, purples, blues, and oranges with nary a cloud to mar it. It was worthy of Monet's *Parliament at Sunset*. The cool breeze teased the tips of my wavy, dark hair. It was such a beautiful evening to waste on worries I had no control over.

The elevator bell dinged.

I turned around, hoping to see the return of my favorite uncle and his boyfriend.

Aunt Evelyn stepped out from the silver doors, and her dark eyes focused on me. Dressed in a long pastel blue sheath dress and beaded jacket, her long hair swept up to showcase a pair of diamond pendant earrings, she approached me with her high heels clicking against the marble floor.

"Hello, Vanessa." Aunt Evelyn greeted me with a genuine smile.

Uncle Michael must have sent her to see me. "Hi," I said. "How have you been?"

We both leaned in for a quick embrace and kiss on the cheek. She smelled of freshly cut peonies and vanilla. In her early fifties, she was still one of the most beautiful women I'd ever seen. She epitomized elegance and class and never allowed her abilities to see the future to hinder her successes or her life. I envied her.

"Busy. We're opening a new tea shop in Paris soon," she replied. "Well done in predicting Johnny's engagement."

I swallowed what I wanted to say: that I had no control over any of it and giving me credit was akin to thanking an automatic door for opening and closing. "He's happy, and Andria is as well. I'm glad it wasn't someone dying or getting into an accident."

Aunt Evelyn's brow furrowed. "You shouldn't always jump to the worst conclusions. Only thinking of the negative causes more of it to happen."

"Just wishing for good predictions hasn't worked." The effort in maintaining the smile I'd plastered on my lips increased.

"You can't talk about something you know nothing about, Vanessa. You haven't bothered to listen to anything I've tried to teach you over all these years. The art of prophecy has specific rules."

"The only rule I'm interested in is one that rids it from my life."

She looked at me with kindness. She always did.

Once my gift manifested, I was Aunt Evelyn's project. I spent weekends at her Victorian in San Francisco. We had the loveliest of afternoon teas in her sunroom, nibbling on matcha mochi, colorful macarons, and egg tarts from a Portuguese bakery nearby. We drank glasses of iced lavender tea lemonade and talked about family history. The idyllic joy vanished when she told me I couldn't avoid this power. The arguments started and never abated, an ouroboros of persistent tension.

"I wish you were more receptive. These rules are meant to be followed, and you might be more adept at handling your gift had you taken my advice. If anything, you're more closed-minded now than when you were younger."

"Aunt Evelyn, please don't start."

She took a deep breath and offered her hand. "Let's go downstairs. I hear Edwin's parents flew the chef and his crew in from Kowloon. His restaurant is famous and was featured in a foodie documentary. The dinner should be spectacular."

I accepted her olive branch and we headed to the elevator, hand in hand.

The wedding banquet was traditionally Chinese with ten courses of the finest ingredients served alongside gossip and business proposals. After all, this was foremost a merging of the Yus and Ngos.

Aunt Evelyn and I walked into a sea of circular tables. Overhead, crystal chandeliers sparkled against the painted sky ceiling while cream-colored drapery flanked the French doors leading out into the gardens. Bouquets of powder-blue hydrangeas, white roses, and blush-pink peonies adorned every table alongside ornate gold lantern centerpieces. The couple's love of yachts and cruises inspired the garlands of miniature international maritime signal flags. The place settings and name cards continued the nautical theme with a ship and anchor design.

Before I could leave Aunt Evelyn's side, my mother stopped in front of me. I recognized her companion: tall, Chinese, short hair, with a propensity to please. The scent of instant coffee and minty mouthwash clung to his suit. He worked at the family's firm. William Chang. She planned on setting me up with the new hire in the tax department. I had administered his job interview. Ma's arrangements had never worked out, but it didn't stop her from trying.

Aunt Evelyn squeezed my hand. "Ah, Linda! I hope you don't mind, but I've asked Vanessa to sit with me. It's been a long time since I last saw her."

"Evelyn, I had plans to . . . ," Ma stuttered. "William here is . . ."

My aunt met my eyes. "Right, Vanessa?"

"Yes, Ma. She has questions about how international tax laws will impact the European expansion," I replied.

"But, but . . ."

"I'm sure there will be plenty of time later," Aunt Evelyn said as she patted my mother's arm, guiding me away.

After we were out of earshot, she leaned close. "You can leave anytime. I don't want you to sit with me unless it's your choice. My intention was only to steer you away from your mother's ambush."

We might have our differences, but I couldn't deny my aunt's good heart. She could have left me standing there in Ma's dating trap and a long evening of awkwardness with William.

"Thank you," I said, grinning.

"No more talk about that thing we disagree on," she said. "And you'll be happy to know that Michael and Jack are sitting with us."

We arrived at our seats close to the head table. These were better than my original assignment a few rows back. Cynthia had mentioned to me that devising the seating plan was an exercise combining diplomacy and puzzle strategy. Her addiction to candy-themed match-three games made her adept at moving pieces to where they needed to go.

"Jack's busy setting up the portrait location in the tearoom," Michael informed us. "I'm afraid he'll be there most of the night. I'm going to help him round everyone up after the tea ceremony by asking some of your cousins to form a human chain around the bar." He reached for the open bottle of Shiraz and poured some into my aunt's empty wineglass. "Your mother is seething in our direction."

"Please pour the wine," I replied, offering him my glass.

Aunt Evelyn kept a serene expression, as if listening to a distant sound. She was focused on Edwin's parents: Ken and Jillian Ngo seated to the left of their son. Nearby, a server wrestled with a wine bottle.

"The glass will break and wine will be spilled, but no one will be injured. The father of the groom will emerge the valiant hero of the night," she declared.

As soon as the words escaped her lips, the server lost his battle with the bottle. As the magnum slipped from his hands, it landed neck first onto the hard marble floor. The glass shattered, sending red wine and tiny shards toward the Ngos. Ken positioned himself to protect his wife. Wine droplets stained his white dress shirt. A collective gasp reverberated throughout the ballroom.

"My valiant hero!" the mother of the groom exclaimed before she jumped up and kissed him on the cheek.

A roaring applause followed the impromptu dinner show.

Uncle Michael grinned. "Evelyn, you really are a treasure."

"Thank you," she laughed. "The real treasure is the coming meal."

The parade of servers ladened with silver tureens of bird's nest soup appeared. My aunt and I may have shared the same gift, but her command of it left me with a mixture of awe and intimidation.

Three

The ten courses of a traditional Chinese wedding banquet tantalized the senses and glorified gluttony. Its true purpose wasn't quantity, but quality, to showcase a variety of ingredients that would satisfy even the pickiest eater. At best, the meal achieved culinary nirvana, and at worst, the quantity of food available guaranteed a full belly. The menu was tailored to the bride and groom's tastes. The guests were treated to a harmonious marriage in edible form.

"The bird's nest soup was divine." I wiped the corners of my mouth with a cloth napkin. "I wonder what the second course is."

"I'm guessing it's the requisite barbecued appetizer platter." Uncle Michael craned his neck toward the kitchen entrance where a stream of servers brought out the next course. The parade of white uniforms stepped in unison and delivered their trays to tables of eager diners. "If the soup is any indication, the rest of the meal should be quite a coup."

I took a sip of the excellent wine. "Cynthia is one of the biggest foodies I know. She once went out with this horrible guy so she could score early reservations at a new Korean noodle restaurant in LA. The sublime guksu jangguk more than made up for the awful date."

"The groom is also a foodie. They kept running into each other at the same places. It's a great match," Aunt Evelyn added.

I smiled to hide the twinge of wistfulness I had growing inside. Every wedding I attended brought with it the weight of longing, seeing all those around me finding and celebrating a union I could never have. It was heartbreaking torture to express such joy for those I loved, knowing all of the wishes I said were those I wanted myself.

The second course arrived in time to save me from any further discussions regarding my preferred partner. The appetizer platter mixed cold and hot items: marinated spicy jellyfish, sliced drunken chicken, roasted pork belly, pickled bamboo shoots, and radishes. The surprise came in bamboo steamers holding plump char siu buns, one of the Kowloon chef's treasured specialties.

The white bun with the dimpled top was warm in my hands as I peeled off the paper adhering to the bottom. The tender bread yielded to the sharpness of my teeth. The aroma escaped, a mouthwatering combination of seasoned pork cooked in its juices. The filling combined sweet with a hint of salt. The shredded barbecued pork swam in thick, reddish-brown sauce, but it was the unanticipated bite of the chilies that delighted me. It sent a tingling buzz on my tongue.

"That spicy kick is wonderful, isn't it?" Uncle Michael remarked, sipping his Shiraz.

Aunt Evelyn wiped her fingertips. "Quite, and so unexpected."

"I'm shocked you didn't see it coming, Auntie," I joked.

As soon as the barb escaped, I wished to cram it back into my mouth like one of my tragic predictions. My aunt's eyes narrowed, and her elegant brows arched ever so slightly. Had I broken the cease-fire and stirred a wasp's nest?

"Vanessa, if you wish to discuss our gifts further, I'd be happy to restart lessons at your earliest convenience."

Uncle Michael flashed me a warning look with his eyes. He turned to his cousin. "Evelyn, I'll be in Munich for a few months in the spring, maybe I can visit you in Paris?"

"That would be lovely. I'll send you the address of the shop later." My aunt returned her attention to me. "Do you have any predictions to make, dear niece?"

"Nothing at the moment," I said into my wine.

The rest of the exquisite courses came out in a blur: spicy giant prawns, abalone, conch and sea cucumber with pea greens, Peking duck, Wagyu beef, Hong Kong–style fried Dungeness crabs, steamed whole sea bass, yin-yang fried rice, and double-layer milk custard for dessert. The endless parade of food acted as a buffer to the growing tension between Aunt Evelyn and me.

I managed to get into a high-stakes game of prophecy poker. She had been calling my bluff since the second course. Uncle Michael tried to be the peacemaker by steering the conversation back to the exquisite food, but after each course the contest resumed. We must have resembled the men in Francisco de Goya's painting *Fight with Cudgels*, trapped in a quagmire of mud, brawling with dull weapons as the world faded away.

"I'd better see how Jack is faring." He stood up and escaped the table.

"The tea ceremony is scheduled next, maybe you'll get a vision then." Aunt Evelyn waved to Cynthia, who was making her rounds to each table.

The bride had performed her second wardrobe change. Out of her Vera Wang wedding gown, she now wore a bright poppy-red qipao with gold embroidery. Cynthia was radiant. She was at a place in her life where I knew I couldn't go. I pushed my personal sadness aside to revel in her joy.

"You two have to come with me," she declared as she offered her hands to Aunt Evelyn and me.

We accompanied her to the salon adjoining the ballroom. Sheer white organza was draped over the tall walls of the long chamber. Tiny twinkling LED lights glowed underneath, giving the illusion of captured fireflies. A large vase of white roses and phalaenopsis filled each corner. Forty-two ivory Queen Anne chairs formed a perimeter reserved for the eldest Yu and Ngo relatives. Cynthia and her husband Edwin served tea in red gilded cups from a batch of high-grade pu'erh they brewed themselves. The order of service was dictated by seniority. The ceremony was a joining of relatives and a symbol of appreciation from the happy couple.

As the youngest in the room, I waited where Jack stood beside his portrait studio setup. Uncle Michael and Aunt Evelyn took their assigned seats.

Jack leaned in and asked in a low whisper, "So this is basically another gift-giving event?"

"Yes, the bride and groom will receive a hongbao—the red envelope—from each of the relatives after serving them tea. In our culture, it's common to dole out cash," I explained. "This is one of the older traditions we've retained. Each generation keeps a set of customs and throws out those they didn't like."

"So that's what Michael was busy with this morning, stuffing an envelope full of hundred-dollar bills." Jack smiled. "It's beautiful. I should be taking some shots."

He fetched his camera and got to work, getting closer to document the ritual. As I watched the ceremony unfold, I felt a pang of envy. I didn't see this in my future despite what the aunties intended for me.

After the ceremony, Cynthia made her way to me. She glanced over her shoulder at the gaggle of aunties congregating in the far corner. "They're so ready to pounce on you. They told me that they tried to track you down earlier, but you gave them the slip."

"I hid. I can't outrun them. At least three of them run marathons," I said before pointing a finger at her. "You were supposed to stay single. We had a deal."

Cynthia laughed. "I fell in love. All bets are off then."

"All kidding aside, I'm genuinely happy for you and Edwin."

"We're going on a foodie eating tour of Asia for our honeymoon. I can't wait to eat everything from Japan to Singapore. I have to show you all the chefs' tables we're planning. There were a few I didn't think I could get into, but Edwin's cousin pulled some strings. You know you married into the right family when that happens." She sipped the last of the tea she was cradling in her left hand.

I caught a glimpse of the bottom of her cup. My stomach churned. I stepped back, reaching for the wall for support.

The prophecy solidified in my mouth, bringing with it the bitterness of raw cacao without the added touch of sugar. I didn't want to open my mouth. I already knew what I was going to say.

In the past, I had tried to swallow prophecies, but the force of the prediction only moved forward, toward its escape through my lips. My jaw ached and my teeth rattled, but I couldn't stop it.

I never could.

"You will be divorced next September. He will break his marriage vows with infidelity. The frequent visits to his favorite sushi restaurant is motivated by more than the hamachi nigiri."

Cynthia dropped her teacup. The sharp shattering sound echoed in the room as it fractured against the floor. She covered her mouth with her hands to muffle her sobs.

"Cynthia, I'm sorry," I whispered as I embraced her. "I'm so sorry."

She pulled away from me.

The aunties crossed the room and descended upon the weeping bride in a protective formation. Aunt Evelyn and Uncle Michael rushed to my side, ushering me into the makeshift portrait studio, where Jack was waiting.

Tears streamed down my cheeks. I dashed them away with the backs of my hands, but they kept coming. I drowned in a tsunami of remorse for having ruined my cousin's wedding and her life.

My right eye pulsed as a sharp pain in my temple intensified. A churning nausea rocked my stomach. I leaned into Uncle Michael and closed my eyes. He held me in his arms and allowed me to soak his beautiful charcoal suit jacket. When sorrow ran its course, I was left hiccupping, drinking in the scent of clean linen, bayberry, and my uncle's aftershave.

He met my gaze and asked, "Are you all right?"

"No." The instant answer unleashed all the resentment I thought I'd locked away. "It's a curse despite what everyone says. Look at what I did to Cynthia."

To supplement my argument, I rattled off a list of incidents. "Remember Mrs. Ferguson, my kindergarten teacher? During my parent-teacher conference, I saw the bottom of her coffee mug and

I told everyone about her affair. And what about my prediction of Logan's ruptured spleen during his championship rugby game? His parents were devastated."

The extended Yu family had grown inured to my unusual talent because of exposure. Outsiders never understood.

My head felt like it was being squeezed in a vise. With each breath the screw tightened.

It hurt. I hurt.

"I don't want this," I whispered. "I never wanted it."

He kissed the top of my head. "I know."

"I can't even imagine what Cynthia is going through right now."

"I'll talk to her," Aunt Evelyn said. "I'll help her assess her options, and she'll need to talk to her husband. None of this was your fault, Vanessa."

"Isn't it?" I said, rubbing my temple. "Aren't we responsible for our predictions?"

"We are the messengers. We're not responsible for the content of our prophecies," Aunt Evelyn explained. "Look around you. No one is blaming you for speaking the truth."

Uncle Michael added, "Cynthia won't hold you accountable for what Edwin might do."

I wrapped my arms around myself. My manicured fingernails dug into my skin hard enough to leave deep, crescent-shaped marks. Despite my family's platitudes, the weight of my guilt crippled me. In the aftermath of the prediction, only the thread of bitterness and a piercing headache remained, which I clung to like a lifeline. I drifted, lost at sea, not knowing when—or if—I'd be rescued.

Four

When Ma arranged for a mani-pedi at Auntie Faye's salon a week later, I couldn't have been more suspicious. Tax season was underway at the firm and I had been too exhausted to decline. She recognized my weak, vulnerable state. I always wondered if Ma's previous incarnation was the editor hovering over Sun Tzu's shoulder as he wrote *The Art of War*.

Ma pulled the salon door open. "This is good for you. I know how stressed you are. Faye suggested it and squeezed us in. She says a good foot massage will take the tension away."

Great. The two women were conspiring.

Auntie Faye had opened her salon and spa in a renovated Victorian thirty years ago. The interior decor adhered to three colors: eggshell white, sky blue, and buttercream yellow. With Lampe Bergers installed in every room, the usual strong odors from the dyes and nail polish were minimized. The majority of the clientele were loyal Asian customers, and on this Saturday morning, it was bustling.

"Ah, Linda, Vanessa!" Auntie Faye made her way from behind the rounded pink marble counter to greet us. She kissed Ma's cheek and then mine. "You made it. So happy to see you."

I smiled. "Hello, Auntie Faye."

"Since you two are VIPs, I'll take you to the special room. Follow me." Auntie Faye's obvious wink to my mother only confirmed my suspicions. I didn't know what the two had planned.

Ma had married into the Yu family, but you wouldn't know it by how easily she blended in. She embraced the aunties with open arms and they, in turn, welcomed her into their exclusive club. Growing up with two brothers, Ma had confided that these women were the sisters she had always wanted.

We followed Auntie Faye upstairs to the third floor. While the second floor was dedicated to private treatment rooms, the entire third functioned as a venue for bridal parties. I'd been here once, for Percy's wedding, as a bridesmaid. Ma and I were supposed to be the only ones booked for a treatment. I sensed an auntie ambush.

Auntie Faye and Ma's conversation in rapid Hokkien kept me in the dark. Cantonese possessed a singsong quality, Mandarin was harsher with crisp *R* sounds, but Hokkien was in between: more concise than Cantonese, but softer in sound than Mandarin. This was one of the few times I regretted not attending Chinese school.

Since I couldn't understand what they were saying, I measured the conversation by inflection and tone. The nervous excitement between them was blatant. "Ma, what are you saying to Auntie Faye?" I asked.

"You'll see." My mother patted my cheek.

My aunt giggled and led us to the twin doors of the suite. With a flourish, she opened the wrought-iron-embellished, frosted double glass doors. "Surprise!"

The immaculate ivory chamber had reupholstered antique chairs painted in white, and a plush velvet lavender chaise longue. A serene floral watercolor-print wallpaper graced the walls framed by Victorian reproduction wainscoting. Intricate copper tiles covered the ceiling, gleaming from the stray sunlight passing through the large bay window.

Every single Palo Alto auntie was in attendance: Faye, Gloria and her rival Ning, Madeline, Suzanne, Annette, the twins Bea and Belle, Rose, Lulu, Jenny, Tina, and the youngest, Holly.

All thirteen of them, excluding my mother.

"It's not my birthday," I said with a forced smile.

Auntie Faye laughed as she took my arm and led me to the high-backed chair in the center of the room. "Sit."

I obeyed with narrowed eyes.

Auntie Gloria picked up on my mood. "Don't worry. No naked man will enter the room and dance for you."

I covered my blushing face as the rest of the aunties burst into laughter.

"We are here to help you, dear niece," Auntie Faye continued. "Your mother and I were talking about how you are the next one to be married. Linda hasn't been very successful when picking from the small pool at the firm. Those accounting men are probably not your type, am I right?"

I couldn't answer. My dear aunt wasn't done with her soliloquy, or sales pitch.

"We decided to help you. We asked around and got in touch with a matchmaker in New York. She has a very high success rate, but her sister in Shanghai is much better. We want the best for you so we got you an appointment with her. Madam Fong is flying in from China in a week to meet with you."

I tried to keep my tone even, but the last word ended in a high pitch. "I can't have a long-term relationship. You all know this, yet you all thought this was a good idea?"

Ma moved to my side and patted my hand. "Her references are beyond reproach. Besides, we never consulted an expert before. She's renowned in China. If anyone can help, it's her."

"Don't you think we should be helping Cynthia first before you start marrying me off?" I protested.

"We are taking care of her. Evelyn is counseling her, dear. This doesn't mean that we can't help you as well," Auntie Faye explained. "Besides, the down payment is nonrefundable."

I covered my eyes with my hands. "I can't believe you all did this. I know I have problems with dating, but this is overkill. You didn't have to hire a specialist. Most of you are accountants or are married to one. You're supposed to be good with money!"

"*Aiyah*, she isn't happy," Auntie Gloria wailed.

Ma blushed. She was a senior auditor at the firm. "This is a smart investment, Vanessa. Good matchmaking is a science. Madam Fong's success rate and statistics check out."

"Did she have a guarantee clause?" I asked.

"Oh, you can't ask for that. This is a very complicated process," Auntie Faye said. She handed her tablet to me. "See. That is her website."

I frowned. The site appeared professional and the picture of Madam Fong seemed real enough, but the website was in simplified Chinese. "You're cheating. You know I can't read this."

"You trust us." Auntie Gloria pressed her hand against her chest. "Would your aunties lie to you?"

The room erupted in outraged Hokkien directed toward my

mother. The absurdity of this situation would have made me laugh if I weren't the crux of the joke. I didn't fault their good intentions: these women would walk through fire for me. Auntie Gloria defended me from a bully at the park when I was in first grade, and encouraged Ma to enroll me in tae kwon do lessons. Auntie Faye snuck me romance novels when Ma banned them from the house.

"You know I love you all," I declared over the din. "I mean, this is sweet in a weird kind of way."

"Why weird?" Auntie Gloria asked. "We want you to be happy. We're only thinking about you."

I sighed. "I know."

"Remember, no refund. If it doesn't work out, then we only paid for the round-trip plane ticket and down payment." Ma squeezed my hand.

The earnestness in their faces made it much harder for me to disappoint them. I was receiving an expensive gift I neither wanted nor asked for. Had this been a sweater, the proper response would be to thank them, wear the hideous garment once in their presence, and then bury it in a closet, ready to be pulled out to refute any accusations it had been tossed or given away. Perhaps one meeting with the matchmaker could be enough to pacify the aunties.

I placed my other hand over my mother's. "Fine, fine. I'll give it a try."

The aunties broke out into triumphant smiles. Of course they'd be pleased: they got what they wanted.

"Does this mean I'm not getting a mani or pedi?" I asked.

"You said yes, so you will be getting one," Auntie Faye laughed. "I'll call the staff. Everyone gets treatments today."

* * *

On the morning before I met with the matchmaker, I researched everything I could find regarding the lore. It had a long history in China. Some consulted zodiac charts, some numerology, but the best matchmakers were guided by their intuition and memory. Reading about the subject reminded me of how much it resembled fortune-telling. People yearned for romance and love as much as they wanted guidance; that was why both professions hadn't died out. I was by no means qualified as a fortune-teller, nor had I any intention to be. The Yu family already had one true clairvoyant: Aunt Evelyn.

Ma provided me with the details for the meeting. She had also gone ahead and sent my picture and description to Madam Fong. This might be the only occasion I didn't mind her interference. Typing up my own bio, measurements, and whatever strange details the matchmaker needed would have been painful.

I spent part of my lunch break traveling from the firm's location near the airport to Linfield Oaks in Menlo Park. Surrounded by palm trees and beautiful gardens, the hotel's classic-style brick and shutters created an old Hollywood feel. The aunties had outdone themselves by hosting the matchmaker at a four-star establishment.

After parking my modest, cherry-red, five-year-old Toyota Corolla, I headed to the lobby in search of the lounge. I knew the layout. Every Yu was well acquainted with every hotel in the Bay Area from the countless family functions: weddings, retirements, anniversaries, and birthdays.

The recently renovated lounge had the aesthetic of *The Great Gatsby*: gold leaf, geometric art deco walls, painted wood ceiling tiles, and interlocking patterned floors. I found the matchmaker in a plush booth third from the back. Given the nature of our meeting, I was grateful for the privacy afforded by her choice.

Madam Fong was a stern-looking woman in her late sixties. Her ears, neck, and wrists dripped with gold and jade. She had the air of a judge of the Diyu with her sharp features and rigid posture. Her goal appeared to be intimidation: potential parents and candidates had no room to question her proposed matches.

She gestured for me to sit across from her. The bracelets at her wrist jingled from the abrupt movement. I took my seat and set my purse down beside me.

She began speaking in rapid Mandarin and stopped when she noticed my look of incomprehension. The matchmaker shook her head and clucked her tongue. Even though I wasn't fluent, I did recognize the one term of derision she slipped under her breath. Xiang jiao ren. Derogatory for those who looked Chinese, but acted American. I could have called the meeting off, but Madam Fong was only one of a long line of Chinese who had disrespected me for not being fluent, for not being Chinese enough.

The older woman frowned. "English it is then."

"Thank you."

"Your relatives enlisted my services to find you a match. Normally, I make matches between families of people I know in Shanghai. Your case is unusual." She narrowed her eyes. "You are a strange girl."

Again, this was a variation on something I'd heard from outsiders. I felt normal, but my peculiar talent for spitting out fortunes marked me as an other. I had spent my whole life wishing to be like everyone else—normal.

"I have consulted numerology, astrology, and zodiac charts, but have come up with nothing. You have no match." Her powdered brow furrowed. "Are you dead?"

Five

The matchmaker ordered a Macallan 25 on the rocks.

She cradled her drink with her left hand. The ice shifted against the clear glass with each breath. We sat in silence, the steady metronome from her drink marking time. After what felt like an eternity, she reached out and touched my hand. Her heavy rose-based perfume teased my nostrils as a dry laugh rattled off her chest. "Well, you're not a ghost. I've dealt with them before, you know. Are you familiar with the red thread of fate?"

I nodded. When I was a child, over bowls of salted duck egg congee on rainy Saturday mornings when my grandmother and I stayed inside instead of heading to the park, she told me stories like these, of how the gods place a thread connecting two people together as soul mates.

Madam Fong sipped her scotch. "As a matchmaker, I can see these threads, and you, Vanessa Yu, do not have one."

"Did my mother tell you that I can see the future?"

She leaned back. "No, she did not."

Ma gave this complete stranger my weight within two pounds, my blood type, my medical history, and probably my net worth, yet she hadn't disclosed my fatal flaw. Was hers a crime of omission? That leaving out what made me different would change my predicament?

Madam Fong's long, tapered fingers tapped the table in a cascading rhythm while she again studied my face. "Your mother sent me all the information I asked for, but conveniently left this out. It complicates matters. I've matched thousands of couples. Every time I get a challenging case, I meet it and that person is paired: the marriage lasts. But you have no thread."

There was a morbid sense of relief in having a matchmaker confirm what I already knew and had been told: I could predict the future, but I couldn't have a normal romantic relationship.

"How your gift factors into this, I don't know. I need to return to Shanghai and consult with my peers." Madam Fong frowned. "For now, I'm afraid you and I will have unfavorable news for your mother."

The aunties and Ma would be devastated. They had invested too much and had pinned their hopes on Madam Fong.

"I'd prefer you tell her that I'm unmatchable," I declared.

Madam Fong sipped her drink. "That isn't what I said."

"I don't understand. You mentioned I had no thread. Doesn't this mean I can't be matched?"

"Right now, you can't."

"You're insinuating this can change?"

She didn't answer. Her mouth formed a thin line while her dark eyes continued to study me. "Tell me about your gift."

"There really isn't much to say other than it's erratic, embarrassing, and if given a choice, I would want to get rid of it."

I no longer cared what the matchmaker or anyone else thought. As a child, I often nodded and agreed when family members patted my head and praised my predictions. Why should I receive accolades for something I couldn't control in the first place?

"Do you believe in fate, American girl?" Madam Fong asked.

Despite spilling others' fortunes, I refused to believe fate dictated my life. I believed in revolt, in breaking away from what was imposed upon me, and my fundamental rejection of my power proved that I rejected destiny too.

"No," I replied.

"I thought so. It's an American mindset, isn't it? The rebelliousness, the entitlement, the thinking you know everything." Anticipating my protest, she held up a finger. "It's not an insult, it's a fact. You are a Yu. You still have family in China. I can introduce you should you wish to visit. But I digress. Others in your family share this gift. Why haven't you sought them out?"

"You mean Aunt Evelyn?" I asked. "We talk."

"Not enough, from what I can see."

I exhaled before taking another swig of my club soda. The matchmaker had changed into a pontificating auntie, which I never asked for.

"Fortune-telling is a simpler art. With the right guidance and discipline it can lead to true clairvoyance. The masters command respect as they have dominion over their talents. Even in China, we know of Evelyn Yu. Why don't you want this for yourself?"

I straightened my back. "It has only ever ruined my life."

"And would you change your mind if I told you they were connected, your gift and your missing thread?"

"You said earlier you weren't sure if they were."

She opened her mouth, closed it, and then paused, appearing to contemplate her words with care. "I'll speak with your mother about the state of this match. I leave you with this last piece of advice: Be true to yourself and to who you are. That is the key to gaining control of your life. If you find your missing thread, you find yourself."

"Thank you, Madam Fong," I said before making a hasty exit.

I wasn't expected back at the office yet, so I invited Dad to my favorite boba tea shop. It's Always Tea Time was a modest corner store that offered an array of drinks and Taiwanese fare. The decor was dominated by wood and glass: stained barn boards covered the walls, and indoor ficus plants stood by the entrance and near the glass takeout counter. Low acrylic chairs, with fake wood grain, filled the remaining space.

My go-to snack here was a sweet custard brick toast. The thick, fluffy bread was slathered in custard and then toasted to perfection. A healthy dusting of cinnamon sugar completed the dessert. Biting into the thin, crispy crust gave way to the marshmallow softness underneath.

This time, I ordered lunch, grilled pork rice bowls and two large taro slushes for us. I took a seat at my favorite spot by the large picture window where I could people watch and waited for my father to arrive.

Dad came in with a lopsided grin. His infectious smile always brightened my day. Gray streaked his dark hair, while his wire-framed glasses carried a slight dent in their top left corner from when he whipped them off his face celebrating the Warriors' first NBA championship in the Steph Curry era. A pressed, lilac dress shirt over tailored dark slacks was his concession to Ma. She insisted on a pop of color. Dad, if he had his way, would choose monotone.

He slid into the seat next to me. "How has your morning been?"

I laughed. His question seemed so mundane given my morning meeting. "Ma would kill you if you didn't ask how the matchmaking appointment went."

"That is your business. I think they should leave you be." He checked over his shoulder and moved to accommodate the incoming server carrying our meals.

"The matchmaker didn't give me anything I didn't know already," I said after we thanked her. "Maybe they'll now accept that me and long-term relationships aren't meant to be."

"I know them. You'll be lucky to get a six-month reprieve." My dad hovered his fork above my tea egg, pretending to steal it.

I covered my bowl with my hands. "Oh, Dad, you're supposed to be watching your cholesterol."

"I can have one; though, we won't tell your mother about this. We'll claim it's another boring egg white omelet." He grinned and stabbed his egg with a fork.

I followed his lead and attacked the tea egg in my rice bowl. The creamy yolk disintegrated in my mouth. Tapping the shell during cooking allowed the marinade to seep in, which created a linear pattern resembling cracked glass in the hardened egg white. Ma and I sometimes made tea eggs on weekends where we boiled the eggs in a secret recipe of spices and Yu tea. It was a calming ritual. The hectic game of keeping it hidden away from my father, lest he eat them all in one sitting, was less so.

A retired couple power walked by, clad in matching lime-green sweat suits. A pair of teens held hands, their shoulders brushing as they sauntered down the sidewalk. Squirrels chased one another up a red Chinese pistache tree. The universe mocked me.

"If I fill my life with other things, can I forget that love is the one thing I can't have?" I asked my father while watching the squirrels.

He set down his fork and placed a hand on my shoulder. "Back in college, I had a crush on your mother. It took all four years to gather the courage to ask her out. I have faith, though, that you will find your match. You have a big heart. You deserve to be happy."

Dad still had hope—a hope I did not recognize. Hope was not for people who halt an evening engagement blurting out a relationship's end, or predicting a home burglary, or revealing future unemployment. Only one date had a happy prophecy: a lottery win. He ran out of the restaurant to start his exciting new life without me.

My teeth grazed the extra-large straw as I sipped my boba slush. The creamy powderiness of taro lingered on my tongue while the chewy tapioca pearls provided a satisfying challenge for my teeth. It was one thing to tell myself that I'd been doomed to be forever alone. It was another for a matchmaker to confirm it. I was twenty-seven, single, and still hooked on boba tea. Only one of those was a problem.

Our conversation moved on to breezier topics, the sports pools he had joined and Ma's chances of winning this year's mahjong tournament. Dad was still terrible at fantasy sports drafts unless his home basketball team was involved. We both agreed that Ma would take the championship tiara and sash this year. She was due.

As he settled the bill, I grabbed my purse. My drink had a few sips left so I gulped them down, careful to avoid choking on the pearls at the bottom. As I chewed my last piece, I pulled out the straw, tearing open the plastic sealing the top.

I gripped the table to steady myself as my stomach knotted. My father placed his arm around my shoulders.

The prophecy formed in my mouth, larger than anything I had ever experienced. It crackled with energy. A taste of Himalayan salt, with a dominating bitterness of burnt garlic, assaulted my palate. The pressure pushed against the bones in my head until it felt like someone had rammed a rod through my right temple in an aborted attempt to release the tension. My hands wrapped themselves around my stomach as I held my breath, willing myself to stay silent.

"Brendan will have a heart attack during the fourth inning of the Angels baseball game. He will die in your arms."

Dad's glasses fogged over. Cupping his hand over his mouth, he sobbed. The gesture did little to muffle his anguish.

He had known Brendan for over forty-five years. They grew up on the same street, played on the same softball team, went to the same high school and college. Uncle Brendan was Dad's best man at my parents' wedding. They went on annual fishing trips. He was more than Dad's friend: he was family.

Dad lowered his hand and wiped the condensation from his lenses. "He took up running. He finally started to eat right. It was so important to him to change." His voice cracked. "He became a grandfather this winter."

Three tears slid into the deepening lines of his pale face.

My heart broke.

I made my father cry.

In the engulfing silence, all that lingered was the sorrow the prediction bore.

"Dad, I'm sorry. I'm so sorry." I repeated my apology over and over as if my words could mend the wound, could take us back to before the damage—before my father cried.

He enveloped me in a tight embrace and kissed my hair as my tears soaked his shirt, mingling with his own.

When learning to roller-skate, I took a hard fall on the pavement. My father ran to my side and carried me back to the house. He comforted me well after the tears had stopped even though it made him late for an important appointment. He placed me above all else.

A sharp, invisible screwdriver slammed into my right temple. My stomach reeled, convulsing with rising nausea. I slumped against my father as my legs buckled.

Dad held me steady. "Are you all right? Vanessa?"

I winced, keeping my eyes closed. "I think I have a migraine."

He rubbed my back and waited. When the intense pain subsided to a more tolerable level, I stepped back. A backdrop of nausea, and the persistent throbbing in my head, remained.

"Migraines don't run in our family. Have you seen a doctor? Has it happened before?" he asked.

"The last one was at Cynthia's wedding. Before that, when I was out with Uncle Michael and Auntie Faye. I'm probably just tired or overstimulated. It's not a big deal. I'm more worried about you and Uncle Brendan."

A shadow crept over my father's dark eyes as he tightened his jaw. "Death is unavoidable. But knowing when it's coming can be a blessing because it gives you time to come to terms. I know you think this is your fault, Vanessa, but it's not. You need to understand that."

I wished I did.

* * *

I had never predicted death in such a blatant manner. Death had only ever been implied as the final verse to a tragic poem. This, though, was visceral, as though I, personally, had condemned Brendan to death.

My hands trembled before spreading upward until I shook like I was shivering from the cold. Dad held me until the shaking subsided into minor tremors. He took my car keys and called Ma to pick up his car while he ushered me into my car and drove me home.

As he drove, my dear father continued to console me. "It won't stop me from trying. I'll call Brendan to check in on him tonight. Vanessa, this isn't your fault," he repeated.

I remained silent. My hands gripped the handles of my purse while my breathing came in shallow waves. I had no control over what I predicted—I was a menace. My fingernails cut into my palms. It wasn't fair that he had to comfort me. Years of wishing the predictions would end had not amounted to anything.

"When I'm upset, I calm myself by figuring out my next steps," Dad said softly as he turned onto the Oregon Expressway.

"I'm so miserable, Dad. I don't want to feel like this for the rest of my life. I don't want to hurt anyone anymore. I'm tired." I drew a pattern on the passenger window. "Aunt Evelyn is in control. I'm a helpless mess."

"Those lessons she tried to give you when you were younger never ended well. You want to try again?"

"I need to." I curled my hands into fists. All my life Aunt Evelyn had tried to help me, and I always fought her.

I couldn't any longer.

* * *

My condo was at the edge of Midtown and Charleston Gardens, about an eight-minute commute to work and ten minutes from my parents' craftsman home in Crescent Park. As Dad pulled into my street, I saw a familiar white Tesla Model S parked before my building. The car's owner waited at the doorway.

Aunt Evelyn.

Six

Aunt Evelyn and I stood in the kitchen of my 1,200-square-foot condo. For the first time in a while, we weren't arguing. Instead, a strident silence stretched between us, a still lake teeming with unspoken thoughts.

Dad had stepped outside to call Ma. I muted my phone. I didn't need any outside distractions. The only person I needed now was with me.

"I saw a death, not some oblique reference to dying: it was one of Dad's closest friends." I met my aunt's steady gaze. "I can't do this anymore. I don't want to live like this. It's too hard. It hurts too much. Please, I need you to help me find some measure of control."

Aunt Evelyn opened her arms. I stepped into her embrace and buried my face into her perfumed shoulder. Tears trickled onto her cashmere sweater, soaking the light yellow silk blouse underneath.

"When I saw my grandfather's death, I felt the same." Aunt Evelyn rubbed my back in small circles. Her peony perfume soothed me as the sobs subsided into silent hiccups. "I was thirteen. We were sitting at the heart surgery clinic together, waiting for his appointment. Ye-ye was recovering from a triple bypass. He was the type that, if he thought no one was watching, would eat all the skin from a crispy, roasted pig. He loved salty and fatty foods. Thankfully, Aunt Charlotte was with us. I couldn't stop vomiting. The emotions we feel are so intense. Death is the hardest, more so when it concerns those we love."

"Can you help me, Auntie?"

"I can. But why did you avoid lessons all these years?"

I began lessons with Aunt Evelyn the week following my third birthday and was, at first, a keen student. However, in my last weekly lesson, I had a graphic prediction of a car accident involving my librarian from first grade, Mrs. Chiang: a transport truck T-boning her car, her right arm and leg amputated, the taste of half-cooked beef liver, metallic.

The vision was intense, and I could not comprehend its details except that Mrs. Chiang wasn't at school the next day, or the following week, or the rest of the school year. Soon, kids in the schoolyard spoke about her with immature callousness and a fascination with the gory details. Only then did I understand the gravity of my words. I vowed never to return to prophecy lessons: they forced me to see visions with a clarity I never wanted. Without my aunt's guidance, my predictions returned to a preferable vagueness.

"I had a vision I didn't want to see. It terrified me," I replied. "But now they're worse. I need your help."

She squeezed me tight. "Come with me to Paris."

"What?"

"You need to be where I am for me to help, and I have to leave for France tomorrow. No one else understands what you're going through." She reached for her satchel purse and pulled out her phone. As her fingers danced across the smooth surface, she smiled. "It's done. I bought you a first-class ticket on the same flight. Being away from everyone and everything is ideal."

"But what do I tell my parents? The aunties? The family? The firm?" I asked.

"Your father is inviting your mother over. We'll have dinner and I'll explain everything."

I frowned. "Leaving tomorrow is so sudden."

"You want my help, don't you?"

"Yes, but . . . you're asking me to put my life on hold and fly halfway around the world. I can't just drop all my responsibilities to take prophecy lessons. I'm not one that resists change, but I'm still trying to process the fact that I saw one of Dad's friends die and I'm expected to go to Paris tomorrow. I don't think this is the best time."

"The time *is* now," she replied, patting my arm. Returning to her phone, she sent another flurry of messages. "I invited Michael. Between us, we'll figure out what to tell the family."

She opened the stainless-steel double doors to the fridge. My fridge was as empty as my cupboards. Auntie Faye and Ma had helped decorate my kitchen to make it appear like it belonged to someone adept at cooking. They had created convincing window dressing. Dinners were spent at my parents', relatives', or out at restaurants with cousins. Ma and my aunties were excellent cooks, but I never learned. I was too busy eating.

Aunt Evelyn glanced under the counter. "At least your wine fridge is full."

"For whites and rosé, yes. The reds are in the rack near the living room," I said with a wobbly smile. "I do have proper cutlery and plates, so there is that."

My aunt laughed. "I'll order dinner. Tonight calls for sushi."

Uncle Michael and Ma arrived at the same time. I didn't entertain often. When I did eat at home, I ate at the quartz countertop in the kitchen. My formal dining room was pristine from disuse. Crystal and sterling silver barware along with bright, colorful cocktail glasses filled the modern hutch near the circular dining table. Each had been gifted by various aunties last Christmas.

I sat between my parents. We picked at the various maki rolls packed in a large round plastic tray. Uncle Michael poured prosecco into flutes and kept the open bottle between him and my father, ready for refills.

"I will ask Gene to manage your work. It won't be a problem. You're due for a vacation anyway. Three weeks is definitely doable," Dad said, sipping his wine.

Ma waved her chopsticks in the air. "If Chester complains, I'll clip his—"

"Linda! Faye will keep him in check," Aunt Evelyn said.

"Not how you expected today to unfold, I'd imagine," Uncle Michael said to me as Ma and Aunt Evelyn continued to discuss their nephew. The wrinkles around his eyes deepened, making him look closer to his true age.

I plucked a piece of the spider roll from the tray. "I'm excited about Paris."

I always wanted to go for the art and food, but I never went because I didn't want to go alone. It wasn't that I cared about what people thought, it was more that I wanted to experience the city with someone. No one else in the family had mentioned any desire to go, and if I had known Aunt Evelyn was interested, I would have been tempted to ask despite knowing that we would quarrel.

"Now is your chance to see the *Mona Lisa* in person." Dad held my hand. "Evelyn knows what she's doing. You'll come back a master fortune-teller."

A narrow scar curved along the base of his thumb from a fishing accident. When I was ten, Dad tried teaching me to fish at Lake Tahoe. In my first attempt to cast the line, I threw the rod back, and the hook caught him. After some iodine and a bandage, he asked me to try again, but I'd sworn off fishing, terrified I'd injure somebody else.

"Also, I'll be in Germany soon and close by if you need me," Uncle Michael added.

"Thank you," I replied.

I popped the piece of spider roll into my mouth. The crunch from the deep-fried soft-shell crab complemented the velvety avocado. Tasty, but not my ideal.

My perfect meal would consist of a platter of sixty oysters on ice and a bottle of Chablis. It would be more perfect if there were a wonderful man sharing them with me, someone who loved and appreciated them as much as I did.

Uncle Michael heaped two more of the spider rolls on my plate. "Where did you go just now?"

"I was thinking about my perfect meal and how satisfying it would be to share it with someone special." I refilled my glass with more prosecco.

Ma and Aunt Evelyn stopped their conversation.

"What did the matchmaker say?" Ma asked.

I told them what happened.

"*Aiyah*, you're going to be alone forever," Ma wailed. She grabbed the wine from across the table and started drinking straight from the bottle.

"Linda!" Aunt Evelyn pried my mother's fingers from the neck.

Ma's teary eyes bore into me. "I want you happy."

"Calm down," Dad said to her as he took the bottle from my aunt. "The matchmaker didn't say she'd be alone forever. She said it was tricky."

Ma nodded. She sniffled and reached for the Kleenex box on the sideboard. Tissues flew out of the box as if my mother was a magician performing an endless-scarves trick. If she weren't so concerned about *my* love life, I'd be laughing right now.

"After I'm in control of these prophecies, then, maybe, we can worry about what the matchmaker said."

Aunt Evelyn set her chopsticks down. "Linda, I told you multiple times to not interfere in Vanessa's love life. She can't maintain a romantic relationship. No amount of meddling from you can change this reality. She is a clairvoyant, that is her future and her fate." My aunt sighed. "I can see where her stubbornness came from."

I narrowed my eyes at Ma before burying my face in my hands.

Ma had always contested this fact, and she, like the rest of my aunts, chose to believe what they wanted. On this point, I felt my mother's maturity was lower than my own.

She stopped dabbing her eyes and waved her hand. "I just don't want her to be alone. It's sad. No one should be alone unless they choose to."

"Did everyone know?" I asked. "Why did they spend so much money on the matchmaker?"

My aunt rolled her eyes. "It isn't a secret. I told them all so many times, but do you think that would stop them once they get an idea in their collective heads?"

I laughed because what she said was true.

Ma shrugged. "I thought your warnings were a mere suggestion."

"If I can help Vanessa, it will change the quality of her life, but not her love life," Aunt Evelyn said. "What's important is controlling her gift."

A resigned silence fell over the meal.

"Had she followed in her education the way I did, she would be in full control by now. Death predictions manifest during the teenage years. To be so delayed is strange," my aunt continued. "We'll find out more in Paris."

The more I listened to Aunt Evelyn, the more I felt that there was so much she was keeping from us. Even when I was a child, she was shrouded in an air of mystery. While the rest of my aunties were clear windows into their personalities, Aunt Evelyn always held a part of herself back. She was like a misty forest where darkness dwells and fairy tales were born.

"We will treat this as a mini vacation. You'll stay with me at my flat and help with the tea shop during the day," Aunt Evelyn said. Then she smiled at me. "It'll be fun to spend more time with you."

"I will help you pack," Ma declared. "We need to make sure you bring nice clothes just in case. They dress well in Paris. You need to impress!"

I covered my eyes with my hand and groaned.

"The flight is tomorrow morning. Everything is arranged. After we land, Linda, you'll need to tell the family, start with the women. They can't, under any circumstances, interfere with this. Vanessa and I need to be given our space. Harry, smooth this over at the firm. They can't suspect anything beyond a sabbatical. Michael, handle the info with the rest of the family. Sell it as a vacation. We all need to work together." Aunt Evelyn refilled everyone's wine flutes. "I promise you I'll do everything possible to help Vanessa."

Uncle Michael raised his glass. "I promise to use my charm and convince everyone that everything is fine."

"I promise not to fly out to Paris even though I really want to," Ma said. "I promise to let you two handle everything on your own and not to call my daughter too often."

"I promise to do my best to hold my wife to her promises," Dad added with a smirk.

I listened to my family and held up my hand like a Girl Scout. "I promise to do my best with my lessons and listen to Aunt Evelyn."

Of course, given our history, that would be easier said than done.

Seven

Impending lessons notwithstanding, I was excited to experience Paris. My parents and I had trotted all over Asia and North America, but we'd never visited Europe. Having studied European art history, I pined to be in the physical presence of these masterpieces. Exhibits at local museums and galleries had only brought a fraction of what I wanted to see. Staring at a Degas for an hour and studying every brushstroke on the canvas was the closest to a religious experience I'd ever had that wasn't triggered by sublime food.

When traveling abroad with my family, the language barrier was our biggest hurdle. Ma was terrified we'd become lost in places where we couldn't converse. I'm not sure why she worried: even without asking, she located every Louis Vuitton store in the vicinity.

When I was younger, Uncle Michael had taken me to a showing of Audrey Hepburn and Humphrey Bogart's classic *Sabrina* at the Stanford Theatre. I imagined myself as the girl in the tree, watching the wonderful life I craved happening below me at one of the glittering Larabee soirees. The scenes of Paris were enchanting, while the grand romance between Sabrina and Linus captured my heart.

Early the next morning, Uncle Michael drove Aunt Evelyn and me to San Francisco International Airport. My parents had made arrangements to meet us there.

"Linda's bringing the battalion, isn't she?" Uncle Michael asked.

"I wouldn't put it past her," I replied.

"They shouldn't interfere," Aunt Evelyn added from the back seat. "We have her promise."

If the aunties were coming, I worried about delays. A requisite lineup of goodbyes with the fourteen women, including Ma, where each was certain to have some piece of sage advice and, possibly, an object of great importance I had to bring.

Uncle Michael laughed as we turned into the airport parking lot. "If Madeline is there, no matter what, don't let her convince you to smuggle her homemade chili shrimp paste across international lines."

We parked and Uncle Michael popped the trunk. We unloaded my aunt's three large suitcases. I had a single one.

"You didn't pack much," he remarked.

After two hours of assessing my wardrobe, Ma had concluded that I worked too much and didn't go out enough. Paris and Palo Alto were comparable in the spring—California was warmer by a few degrees. I brought the few dresses I loved. As for shoes, Ma insisted better footwear was waiting for me in the fashion capital.

"We agreed it's better to shop in Paris. Ma didn't approve of all the work wear in my closet," I replied.

Aunt Evelyn smiled. "It'll be fun to get a new trousseau for you. I can't remember the last time you took an extended vacation or sabbatical."

This last-minute trip seemed normal, almost.

My most recent time away had been to Barbados with the cousins for a week the previous spring. It was a fun, last-minute getaway to lounge and work on our tans by the beach after a grueling tax season. Before that, a winter vacation with my parents in Hawaii. Family activities and special occasions populated the calendar, making vacations difficult. Getting out of a family affair required multiple permission slips, which the aunties were reluctant to grant. Attendance reflected both duty and love: these were not mutually exclusive.

"These three weeks will be so different for you. I think you might enjoy being an ocean away from the family for a while," Uncle Michael said as he corralled two of Aunt Evelyn's suitcases.

"Maybe, but I won't be alone," I replied, tilting my head toward my aunt.

We stepped through the doors of Terminal A before being engulfed by the colorful mob of Yu women clustered near the Air France ticketing desk. My father was the lone male among them.

I was greeted with a flurry of kisses and embraces—little pats and touches borne out of familial intimacy. They cooed over me like it was my first day of school. These women treated their nieces and nephews as their own children: second mothers, watchful guardians, lovable meddlers. I would miss this irresistible chaos.

Ma and Dad waited at the end of the group, his arm wrapped around her shoulders. They still held hands on their evening walks. This must be what the matchmaker meant by red threads connecting two people.

Ma held me tight before giving me to my father.

Dad smiled, and gathered me into his arms. "I'll miss you."

I breathed in the scent of French-press coffee mixed with the subtle cologne Ma picked out for him.

"I love you, Dad," I murmured into his shoulder. "Don't worry. Aunt Evelyn will fix everything."

The gathering of aunties moved to enclose me once again. Auntie Faye, the group's designated speaker, stepped forward. "We all decided to go with a theme for your going-away present."

I braced myself. I'd anticipated this, but I couldn't begin to guess what the ladies had planned. They all appeared to be quite pleased with themselves. In unison, they reached into their purses and pulled out . . . books?

Ma withdrew one as well. She placed it in my hands. "Romance novels. To get you in the right mood for your trip to the city of love. A thirteen-hour flight is perfect reading time."

"I thought you didn't like these." I grinned, recognizing the title.

"Faye made me a convert years ago. She said I was too uptight and made me join the book club. Gloria double-checked your Goodreads account to make sure we didn't get you anything you've already read."

One by one, the women handed me a paperback until I carried a sizable stack. Auntie Faye took out a cute cat-print tote bag, shoved the books in, and handed it to me. "We'll miss you, Vanessa." She gave me a quick peck on the cheek. "Have a wonderful time in Paris."

"Thank you," I said. "I'm going to miss you all."

Aunt Evelyn cleared her throat. "It's time. We have to go."

Uncle Michael handed me a ribboned package. "It's not a romance novel."

"You too?" I asked. "You didn't have to get me anything."

He shrugged with a sheepish smile. "I didn't want to feel left out."

Uncle Michael had given me a large leather sketchbook along with artist pencils, watercolors, and chalk pastels. As a child, I'd taken lessons on weekends and went to art summer camp. My uncle picked me up when my parents were working. He praised my sketches and paintings over burgers and fries at our favorite roadside joint.

"Thank you," I said, hugging him. "I'll show you when I get back."

Uncle Michael returned his attention to the two pieces of luggage by his side. "We'd better move. Evelyn's already waiting at the counter."

My aunt waved me over. I bid a quick goodbye to the family and joined her. Soon, Uncle Michael left, ushering the others out of the airport.

Aunt Evelyn and I remained.

The ensuing silence was palpable as the attendant oversaw our passports, checked in our luggage, and issued our tickets. The handsome fortysomething admired my elegant aunt. It was in his careful manner and lingering glances, a quiet, respectful kind of appreciation.

Aunt Evelyn was stunning and intimidating at the same time. The other aunties mentioned a failed relationship once, but they respected her too much to gossip. My aunt chose to keep her own company, owning her single status without shame. I coped with the lack of romance in my life by developing an addiction to romance novels. We were related, but we couldn't be more different.

I glanced down at my printed ticket.

"It's a long flight," Aunt Evelyn said. "I had to justify the upgrade to your mother as she was appalled by the extravagance. You can see that I won."

Every time we traveled, we were in coach, even on long all-day flights to Asia. Ma saw no point in paying more for a seat closer to the front of the plane. "This is going to be a new experience for me," I confessed.

"You'll enjoy this trip, but, remember, this is a working vacation first and foremost even though you're not working for the tea shop."

"The lessons?" I asked.

My aunt hadn't divulged any details yesterday. She'd been tight-lipped about it despite my stated desire to learn. Given how my final childhood lessons had ended, her caution might be warranted.

She nodded. "We'll start once you've settled in. I need you to be receptive. It won't work otherwise."

"Did you see this coming?" I asked. "I mean, your sense of clairvoyance is much more powerful than mine."

"Yes. It was why I was waiting for you at your condo yesterday." We stopped before the security gate. "I will teach you, but if you don't give in to the process, it won't work. I want to make this clear before we leave."

Going to Paris wasn't meant to be some sort of miracle cure, but a part of me wished it could be. Still, I didn't expect her to be so explicit in her assessment of the situation. To anyone else, I appeared to be going on a wonderful trip with my aunt to one of the most beautiful cities in the world.

"I didn't expect a quick or easy fix."

"Good. I want you to have realistic expectations. This is going to be equal parts wonderful and painful, depending on how you take to my guidance. The more you fight, the worse the situation. I need you to promise that you will put as much effort into the lessons as I will."

"I'll do whatever it takes, Auntie."

I wanted to change my life. Nothing I could say to her would prove my intentions more than showing her that I was up to the task.

Eight

Stepping off the plane, I half expected to hear the first chords of Édith Piaf's "La vie en rose" on a whimsical accordion. Paris in the springtime—a magical time to visit, according to the tourist guide I devoured between romance novels. I skipped the parts about helpful phrases; that path only led to me butchering the language. My seventh-grade Spanish teacher once accused me of making his ears bleed. Ma talked to him, and after he made me demonstrate, she concurred. Besides, I was more fascinated with the pages in the guide detailing the restaurants. Delicious food and astounding masterpieces awaited me in the ancient City of Light.

Terminal 2 at Charles de Gaulle Airport was crowded. Despite a first-class seat on the long flight over, I hadn't slept. My aunt was in better shape. She had put on an eye mask as soon as the wheels retracted, and slept until we landed.

"Jet lag?" Aunt Evelyn asked as grogginess and exhaustion tugged at me with every step. We had arrived in the morning, but running on California time, I felt every second of the nine-hour difference, and all 5,571 miles.

"Yes and it's bad."

She patted my hand. "When we get back to the apartment, sleep. Paris can wait until you feel human again. The travel from west to east is always the hardest. One of the downsides of traveling to the future."

"I feel like I could sleep forever." I craned my neck and squinted at the lights overhead. "How long before my lessons start?"

"A few days. When you feel better, we'll go out to dinner and then shopping. I'll be busy preparing the store after that. The upgrades to our flat finished last week. I can't wait for you to see it."

My aunt strolled to the baggage carousel and checked the screens for our flight. "The family's tea company purchased the building in the Saint-Germain des Prés area fifteen months ago. The renovations took about a year. I was quite specific about how I wanted the shop and the apartment to look."

Aunt Evelyn's tastes had always been exquisite. Her Victorian in San Francisco was decorated with a sense of period drama, bold colors tempered with textiles and accents evoking the era she wanted to capture. My aunt re-created the aesthetic of *Alice's Adventures in Wonderland*, but without the modern outlandish and garishness associated with Carroll's books. Her keen eye for pristine antiques matched her need for fresh flowers every week: tea roses, hydrangeas, pink carnations, orchids, and of course, peonies.

"You were always comfortable at my place when you visited," she said. "It'll be similar in feel and decor. I had some of my favorite pieces flown in from the old house."

"It sounds like you're moving here. Are you?"

"I haven't sold my Victorian yet."

She hadn't answered my question. I wasn't sure if she didn't want to respond or didn't know the answer herself.

We claimed our luggage and made our way outside. It was bright. My bloodshot eyes hurt from the glare inside the taxi. As we drove away from the airport, the driver placed a notepad over the steering wheel and began scribbling notes. The car lurched and swerved. My aunt and I held on, thankful for our seat belts. After the driver almost collided with a road barrier, Aunt Evelyn blasted him in French. I didn't need to understand to know what she said. Her frostbitten tone conveyed the message.

The driver tucked his notepad away, apologized, and stared straight ahead.

Aunt Evelyn checked her phone for messages. "I've spoken to Cynthia. She is working things out with Edwin. For now, they're staying together and talking. It's a start."

I'd been in touch with my cousin. We'd spoken a few times, but the awkwardness from the wedding carried over and ruined the natural ease of our friendship. She told me, "Talking to you is futile when the only thing that comes out of your mouth is guilt."

"I've apologized so many times," I said, "but it doesn't make it better."

My aunt shook her head. "She doesn't want an apology from you. What are you trying to get from her? Forgiveness?"

"I don't know. My mouth is a loaded weapon with prophecies that injure and harm. How could I not feel responsible?" The dimness of the cab's interior hid my blushing cheeks.

"You've turned your gift inward and made it a weapon. I'm more worried about you than your cousin." Aunt Evelyn tucked her phone away. "There is a wonderful bistro I can't wait to show you. The menu is sublime. I am in love with their risotto."

In my family, the promise of food was the first step in resolving potential arguments. To quell an existing one, it had to be *good* food. You could bribe others with money or fame, but a Yu would only accept exclusive reservations or admittance to a chef's table. Discerning palates were hardwired in our genetics. Stampedes at the family buffet tables still occurred: regardless of age, we sought out the best piece, which remained the ultimate goal.

My stomach groaned. It had been a long flight and I was famished, but the lure of a comfortable bed trumped all else.

I mustered a smile. "Please tell me more about the food scene here." And with those words, the building tension escaped the cab like a whistling kettle taken off a stovetop.

A minute's walk from the tea shop, Aunt Evelyn's luxe two-bedroom apartment was bigger than those in San Francisco. Her Victoriana tastes underwent a subtle change with the infusion of French Romanticism. Against muted cerulean walls, giclée reproductions of *La Grande Odalisque* and *La Source* by Ingres in gilded frames hung in the living room. A bouquet of white roses with lilacs stuffed in a Lalique crystal vase adorned the small, rectangular cherrywood dining room table. Our bedrooms overlooked rue de Montalembert, a small street off the much larger and busier boulevard Saint-Germain to the south.

My aunt instructed me to emerge whenever I was hungry and ready to move. I collapsed onto the fluffy bed waiting for me.

Later that evening, I awoke famished following a zombified sleep.

The apartment kitchen was small as compared to the one in her spacious Victorian. Dark blue cupboards with glass panes and wrought iron hardware highlighted a mosaic herringbone-tile backsplash. Her impressive tea collection shone like jewels—rows of colorful tins from all over the world containing her favorite blends. If I didn't view the beverage with such hostility, I'd want a proper introduction from an expert such as my aunt.

A set of gorgeous milky, pastel ceramic jars perched on the gleaming white counter. I recognized them from her home in California; they contained cookies. My aunt's sweet tooth was as potent as mine.

Aunt Evelyn was seated at the round table in the kitchen, browsing a stack of forms in a manila folder while sipping tea. "How do you feel?" she asked.

"Starving."

She tucked her forms away and fetched her purse. "Then let's eat. I made the reservations hoping you'd be up to enjoy them."

We headed for dinner at a lovely bistro in the fifth arrondissement, near the Panthéon. All the beautiful lights highlighted the historic, stunning architecture. The clouds thinned into wispy columns revealing the dark sky overhead. Above us, the stars twinkled, flashing bright in their vanity. The restaurant was crowded: locals dined outside on the patio, and inside, the booths and tables were full.

"Parisians love to eat late and they tend to take their time. It's a wonderful trait. As for this place, it's pricey, but for your first night, this is perfect." Aunt Evelyn winked, then spoke in immaculate French to the hostess behind the podium.

The handsome hostess led us to our reserved booth.

I opened the leather menu cover and then closed the portfolio with a sigh. Of course it was all in French.

My aunt laughed. "You can get by with English in the city.

There's enough tourists around to keep everyone bilingual. You'll fit right in."

"I didn't even know you spoke French."

"You should hear my German. It's getting there." She blushed and reviewed the menu.

I'd known her for years, yet the woman before me seemed like a stranger. My aunt had so many secrets, which tumbled out like errant breadcrumbs. Where did the trail lead? What lay at the end? I was curious, but nowhere near Auntie Faye's level.

"Why expand to Europe now?" I asked. "And wouldn't London have been better?"

"The competition in London is fierce. Here, coffee is king; therefore, we can start small and grow our customer base. It's why I picked this area. It has enough tourists. Plus, I fell in love with this part of the city. Once you see it during the day, you'll understand why. There's a friendly community here."

My aunt caught the attention of our server and placed our order. I was curious to see what she had in mind.

"Michael mentioned you're a fan of Audrey Hepburn. We'll go dress shopping tomorrow. I know a few charming shops that carry her style. Some are vintage. Will you cut your hair to match?"

I'd had long hair all my life. Even with my usual high ponytail, the thick waves fell past my shoulders. I did, however, indulge in auburn highlights during a recent salon visit. "No. I don't think a pixie cut works with my bone structure."

Aunt Evelyn laughed. "You'd be lovely if you chose to get one. I think the city will suit you."

"I don't know. Paris might be too elegant for me." I smiled.

The server returned and placed two appetizers on the table.

The first was a sumptuous salad laid out in a lush line on a round plate. Among the green were dots of color: pickled vegetables, golden cassava curls, slices of decadent black truffles. Dabs of cumbawa cream added rich acidity. The fragrance of spring drifted up from the fresh ingredients.

The second was more-familiar fare. On one side, thin slices of smoked salmon layered over each other as if they were a continuous peach-colored ribbon. On the other was a small arrangement of mango chips interrupted by hints of red chilies. An intriguing bumblebee-yellow sauce separated the two.

With food like that before me, I was sure the city and I were destined for a passionate love affair.

The following day, Aunt Evelyn fulfilled her promise and showed me the city's best dress shops in le Marais. I came away with enough clothes to last a month. My aunt took doting to a new level: extreme generosity, without crossing the line to overkill.

We returned to the apartment, hauling armloads of bags. I spent the entire time thanking her as we climbed the stairs from the courtyard.

"Drop everything off in your room," Aunt Evelyn instructed. "We're not done yet."

"This is more than enough clothes, Auntie." I deposited the purchases into my bedroom and returned to the hallway. "I don't need anything more."

"This isn't about clothes. I'm talking about fragrance. You're in Paris—you need perfume. It's essential."

The beautiful Parisian women we walked past smelled lovely, with a subtle perfume that was unique and unlike the wall of sheer suffocating fog I had encountered from an auntie or two. Aunt Evelyn's scent, I realized, was like a Parisian. It had always been.

"Wait, is your perfume French?" I asked her.

She smiled. "You've discovered my secret. Your aunts have been forever guessing what I wore. My favorite perfumer is based in Paris. I've been having it imported for years. Until now."

My aunt locked up and we made our way back downstairs and onto the street.

Along rue de Montalembert we walked past jewel-like shops as shafts of sunlight peeked through the leaves of the trees overhead. A church bell rang in the distance. My aunt identified it as belonging to the Saint Thomas Aquinas Catholic church. It rang every hour, and it amused me to no end that a person could be responsible for the task.

The classic architecture of the buildings enthralled me, and the ornate doors held me spellbound. Each exquisite door represented a physical manifestation of possibilities. The allure appeased both my aesthetic and whimsical sensibilities.

As I walked around this neighborhood, it became clear that the beauty, elegance, and grandeur of these old, majestic cream-colored buildings with their wrought iron balconies, capped dark-colored roofs, and dormer windows were as much Aunt Evelyn as was her old Victorian back home.

My aunt stopped by an aquamarine-painted storefront. The gold letters sparkled against a blue-green background. The window display contained round perfume bottles encircling a bountiful arrangement of tiny fuchsia orchids in a milky rose-glaze vase on an antique oval cherrywood table.

She held the door open for me. "We're here."

I was surprised when the scents didn't assault my senses the moment we stepped in. The store was small, although the eggshell walls made it appear larger. Aside from the orchids by the window, the only source of interior color was the perfume bottles.

The lone Asian saleslady, close to my aunt's age, at the counter greeted us. Aunt Evelyn spoke with her, and soon I was presented with a velvet tray of five options.

"Try those. Clemense and I narrowed it to floral and citrus notes. If you prefer musk or something else, let us know."

Clemense smiled at me and made a gesture. It was clear she didn't speak English. She picked up a lilac bottle, sprayed it on a tester strip, and handed me the paper.

I brought it to my nose and closed my eyes. Subtle, floral, and clean. Jasmine.

"I love this one," I declared.

"Try the others anyway. You might find something better." My aunt said something to Clemense, who nodded, and retreated to give us some privacy.

I picked up an orange bottle and sprayed a tester. "Who were you with when you bought your perfume?"

Aunt Evelyn traced the side of the sky-blue perfume bottle on the tray. "A dear friend who showed me the beauty of this city. It was a time in my life when I wanted nothing more than to stay here. Back then, I walked these streets every day and spent hours sitting at a café watching the world unfold."

I reached for the yellow bottle, spraying a new tester. "Have you gotten in touch with that old friend of yours?"

"Not yet."

I yearned to pry, but I didn't want to risk ruining the enjoyment of the past two days. I couldn't remember the last time my aunt and

I spent this much time together without quarrelling. She had never revealed a kernel of herself to me before. The need to connect with my aunt on a deeper level overrode my curiosity.

I waved the tester under my nose. The yellow bottle contained both floral and citrus notes. It wasn't for me. I reached for the pink bottle, which was roses, next.

My aunt released her grip on the blue bottle. "You're still leaning toward the jasmine, aren't you?"

"So far, it seems to be the winner." I sniffed the rose perfume and shook my head. "What are we doing tomorrow?"

"*We* are not doing anything." She sprayed the blue bottle onto the tester and handed the paper to me. "I have work in getting the tea shop ready for its opening, but you are free to explore the city solo."

"I'll miss your company." I sniffed the final option and shook my head.

"There was a time when I thought I would never hear you say that."

"I mean, you did spoil me today."

She arched her brow and let out a girlish laugh. "That I did. Do me a favor: don't tell your mother. Linda would ask me for a spreadsheet breakdown of every item."

"She totally would," I laughed.

The next morning, as we sat down for breakfast, my aunt prepared me for exploring the city. She handed me a Paris Museum Pass along with a carnet of metro tickets.

"Your first day out on your own." She nibbled on a buttery croissant. "You'll be an excellent *exploratrice*. Don't worry, you'll be perfectly safe."

"A wonderful city for tourists, right?"

She nodded. "The nearest station is rue du Bac, a three-minute walk away. Take Montalembert south to boulevard Saint-Germain and you'll see it. The metro system is easy to navigate and, you know, I'm only a text or call away if you need me. Enjoy these precious few days before you have to start your lessons. You're young and you've never seen Paris before. It'll be exciting."

"There're so many museums and galleries on my list. I don't know where to begin."

"It's beautiful out. The Musée d'Orsay is nearby, as is the Louvre. I do think, though, that you should head to Luxembourg Gardens first. There's nothing like seeing the flowers in bloom. The Eiffel Tower isn't going anywhere."

"Thank you. I'll take my coat." We had picked up a fitted trench coat yesterday and, with the cooler spring weather, it was perfect for this morning's outing.

My aunt sipped her tea. "You'll need a scarf. It complements your outfit. Go into my closet. There're a few hanging there. I want you to pick one."

"Auntie, you already gave me too much," I protested. "I can't raid your closet."

"You can and you must. I'd love for you to have something of mine. Go on."

There was no use in arguing with an older relative.

I headed to her closet. The bedrooms were of similar size. Rose damask curtains hung beside tall windows, contrasting against creamy white walls and their decorative plaster molding. The ivory Venetian rococo hand-painted commode was the centerpiece of the room. This had been my favorite piece of furniture in my aunt's home. Delicate royal-blue butterflies fluttered between the bright painted roses, shifting as if they could fly into the air at any moment. It was as I remembered from wandering upstairs in my aunt's house when I was six. I touched the moving butterflies on one of the drawers. One leaped into the air, fluttering until it faded into nothingness.

I tore myself from the mesmerizing cabinet, walked to the closet, and opened it. I always admired my aunt's exquisite tastes: everything was tailored and stylish. After scanning through her curated collection of clothes, shoes, and handbags, I found the scarves: all Hermès and pricey. It would be a grave slight to my aunt to choose the cheapest option, not that there was one I could see. I selected the Faubourg print in pinks.

Before I put everything back, I spotted a stack of papers at the corner of her dresser.

I didn't want to pry, but the top sheet caught my eye.

It was the real estate listing for her Victorian back home.

She was leaving San Francisco and moving to Paris.

Nine

I scanned the sheet for the opening date. Aunt Evelyn listed her home in San Francisco yesterday. The way the market worked, it wouldn't be surprising if she was already fielding offers. It might explain why she'd been glued to her phone the past twenty-four hours.

Curiosity was a classic Yu trait. Auntie Faye had built a business around it. Aunt Evelyn, though, had mastered secrecy. Her decision did not require my approval, but why keep it a secret? She had yet one more secret and now, by not confronting her, I did too.

I picked up the scarf, returned the sheet to its place on the pile, and headed back.

"Ah, the Faubourg. Great choice," she said, tying the scarf around my neck. "It will look better on you than it did on me. These spring breezes can be quite cool. Best to have your neck covered. Promise me you'll start at the fountain and make your way out from there. There is no better place in the city to begin your adventure."

The simple act of readying for a day out reminded me so much of

Ma that a wave of homesickness constricted my heart. We hadn't been apart for too long, yet I already missed her. She had sent numerous messages through the electronic umbilical cord tying the two of us together, but it wasn't the same.

"Try and enjoy the city before I make you miserable with my teachings," Aunt Evelyn said.

I laughed and focused on my first day out. "Where is this garden you were talking about and how do I get there?"

Growing up in California, I had become conditioned to drive everywhere, but Paris traffic was intimidating. The city's rhythm rocked like an offbeat song. Until I could acclimatize, I exercised the same level of caution young children make when learning to cross a street for the first time. One of the thrills of traveling was discovering the soul of a city, which could only be accomplished on foot, slowing down to know how it danced to its own pace: walking by the buildings and art; tasting its foods through its stalls, shops, and restaurants; and meeting its locals.

Luxembourg Gardens was located in the sixth arrondissement, a twenty-minute walk away, near the district where we had dinner. At my first dinner in Paris, I had glimpsed the palace in the distance and fallen in love, but now, during the day, the castle appeared more magical and splendid with its fairy-tale charm. A pleasant breeze teased my unbound hair and ruffled the petals of the flowers and blades of grass nearby. Blooming rainbow flower beds accented the sea of emerald lawns. English and French gardens stretched out around me, close to twenty-three hectares, according to the website. Runners and families with strollers walked by, along with fellow tourists.

Aunt Evelyn had mentioned a landmark, the Medici Fountain, as the perfect first subject to capture on paper before I made my way through the gardens and its numerous statues. I threaded north through the throng of tourists mixed with trendy locals. The perfect weather ensured a healthy turnout for this idyllic attraction.

I took in the fountain, framed by a canopy of trees, and my heart swelled as I approached the large rectangular reflecting pool and its collection of ducks leading to the monument. The landmark was unapologetically Italian. Named after Maria de' Medici, the mother of Louis XIII, it reminded me of the Trevi Fountain in *Roman Holiday*, but on a much smaller scale.

I chose a metal chair with a great vantage point of the three main figures, a giant spying on two lovers below. Which myth did they belong to? I hadn't had a chance to look up the history of the fountain yet.

A strong gust swept through the area, stirring the branches from the trees into an animated clatter. Stray leaves cascaded in an unexpected rainfall as the people below clung to their belongings. I reached for my purse and held it against my chest. The wind whipped my hair and stripped the scarf off my neck, sending it flying like an errant ribbon into the sky.

I slung my bag onto my shoulder and took off in pursuit.

The pink scarf seemed to change into a bird with fluttering silk wings as I tracked it. I couldn't lose my aunt's possession on my first day. It would be a sign of disrespect, which would cloud my lessons. The background blurred as I focused on the silk bird flying away from me.

I collided with a beautiful man who smelled of espresso, vanilla bean, and toasted sugar.

"Je m'excuse," he said in a deep voice. Tall, Asian, with dark hair and sparkling brown eyes.

"My scarf!" I blurted.

He followed my gaze and took off running. I was wearing heels. The grass might as well have been quicksand. The traitorous gust died as if its purpose was spent. The stranger caught the scarf when it dropped a few steps in front of him.

Scarf. Fountain. Beautiful man. Aunt Evelyn. She might as well have orchestrated the elements of nature to do her bidding. My favorite romance novelist, Ingrid Ing, could not have crafted a more glorious beginning.

He returned, scarf in hand.

"Thank you." I accepted my scarf and tucked it into my purse just in case it had any other ideas of taking to the skies.

"American?" he asked, switching to English.

He had dimples. I died a little inside.

"Yes, from Palo Alto. You?"

"Canadian from Montreal."

We stood together, staring into each other's eyes with a familiarity we hadn't earned. It was the type of study an artist would do, the appreciation of beauty in all of its forms and nuances.

"Marc Santos." He held out his hand.

I reached out and grasped it. The heat of his skin tingled against mine. "Vanessa Yu."

"Are you planning to go back to the fountain?"

I nodded. "Yes, it's my first day out and I wanted to break in my sketchbook."

Marc pulled his canvas messenger bag open to reveal numerous sketchpads and notebooks along with art supplies. Beauty, indeed.

My aunt and her clairvoyance seemed to have outdone themselves. If Aunt Evelyn and Madam Fong ever decided to join forces, nothing could stop them.

"You're an artist?" I asked.

"No," he replied with a boyish grin. "Not quite."

"I'm an amateur artist and an accountant back home."

"We have the amateur artist part in common," he replied. "As for my career, how about you guess? You have unlimited chances."

I bit my lower lip. Unlimited chances meant he wanted to spend more time with me.

"Deal."

We made our way back to the fountain. I took my task seriously and began peppering him with questions. "Is your job something you can tell your grandmother about and she'd approve?"

Marc laughed. "My lola knows what I do. She's proud of it."

This ruled out a small list of occupations that ranged from escort to hit man. I needed more clues. I prided myself on being right on the first try, even if it took more time and effort.

We found two unoccupied chairs to the left of the fountain. He scooted his chair closer to mine and we worked side by side. I used graphite pencils, focusing on capturing the figures of the lovers. My pencil glided across the page to break the figures down to their basic shapes and proportions. I had always sketched for myself. On occasion, I would show my parents or Uncle Michael. Now, I had an audience: I couldn't help but feel self-conscious about my skills.

I checked on Marc. He worked with ink. Instead of sketching the entire fountain or the figures, he concentrated on the architectural details: the crest, the arch, the columns. Two pages of vignettes.

"Can you tell me who they are?" I asked, gesturing to the sculpture.

"The lovers are Acis and Galatea, and the Cyclops, Polyphemus, is the voyeur."

As I suspected, the subjects were from Greek mythology. When I was younger, I loved reading about them, problematic gods and mortals with messy lives creating a swarm of dysfunctional relatives. It was familial stress I could consume for entertainment.

"Isn't Polyphemus the Cyclops who Odysseus tricked?" I asked.

"Yes, the same one. After he found the two, he crushed Acis with his bare hands. Galatea saved him and turned him into an immortal river spirit like her. A rare happy ending."

Inspired by the story, I flipped to the final page of the sketchbook and listed the names and location. It was a habit I acquired when I visited museums with my family, collecting Greek mythological figures and references and keeping a running tally.

"Have you seen the Panthéon?" he asked. "It's nearby."

"Not yet. This is my first Parisian attraction." When I realized I'd been staring at him when I said the last three words, I blushed. Classic Freudian slip.

The corner of his mouth tipped upward. "I have a few days off. If you want, I can help you add more names to the list you started."

I waited five heartbeats before saying yes.

We visited the palace on the grounds, marveling at the architecture. Maria de' Medici's taste at the fountain extended here to the ceiling murals and ornate doorways. Though the building had changed owners and functions, and was now where the French Senate convened, it kept its name. Her influence endured.

"How about lunch before we head to the Panthéon?" he asked as we walked back outside to the gardens.

"Please, show me where the good food is."

"You're a foodie?"

"Yes. A huge one. Are you?"

His answer would determine whether I'd be interested in seeing the city through his eyes. Lack of appreciation for good food was a deal breaker. I once tried to date a charming guy who worked at a car dealership. He took me to a greasy spoon. The meal was as horrible as the date. It ended when I predicted he would be denied a promotion, a rare time when a prediction helped me. I wanted to walk out. Instead, he stormed out in a huff, denying me the opportunity.

As long as I didn't call this a date, I could avoid all the mishaps associated with a Vanessa Yu classic. Marc was a nice stranger offering to show me around the city. A polite Canadian showing this American tourist around. It was nothing more than a kind gesture; though, if I was honest with myself, I wanted more.

"Yes. Why don't I show you one of my favorite cafés in the sixth arrondissement?" he asked.

"I'd love that." I tucked a stray strand of my hair back into place. "How long have you been here in Paris?"

"About three years. Long enough to explore the city on my own," Marc replied. He withdrew a mini Moleskine notebook from the side pocket of his bag. "This has all my secrets and tips including the best places to eat. If you guess my job, you'll get to see it. I'm surprised you haven't made an attempt yet."

"I need more data and time. I don't want to guess unless I'm sure." Game nights with the cousins, along with the softball tourney every summer, guaranteed my generation's spirit of competitiveness. Plus, guessing the right answer too early wouldn't be in my best interests.

Ten

"This is the best sandwich I have ever tasted," I declared before taking another bite.

Marc grinned. "Croque monsieur is one of the many local delicacies. It's a simple sandwich with three vital components: great bread, ham, and melted cheese. Simple, but fantastic."

The crisp, buttery bread contrasted with the spicy, textured Dijon, salty paper-thin slices of smoked ham, and scorched, melted Emmentaler over it all. The extra ingredient was arugula, which added a touch of peppery bitterness. I'd never been a sandwich person, but today I was converted. The quality of the bread was the catalyst. It was fresh and thick. Everything before had been on the chewy side, reminding me of glorified masticated leather.

The crust on this bread crumbled under the perfect pressure, and the delightful crackling noises it made in my mouth were culinary fireworks. The distinct aroma of it being freshly baked added to its allure.

"That's about how I reacted when I had my first sandwich here. I'll have you know that this is good, very good even, but not the best."

I wanted to protest, but I kept my mouth shut for fear I'd lose the delicious contents inside.

"My job is what brought me here. What brings you to Paris?" he asked.

His career was creative and required specific relocation. I filed the tidbit away. "I'm keeping my aunt company. She is opening up a tea shop on rue de Montalembert."

"That area has a ton of tourist traffic. She should do well there. Is she making her own or importing?"

"The family business is tea imports. I think she also makes her own blends because my aunties keep asking for custom mixes."

Auntie Faye and Ma would often consult with Aunt Evelyn regarding special blends for a host of ailments, from something as innocuous as a unique iced tea to serve to important guests to embarrassing cures for problems I didn't even want to know about. My aunt had kept business talk to a minimum. I imagined she would open up more once I started helping her out at the shop.

"There are more food places to try tomorrow," he said. "I can also take you to more attractions."

I wiped the corners of my mouth. "You're being awfully nice. I can see why Canadians have the reputation."

"I'm supposed to keep my mind off work right now, and this is the best distraction. You are doing me a favor. Besides, I wish I had a tour guide when I first arrived."

I added *stressful job* to my mental list of clues. Marc tapped the tabletop with his long, slim fingers. He had a few calluses along with a thin, faded mark on the side of his thumb pad. Not a desk job, I concluded. The air of mystery around him thickened like the celestial clouds of Bouguereau's paintings.

"You at least knew the language." I kept my eyes trained on his face and away from his espresso to avoid any spontaneous predictions. I didn't want this, whatever this was with Marc, to end yet.

"It helps," he laughed, tapping a rhythm on the table. "We should do Versailles tomorrow and Giverny the next day, and leave the huge attractions for the last day. What do you think? Is there anything you're dying to see first?"

"I'm open to anything. You won't be bored seeing these places again?"

"Not at all, and I needed the time off anyway. My boss was getting a little too cranky. It's been building for a few months, but it's been terrible lately. Something set him off. Everyone at work has been trying to figure out what. We're even running a pool." Marc frowned and his dark brows knitted together. "He's one of the kindest people I know, but he's criticizing everyone for the smallest offenses, and his dark mood is ruining everyone else's."

"Did he suffer a breakup?"

"I don't know what his problem is. All I could do was take a few days to get away for a while." He leaned back in his chair. "I'm going to leave the unpleasantness behind and enjoy my short-term tour guide stint instead. How about we meet by the rue du Bac metro station at 8:00 a.m. tomorrow? We can start our adventures there."

Marc dropped me off where we agreed to meet the next morning. As I made my way back to my aunt's apartment, I couldn't stop thinking of the cute Canadian who offered to be my guide to the city.

Today's excursion wouldn't have been possible without Aunt Evelyn's intervention. She predicted all of this. If I hadn't resisted so much over the years, what could she have taught me and how different would I be now? I pushed the thought away: I didn't want to live my life with regrets.

My aunt had given me a key to her mailbox so I could bring the mail in for her. She had also pointed out where the post office was in case I wanted to send anything home. It would come in handy, as I had spotted a few antique stores on this street and, knowing my aunties, they'd want me to check them out.

Inside the mailbox was a lone, cream-tinged envelope. The addresses bore the indentations of an old typewriter. Neither the sender nor the recipient was from here. There were no signs of a postage stamp. I tucked the envelope into my purse.

Aunt Evelyn stood in the kitchen, minding the kettle on the stove.

"I'd love to tell you how my day went, but I think you already know." I placed my bag on the half-moon table by the door.

My aunt winked. "Beautiful, wasn't it?"

"The man or the fountain?"

"Both."

The teakettle whistled. Aunt Evelyn refilled a chintz-print teapot and brought it to the table. I grabbed matching teacups with saucers from the cupboard. A lavender box with a cursive font on the label awaited us at the table.

"I picked up a tarte tatin from a nearby bakery. It might take us a few days to finish it though." Aunt Evelyn grabbed some plates and cutlery. "It's a French version of an apple pie or cake."

When we were both seated, she pulled the box open and withdrew the pastry. As with everything else I had encountered in Paris, it was lovely. Caramelized apple slices arranged in a floral spiral pattern covered the top of the tart. The golden crust crumbled under the pressure of my aunt's knife.

"I've had the softer-crust version, and the more firm version. I opted for the firmer one today. We can try the other next time." She transferred a generous slice to my plate and cut herself a more modest portion.

My preferred pastries are on the savory side: meat pies, empanadas, patties, potpies, stuffed rolls. My aunt, however, had a famous sweet tooth. The dripping, sticky slices melted on my tongue while I chewed on the crust. The sharp tang of fresh apples melded with the sweetness of toasted caramel.

"I usually eat this with vanilla ice cream." My aunt smiled before she ate another forkful.

"This is really good," I said with a mouthful of tart. "The food here has been marvelous."

"Yes, it is. I was hoping you'd mention the man whose name began with an *M*."

If I had harbored any doubts about my aunt's meddling in this morning's surprise, they were gone. "Marc Santos. He's very cute and offered to be my tour guide. Did you set us up?"

"Not exactly. I saw what was going to happen and I gave it a little push." She winked and placed the rest of the tarte tatin in the fridge. "I'm so busy with the store and I felt guilty that I can't show you around."

"How is the store doing?"

"On schedule. We'll open in a few days. Don't think about the tea shop until your sightseeing tour is over. Women like us need to enjoy romance while it lasts."

She said those last words with a sense of wistfulness I'd never heard before from her. Aunt Evelyn was never one for regrets. She'd never expressed any to me, or to anyone, as far as I knew. Again, I was struck by the realization that I didn't know much about her.

"I found a letter in our mailbox with the wrong address. I think it was misplaced. The post office is down the street. Do I just mail it?" I asked.

"Yes, this happens all the time. I'm sure the recipient will be grateful," my aunt replied. "Sometimes, lost things find their way, but they need a little help. The world is full of wonders. You just need to trust in it."

"Easy to say for someone who is clairvoyant."

She gave me a playful swat on the arm. "Go now before we head out for dinner. I'll finish up downstairs at the shop."

I placed my plate and cutlery in the sink, grabbed my purse, and headed out the door.

Late afternoon sun reflected off the buildings as I walked the block and a half to the post office. With thousands of shoppers and tourists visiting the area, I was sure some end up mailing items back home. The modern post office was on the ground floor of an old seven-story building with a bright navy-blue door.

I slipped inside and felt at home stepping in line with the American tourists. I waited with three couples ahead of me. An elderly couple at the counter were negotiating to send three items to upstate New York.

"The antiques were pricey," the husband in front of me drawled in a midwestern accent. "I can't believe how much you paid for that clock."

"It's worth it," his wife retorted. "I would have paid more if I bought it back home. It's too bad that tea shop with the blue butterfly on the sign wasn't open. I loved the design. We might have found a teapot for Sue."

My aunt's tea shop was closed, but people were already paying attention.

He lowered his voice. "The tour director mentioned it was a Chinese triad front."

My hands curled into fists. Ignorant lies. I dealt with this kind of ignorance and racism back home, but somehow didn't expect it here.

"Excuse me," I said, "but whomever you're getting your information from is wrong."

A deep flush crept from his neck to his face. His wife placed her hand on his arm and turned to me. "I'm sorry, dear. It's what the director told us. We'll talk to him."

"Thank you, I'd appreciate that." I kept my voice even, but my hands didn't uncurl until I reached the counter.

Eleven

As we dined at a nearby Italian bistro, I recounted the incident at the post office to my aunt.

She twirled her fork into her cacio e pepe. "We deal with this all the time, Vanessa. Sadly, it's everywhere. We will be fine. No one can deny what we have to offer. My shipments have arrived, and I'm on schedule."

I was more upset about the exchange than she. Aunt Evelyn was from the previous generation: they bore the societal injustices of misogyny and racism. But they raised their daughters to not accept the world's limitations. They fought for us and taught us to fight. These were women I wanted to be. As a pack, my aunties could conquer a small country.

"I heard from Michael," my aunt continued, placing a considerable heap of her pasta onto my plate, while plucking two slices off my arugula and prosciutto thin-crust pizza. "He hopes to visit within the next couple of weeks. Your mother also called. You missed your twelve-hour check-in."

Absorbed in my walk with Marc, I had missed the buzz of my phone. Ma would appreciate my spending time with him rather than taking her call and killing the mood. I'd return her call after dinner.

"Where are you headed tomorrow?" my aunt asked.

"Marc mentioned Versailles. Monet's garden at Giverny the day after."

My aunt opened her mouth, but I stopped her.

"I don't want any spoilers, Auntie."

She winked, and pressed her finger against her lips.

"Today was fun, but I can't get too excited. It can't mean anything. A prophecy will eventually ambush me and that will be the end."

Wanting something I couldn't have was a form of self-torture—one I had inflicted for years.

"There isn't anything wrong with knowing that something will expire. It focuses you: treasure the time you have together." She paused and then changed subjects. "What do you think of the pasta?"

Cacio e pepe contains three main ingredients: noodles, cheese, and pepper. The chef's execution elevated the elements into a delicious blend of cheeses (in this case, pecorino and Grana Padano) with a spicy bite from the cracked peppercorns. The tagliolini was made fresh in the kitchen.

"As amazing as the pizza," I replied.

Aunt Evelyn nodded.

The arugula and prosciutto pizza had a simple yet tasty tomato sauce as the first layer on the crispy crust. Strips of translucent Italian ham interlaced with a pile of rocket greens on top. My aunt and I agreed to douse it with the provided house blend of chili oil.

"The food has been a revelation," I said, "and I've only been here for two and a half days."

"Yes." My aunt sipped her glass of Casavecchia. "Paris has its charms: the food, the sights, the people. Anyone can imagine themselves living here."

The way she spoke, I felt she was talking about herself. Aunt Evelyn was selling her home in San Francisco. The rest of the family couldn't have known, otherwise the pageantry and procession at the airport would have been bigger.

"I couldn't live here," I said. "It's beautiful, but our family is back home. I'd miss too many things about California, like the convenience of driving my car."

"You're already tired from walking?" Aunt Evelyn asked.

My feet were sore, but not painful after a day out sightseeing. However, switching to more comfortable flats for the next two days would be best.

"Not quite," I admitted with a laugh.

"As long as the company is good," my aunt said with a smile, "I'm sure your feet will feel fine."

After dinner, I called Ma and asked if she knew that Aunt Evelyn was selling her house. The gasp from the phone indicated she didn't. She promised to use the auntie network to find out more details, before reminding me to call the next day.

Deep sleep enveloped me as I dreamed. A scarf. A chase. Lovers in an embrace.

* * *

Marc was waiting for me at the top of the stairs leading down to Rue du Bac Station. He wore a tan leather jacket, dark denim, and the same messenger bag from yesterday. I didn't think it possible, but he appeared even more handsome.

His eyes brightened when he saw me, followed by that dazzling smile.

"Are you ready for today's adventure?" he asked.

"Yes."

His phone beeped. He ignored it. The beeping persisted until it escalated into rings. He sighed and checked the screen.

"Work?" I asked. "It's okay, you can take the call."

Marc rolled his eyes while the ringtone trilled on. "Yes, it's work. I'm sorry. Please excuse me."

Brief pauses in the ensuing conversation were interrupted with rapid French.

I'd been hoping to eavesdrop, but I couldn't understand any of it. Judging by his tone and body language, I could see that whatever was happening at work was stressful. I ruled out a few more careers in my list of his possible vocations.

Marc hung up three minutes later. "I'm really sorry. I told them not to call again."

"It's all right. I understand."

He tilted his head and admired my cap-sleeved dress. "You certainly dressed for the palace. You're the embodiment of spring."

I twirled in one of the new items I had picked up while shopping with my aunt. The movement of the knee-length skirt highlighted the colorful butterfly appliqués pressed against a sheer lace overlay.

The garment was a decadent, romantic confection of embroidery. Aunt Evelyn suggested the outfit this morning because of Marc's plans for the day.

"Thank you." I smiled.

The tension in his shoulders disappeared and his dimpled smile returned. "It's less crowded at this time. We can afford to grab some breakfast before taking the RER to Versailles. Are you hungry?"

"Yes. I'd love breakfast."

We walked to a boulangerie near the Musée d'Orsay. He went inside while I selected an unoccupied table outside in the sun. Marc emerged with a baguette and two coffees. Reaching inside his bag, he took out three small jars along with a cloth-wrapped parcel.

"This," he said, leaning over the table to showcase the bread, "is important for your foodie encyclopedia." The crinkle of the paper reminded me of opening presents on Christmas morning with the same levels of nervous excitement and anticipation.

Unraveling the cloth, he revealed a small, serrated bread knife and three metal teaspoons. Marc cut the baguette into a stack of slim slices. "Most locals don't often eat decadent breakfasts. They love spreads and preserves—especially Nutella. I didn't bring that, though, because you have it back home."

I reached for the jars and unscrewed the tops. "So this is jam and toast?"

"Yes. Carrot and ginger, raspberry rhubarb, and blackberry vanilla," he said, placing the spoons in each one.

Marc planned our breakfast like he had planned our day. Thoughtfulness like this did not exist on my dates—not that this was a date, I chided myself.

"Taste the jam first before I put it on the bread." He dipped the spoon into the golden jar.

"Before I do, I have to ask: Did you make these?"

"Yes, preserves making is a hobby," he replied. "Apparently, it's common around here."

I closed my eyes as he fed me the first flavor. The carrot and ginger jam was smooth with a hint of bitterness, which only helped balance the sweet notes. Delicious.

"You sure you don't want to quit the day job to make artisanal jams instead?" I asked.

He laughed. "I have no plans to do that. This is something fun for myself."

"I still think you should consider it as a backup. I can't wait to try the next two."

We took the RER to Versailles-Château Rive Gauche. A steady rain greeted our arrival at Versailles. We ducked inside before the downpour.

"The palace is incredible and the gardens, massive. If the weather were better, we could have walked along the Grand Canal to Grand Trianon and Petit Trianon. You can't really get the scale of how big the estate is unless you walk it." He ran his fingers through his hair to shake off any stray rain droplets.

The grandiosity and scale of the palace was matched only by the gilt. It inundated the senses until it became common—the irony of reducing its worth to the banal and the ensuing ennui that inevitably followed. The opulence didn't intimidate; rather, it radiated the reason the population revolted. This was beauty at a price—viewed with equal parts caution and awe.

"This place has a ton of mythological references in the murals and names," Marc leaned in and whispered over my shoulder. "You'll be very busy writing everything down."

I pulled out my pen and sketchbook as we trailed behind the tour guide. The ceilings gave my craned neck a workout—murals and panels, without an unpainted inch in sight.

"Why are you here in Paris?" he asked. "What made you pick this city?"

"My aunt kind of sprang the vacation on me."

"Like a present?"

How could I explain the weird truth? I had to take lessons to control the prophecies I see, and my clairvoyant aunt abducted me to Paris because only she can teach me. A little too much information for a second day together. Better to be vague before I lost my guide.

"Yes, a last-minute one. I'm sure she'll appreciate my company when her tea shop opens, but it's also an opportunity to see the art in person. The textbooks can't do it justice."

"When I went to see *The Night Watch* at the Rijksmuseum in Amsterdam, I stood there, staring at it for what seemed like hours. It's huge and you feel as though you're in the square with the men. No photo in any book could re-create that experience." Marc tightened the strap of his messenger bag.

"I'm jealous. Most of the traveling I've done has been to all-inclusive resorts in the Caribbean with my cousins, or eating and shopping trips with my parents in Asia. I need to travel more with an art-food itinerary in mind."

Our group moved into the War Salon. Murals covered the arched ceiling. The guide explained the planned art was mythological until King Louis XIV's decision to depict his military prowess instead.

The tourist experience wouldn't be complete without being herded as human cattle from one attraction to another.

A British couple in front of us carried a small drinking thermos. "Is that allowed in here?" I asked in a low whisper.

"If it's alcohol, I don't think so," Marc whispered back. "Security inspected our bags twice. They must think it's okay."

The brunette struggled with the cap. I didn't need my aunt's clairvoyance to know this wasn't going to end well. She handed the bottle back to her partner, who strained to open it. The lid popped off, hitting Marc in the shoulder. The thermos gaped open for me to see the dark liquid inside.

My stomach clenched. A prophecy formed like a gumball in my mouth.

Please, not now.

Twelve

The taste of chewy caramels flooded my mouth—sweet and sticky. The pressure built against my teeth until the only way to relieve it was to allow the prediction to escape.

"He will propose with his grandmother's ring. The one you've coveted since last year's meeting."

The brunette gasped. His shaky fingers tightened the lid into place.

"You're proposing?" she asked.

"Yes." He blushed. "It was supposed to be a surprise, Clara."

She screeched, threw herself into his arms, and sprinkled his face with loud kisses. He dropped their pack and kissed her full on the lips. Clara's name was inscribed on the canister. It was her future I foretold. The thread of joy from the prediction sang within me as the residual physical reminder.

Beside me, Marc clapped his hands with the rest of the tour group. The applause prompted another set of kisses from the happy couple. I picked up the forgotten container, which had rolled near my feet. I handed it to them when the cheering died down.

Clara embraced me before skipping off with her beloved.

The thread of happiness bubbling inside was tempered by my rising embarrassment from the impromptu fortune-telling. I'd been so focused on the couple that I missed Marc's reaction.

An acute piercing pain bore into my right temple. I stumbled back. Gripping the side of my head, I closed my eyes and sucked in my breath, trying to push down a rising nausea.

Marc reached out and helped steady me. "Are you all right?"

"I need to stay still for a bit," I whispered. "Migraine."

The pounding headache ebbed into a manageable dull throb. Marc offered me one of the bottles of water in his bag. I unscrewed the cap and took a healthy swig.

"Better?"

"I think I know how Zeus felt when Athena was in his head," I replied with a wobbly smirk.

Marc laughed.

"I'll be okay. Migraines have a trigger and I know I tripped mine." I twisted the cap of the water bottle shut and handed it to him.

"My cousin gets really bad ones. His are caused by barometric pressure. There isn't much he can do prevention-wise." He took the bottle and tucked it back into his bag. "Is there anything I can do to help? Are you on any meds that you need to take?"

"Nothing I can do but avoid the trigger. I guess the situation is similar to your cousin's." I took his hand in mine. "I'm going to be okay."

He squeezed my hand before leaning in to ask, "What happened before with the Brits? How did you do that?"

The question I'd been asking myself all my life without an answer. In the past, whenever pressed, I'd give a joke response and change the subject. Now, though, I felt a genuine friendship with Marc, which demanded honesty.

"It's sort of like intuition dialed way up."

"You remind me of one of my aunties, Tita MaryJo," he said. "She knows everything. She has great detective skills."

"That's a polite way of saying she's nosy. Are you saying that I am?"

Marc blushed and then coughed. "I said that wrong. I guess what I'm saying is that intuition is based on observation and empathy. You could have overheard or seen something." He covered his eyes and shook his head. "I can't believe I compared you to my aunt. That's not what I was aiming for."

His embarrassment was adorable. Marc had nosy aunts like I did. "All I heard is that you called me a great detective."

"Thank you," he sighed.

We entered the Hall of Mirrors. The corridor seemed to stretch to infinity. Mirrors flanked one side while tall windows faced the other, strengthening the illusion that the large corridor-like chamber was outside. Cloudy skies and the steady rain darkened the atmosphere. The forest of crystal chandeliers overhead, and those near the windows, reflected against the polished floors, creating a sensation of walking through an endless, sparkling sky. A symphony of soft thunder and rhythmic raindrops echoed from outside.

Very romantic.

Marc craned his neck and admired the murals on the ceiling. "Want to stay a little longer? The last time I was here, it was always onto the next spot."

"Is this your favorite room in Versailles?" I asked.

"It is. You haven't seen the rest of the palace though. I feel selfish asking you to stay."

Our reflection glowed in one of the many large mirrors on the wall. I liked what I saw.

"Yes, this is where I want to be right now."

Marc approached a staff member near the entrance and returned to my side. "She said it was fine to leave the tour group. We can stay here for a bit and rejoin them later if we want."

He took off his leather jacket and laid it out on the floor. "There're no chairs around here so we'll have to make do."

I sat down on his jacket, cross-legged on the floor. "If they had chairs, no one would leave the room."

He lowered himself onto the floor next to me. "I checked the forecast. There is no rain tomorrow for our trip to Monet's garden in Giverny."

"Tell me, why is this your favorite place?"

He rifled through his messenger bag for his sketchbook and ink pens. "Because this room, to me, encapsulates the ideal fairy-tale castle. Reminds me of the ballroom scene from *Beauty and the Beast*."

"I see it." I brought out my art supplies. "Is this one of the reasons why you wanted to go to Paris?"

"Yes. This was the best place for me and my career. Let's just say that when I told my family I needed to come here, they weren't surprised. That was two years ago, and I feel like I'm ready to move on. I've learned what I can in Paris. I might come back again in the future."

More clues. I tallied up the ones I had, and I still didn't have enough to make a good guess. "I don't have a clear idea of what you do yet, but I'm narrowing it down."

"Do you want a hint?" A playful smile teased his lips.

I laughed and shook my head. "That's cheating."

His nearness strengthened the scent of coffee, vanilla, and sugar. My pencil slipped from my fingers and rolled onto the floor. I leaned down and reached for it, only to have his hand meet mine. The warmth of his skin sent blood rushing to my neckline and up to my cheeks.

Marc's fingers lingered over mine for two more heartbeats before he pulled away.

"Look." He pointed to the windows.

The rain had stopped and the darkened sky was cleaved by the golden blades of the sun. Emerging columns of brilliant light bathed the Hall of Mirrors. Gilt and crystal blazed.

In the middle of it all was him.

"And this is why this place is magical." Marc's dark brown eyes met mine. I wasn't certain if he referred to the room, or me.

"Did you plan this? Like you did with those delicious jams this morning?" I asked.

"If I had, I would have met you years ago."

I bit my lip. It had only been two days, yet I was falling.

We spent the rest of the hour drawing in relative silence, the sounds of our pen and pencil scratching across the page, the absence of words replaced with the steady rhythm of our breathing and furtive glances.

As we continued our tour of Versailles, I took the moments we shared in the Hall of Mirrors and tucked them away, as if they were a precious family heirloom like my grandmother's jade bangle.

The matchmaker said I had no red thread.

Marc couldn't be mine, no matter how much I wished it.

At best we could remain friends. The time we had left together seemed both an eternity and an instant.

We walked the beautiful gardens Marc had described and, after a time, arrived at Grand Trianon, Marie-Antoinette's pink marble palace. The gardens were larger than I had expected, and my feet protested with every step. I tugged on his arm to stop.

"The spirit is willing, but my feet are killing me. Unless there's a helpful little carriage to get us to our next destination, I don't know if I can make it."

"There isn't a carriage, but there is a little train." He led me into the parking lot near Grand Trianon to a stop where a couple waited. "I'm sorry. It is a lot of walking. I walk everywhere, and like to walk, so it never occurred to me that you might not be used to it."

"I should have learned and worn better shoes." I bit my lower lip. "Back home, I drive everywhere."

"Paris is a such a walkable city that I got in the habit here. I didn't walk this much in Montreal." He offered his arm for stability as I adjusted my shoes.

When I glanced up, I noted the twinkle in his eyes.

"You're lying to make me feel better," I accused.

"Did it help?" he asked.

"No."

"The little train goes to every stop. It'll take us to the Temple de l'Amour and back to the main palace."

I almost squealed with delight. "*That* helps. Thank goodness for modern transportation."

The little train was really a beefed-up golf cart pulling along three caravans of shaded seats. Marc paid for our tickets as he found us seats in the first car.

"The way you talk about this monument, it sounds amazing."

"When we go to the main building, I believe you can see it from Marie-Antoinette's bedroom window."

Six minutes later, we walked out into the gardens of Petit Trianon. Against the green meadows and flowers, the domed marble gazebo lured me in from a distance. We crossed a bridge over a tiny brook to reach our destination. It was as romantic as its moniker:

slender columns held a small dome while inside was a lone statue of Cupid. A geometric pattern of squares containing a rounded seal decorated the rounded ceiling. The central medallion featured a torch and a bundle of Cupid's arrows.

"This is all so beautiful." I craned my neck to admire the statue. "I've seen many homages to this back home: they were treated as wedding centerpieces."

"I'm guessing you've been to your fair share."

I sighed and leaned against one of the pillars. "Too many. Don't get me wrong, I'm happy for my cousins and all."

Marc studied my face. "The race to get there isn't as important as what happens after the finish line. That's what my parents keep telling me. They've been married for thirty-three years."

"Same. Mom and Dad still go on dates. It's what I aspire to have." I twirled and watched the beautiful gardens blur into shades of the rainbow. "This place is magical."

He grinned. "We can stay here as long as you like."

An hour later, we ate ice cream on the bumpy ride back. Beauty was bountiful today. I didn't want to take it for granted.

We took a train the following day from Gare Saint-Lazare to Vernon, the closest stop to Giverny, and spent the hour ride debating which was better, the impressionists or the Pre-Raphaelites. Marc loved art as much I did.

Bypassing shops, a café, and the impressionist museum, we made our way to the main house. Entering the two-story building, we were funneled into its most fascinating room, Monet's studio. Paintings hung floor to ceiling in the large room, and yet the space was peaceful. There was plenty of room for seating, and a working area where Monet probably also entertained guests and fellow artists.

Light flooded in from the big picture window facing the gardens. I was drawn to the gardens. Standing where the master's inspiration flourished would nourish my artist's soul.

Leaving the house, we snapped a few photos of the chickens for my cousins, and wandered the main garden before descending through an underground passageway, and then ascending to the water lily garden. Yellow irises, tulips, and lupines exploded into color against the grass and the glass-like pond. A perfect location to use the watercolors Uncle Michael had given me.

Marc and I found a spot near one of the green Japanese bridges with an overhang of pinky purple wisterias in the shadow of a small bamboo grove. He helped me set up my paints but didn't open his sketchbook, opting to watch while I captured the idyllic scene before me.

"You're not going to see a master class by any means," I warned him.

"I like watching you work. It's soothing. You're very methodical." Marc leaned over and pointed at the pinks I'd been blending. "You need patience to work with watercolors."

"I wish I painted more, but between work and family, there isn't much time left."

"You're on vacation. You're supposed to be having fun and relaxing."

A gentle breeze carried the fragrances of the garden to us: the heady bouquet of florals along with a few stray petals. Marc reached out and plucked a pink one from my hair. The way he looked at me made me wish for everything I couldn't have.

"Are you sure you don't want any hints?" he asked.

"No. I want to win this my way."

Thirteen

After helping me pack, Marc escorted me to a nearby crêperie in a beautiful late-nineteenth-century two-story manor for lunch. The manor had been converted into a hotel with an adjoining restaurant. Marc requested a table on the open terrace to take advantage of the gorgeous weather.

We settled into emerald-green metal chairs under a matching umbrella. The server appeared and, after speaking with Marc, brought a carafe of peach iced tea.

"I picked out something sweet and savory. I hope you like it." He unrolled his cloth napkin.

"We're sharing like last time?" I asked.

"Of course. Best way to eat is to share. You get to taste everything, and it shows you like the company you're keeping."

I studied his hands with their elegant long fingers and clean, trimmed nails. I couldn't forget how the rough calluses felt against my smooth skin. He could be a sculptor or musician.

"What are you thinking right now?" he asked.

"Your job. I'm fairly certain you work with your hands, and you work in the creative field. I don't have anything else."

He smiled. "You're right on both counts. You have one day left. Do you think you can solve it?"

"Auntie Faye once figured out who my cousin Deanna was secretly dating: who he was, who he worked for, and where his family was from. Keep in mind Deanna was vacationing in Marrakesh at the time and, even with the seven-hour difference, my aunt knew what they ordered at the restaurant." I lowered my voice. "The same detective blood flows through my veins."

Marc laughed. "Are they spying on you now? These aunties of yours?"

"No, because I'm staying with Aunt Evelyn. She's one of them."

The server arrived with our meal. On my plate was a dessert crêpe. Slices of banana rested on a lake of Nutella along with a large scoop of vanilla ice cream. Three pom-poms of whipped cream dotted the corners of the golden, folded triangle. Marc had ordered a galette, which had been folded into a square. The savory crêpe's lacy edges framed a cream sauce with chopped chanterelles and diced smoked ham.

"Which should we eat first?" I asked.

"Dessert, of course. The ice cream will melt otherwise."

Before I finished dividing the crêpe into two equal parts, my phone rang. Only three people knew my new number: Aunt Evelyn, Uncle Michael, and Ma. I grabbed the phone from my purse and checked the screen. Auntie Faye.

Marc took over and separated the dessert crêpe into two. "Do you need to take it?"

"Yes, I'm sorry." I answered the call. "Hi, Auntie Faye! I'm surprised to hear from you."

My aunt tsked. "Ah, Vanessa, you're not busy, are you?"

"No, not at all." I mouthed another apology to Marc, who watched me with amusement.

"Linda called asking about Evelyn's house. I talked to Zeny Chieng, big real estate agent. She's a client of mine. Zeny tells me that the house went on the market right when you flew out. I went with Zeny and got inside. The house is empty! There's nothing left. Even her car is gone."

"You're saying she planned to move here without telling anyone? Even you didn't know?"

"No, I thought she was redecorating when she did a furniture purge earlier this year. Your uncle Damon told me about the tea shop expansion, but he mentioned it was complicated. I didn't ask at the time what he meant, but I'll invite him to lunch tomorrow."

"What do you think is going on with her?" I asked.

There was a short pause followed by a sigh. "Evelyn always did her own thing. I still remember how shocked we all were when she left for Paris after college. The evening of her graduation she boarded a plane and was gone! No one knew she was leaving."

"What was she doing?"

"I don't know. No one talked about it. I can try and find out, but I can't guarantee anything. I'll call you again when I have something. Have fun on your date, Vanessa," she said with a giggle before hanging up.

"One of your infamous aunties?" Marc asked.

I nodded. "Yes. She's the equivalent of a Chinese godfather."

Marc lifted a spoonful of the vanilla ice cream to my lips. I obliged. It melted on my tongue, and the hint of citrus at the end surprised me. "This is really good."

"I'm pretty sure they make it in house." He paused. "I couldn't help but overhear. Sometimes, people keep things quiet for a reason, mostly to prevent collateral damage. Compartmentalizing lets some folks function better than facing whatever it is they're hiding."

"Is this your professional opinion?" I joked.

His serious expression faltered when he laughed. "No. My mom is a clinical psychologist. I absorbed a bit of it over the years by proximity."

"My parents are both accountants, and I 'absorbed' that so much that I became one myself."

Marc heaped a generous portion onto my plate. "Have you thought of doing anything else, or is that what you want to do?"

As a Yu, I was often asked if I was in the tea export business, or the accounting and law firms that supported it. I didn't mind accounting. I'd been good with the language of numbers without much effort. Like a comfortable dent in the couch, I fit into my job with the ambivalence associated with doing the laundry.

"I like it, but I don't love it," I replied. "Do you love your job?"

"I do. It is why I came here. I woke up every morning looking forward to doing what I love. Well, that's not completely accurate. I've had a different and amazing reason to wake up the last few days."

He lifted a dark brow and stared at me.

I blushed.

Auntie Faye called it a date, but I wouldn't—couldn't. Like Cinderella at the ball, we had tomorrow, and then my fairy tale would end. I didn't want to think of anything else but enjoying the present.

Marc dropped me off at our usual spot. We agreed to meet at the same time tomorrow morning. As I made my way along rue de

Montalembert, I stopped to admire the wares in one of the antique shops. Several beautiful paintings caught my eye: an oil still life of roses in a vase, a watercolor landscape featuring a scene in the city, and a spring garden pastel. The prospect of haggling in a foreign tongue curtailed commerce. Ma and the other aunties loved to negotiate, to bargain until the item was won, and to walk away with their prize secure in the knowledge that no seller was satisfied with the price. Sellers were always satisfied in their dealings with me. Too satisfied, to the dismay of my aunties.

Aunt Evelyn had picked a wonderful location for her new tea shop. Kraft paper covered the glass panes of the front doors and picture windows. The painted wooden facade was a soothing shade of deep violet. Gold-painted serif letters spelled out *Promesse de Thé*. The logo was a teacup and a tiny ring on a saucer. Interesting.

Like yesterday, I checked the mailbox and found another envelope: no postage, the addresses identical to the first one. The paper was yellowed by age.

I turned around and headed for the post office. It wasn't a sense of duty so much as helping someone out there who might be expecting this letter. I couldn't imagine the patience involved in waiting for traditional mail when technology facilitated instant communication.

As I returned from my errand, the aromas coming from the kitchen enveloped me in a thick blanket of homesickness. Aunt Evelyn was cooking lo mein noodles in a wok. Hisses of steam released the fragrances of sizzling onions, slices of beef, and ginger into the air. The table held a plate of stir-fried prawns with bright red Thai chilies.

I started setting the table. "This looks so good. Thank you, Auntie," I said as I took down additional plates from the shelves.

"I figured we both needed a dose of home."

But which home? San Francisco or Paris?

"Who is looking after your house while you're here?" I asked.

She stopped stirring for a second. "It's taken care of."

Not quite a lie yet, but not the whole truth. I hoped she would reveal more once we'd reached a deeper connection during my time here. I wanted her to trust and confide in me, to know I had her best interests in mind.

Aunt Evelyn turned off the heat, pulled a large ceramic bowl from the cupboard, and transferred the noodles from the wok to it. "I need to focus on the store here. I have too much invested in its success."

"I figured you're operating it like a franchise. It's a part of the family business, right?"

She shook her head. A shadow fell over her beautiful face. She banished it with a mustered smile. My aunt guarded her secrets. Disclosure would come only on her terms.

"What's wrong?" I asked.

"Oh, it's nothing." She helped herself to the prawns. "What's important is that you have one more day with Marc. And yes, I had another vision about you two."

"What did you see?" I asked.

Aunt Evelyn pressed a finger to her lips and winked.

Fourteen

I checked in with Ma after dinner. She received her assignment from Auntie Faye. The Yu women were rallied under one cause: to investigate one of their own. I acknowledged my guilt in starting their crusade. My only comfort lay in the certainty that the aunties would have found out anyway. They always had.

Aunt Evelyn greeted me in the morning surrounded by a stack of papers.

"Bring the umbrella."

"Another prediction thing?" I asked.

My aunt smiled. "No, a weather thing. It'll rain today and you'll miss climbing the Eiffel Tower. Don't worry, you'll get your visit another time."

I opened my mouth to ask her for hints, but decided against it.

She watched me with avid interest, leaving her work aside for the moment. "Do you want to know anything more about today? Aside from the weather forecast, that is."

"I do. I like Marc, and I feel like I'm getting attached. I'd rather know now that this is really the last day I'm spending with him. Is there a chance for more?"

Madam Fong said I had no red thread. Pursuing a long-term relationship with Marc was impossible, yet I wanted it. My romantic history was littered with shattered possibilities. For once, I would have loved to see something survive.

"Be careful what you wish for." Aunt Evelyn folded her fingers together, resembling a church steeple. "You and Marc aren't meant to be long term. Today will be memorable for both of you. After that . . ."

I allowed myself a twinge of disappointment. To wade deeper into the lake of self-pity would tarnish any joy on the horizon. "Thank you."

"Oh, dear one"—her voice softened into a whisper—"be thankful you at least have today."

I crammed my emotional baggage back into the closet and headed out the door.

Marc was on his phone when I arrived. His shoulders were hitched high to his ears, and if the muscles of his body were a string, they would be tangled into a Gordian knot. His harsh, clipped tone harnessed his command of French into a weapon.

I couldn't catch anything from the conversation except from the clear body language: it must be another call from work.

His hand clenched into a fist around his phone. He'd been so locked into the call that he only noticed my presence after he hung up. "I'm sorry. Things are blowing up at work."

"If it's that stressful, can you find another job?"

"I can, but I have too much at stake where I am right now. My field is competitive. I'd rather leave on good terms. Recommendations are important." The tension he carried melted away. Marc flashed a smile. "This would be easier if you already knew what I do."

I hadn't made much progress in our little game. If I'd been fluent in French, I'd have known what his job was after the first phone call. He carried no physical signs other than the faded scars on his hands. He wasn't a contractor or a freelancer because he had a boss, not clients. The elevated stress levels at his work environment indicated he worked with a team.

"I promise you that I'll guess by the end of the day."

He stuffed his phone into his leather bag. "We never talked about your reward, did we?"

"I thought having your services as my tour guide was my prize."

"No," Marc laughed. "You get to win something." He held out his hand. "Come on, let's get our day started."

I placed my hand in his. He squeezed. Feeling our hands together, fingers intertwined like woven reeds in a rattan basket, I longed for what I couldn't have. Tomorrow was for worrying, but today was for living. I was a carefree tourist out on a date with a charming chaperone.

Marc and I headed up the stairway from the Champ de Mars station. Rain descended in steady curtains, obscuring the Eiffel Tower in the distance. The panorama was Gustave Caillebotte's oil painting *Paris Street; Rainy Day* come to life.

The sound of the drops hitting metal surfaces reminded me of constant applause by unseen hands. We ducked into a nearby café to escape the downpour. It had been sunny when we left Rue du Bac Station.

"No worries. We can go another time. The rest of the day is going to be spent indoors anyway at galleries and museums." He reached into his pocket for his tiny notebook and scratched something off. "We'll head to Voltaire Station next."

"You're not bothered by the change in plans?" I asked.

"Why would I be? It gives me a great excuse to see you again later. Besides, I have a backup plan." He waved two tickets before me. "I always come prepared."

"Meticulous. Must be a helpful trait in your profession."

"It is," he replied. "Details are very important. Everything has to look right."

A visual artist or designer, or even an architect to place such an emphasis on aesthetics.

"Your job is hands on, right? I have a hard time seeing you parked in a cubicle in front of screens all day."

"A desk job would be a nightmare. I never could sit still, even as a kid. I needed to focus and channel all that nervous energy into something productive. My family helped me do that."

I pictured Marc as an adorable seven-year-old running through the schoolyard: thick dark hair spiking in the breeze, little legs pumping, powered with boundless energy, arms outstretched with hopes he could launch himself up to the sky.

"Are you in the family business? You told me your mother's a clinical psychologist. What does your father do?"

"He's a . . ." Marc laughed. "Can't say. It's related to what I do."

I arched my brow.

"You're getting much closer to the answer. I have no doubt that you'll figure it out soon."

* * *

Half an hour later, we arrived at the Atelier des Lumières for the Gustav Klimt exhibit. *The Kiss* was an iconic piece, two lovers entwined in an intimate embrace. The bursts of golds and gilt contrasted with the dots of pinks and purples of the flowers at their feet. This was one of the most romantic pieces of art I'd ever seen in my art history textbooks. The painting itself was a part of the permanent collection in the Schloss Belvedere in Vienna.

"This isn't a traditional exhibit, is it?" I asked Marc.

He took my hand and led me in. "You'll see."

The space was dark, but only for a moment. Klimt's paintings splashed against the cavernous walls: beautiful figures and faces were highlighted by gold and luminous colors. The atmosphere reminded me of the cave paintings in Lascaux and the sense of wonder they must have invoked in the firelight for those primitive painters thousands of years ago.

Marc led me to an empty bench before a projection of *Portrait of Adele Bloch-Bauer I*. The dark-haired woman in the piece had sorrowful eyes and lips quirked as if ready to spill a secret or a prophecy. This detail brought us together in kinship.

"This reminds me of being in a church on a rainy day," he said. "The paintings are the stained glass windows. Sunday masses gave me time to think and reflect."

"Do you still go?" I asked.

"Not as often as I should." He rubbed his neck. "You're not religious, are you?"

"Unless you consider superstition a religion. My family has its own beliefs. It's cultural. There's a mishmash of Buddhism, Daoism, and Confucianism in there that's been diluted by generations of being in America. Think of it as the light Gatsby sees across the water. It's there, not as bright or potent as it could be, but it's still there."

We took our seat on the bench. He scooted closer, stopping when our thighs touched. Marc draped his arm around my shoulders and whispered, "What do you think she's thinking about?"

I leaned my head against him. The closeness was as natural as his warm touch on my skin.

"To me," he continued, "she looks like she's staring at the man who she might have had an affair with."

"So you're in the scandal camp."

"And you're not?" he asked.

"They could have just been close friends, you know."

"That is not how you draw a friend."

I laughed. "Art is art. You draw what you see. An artist translates their environment or ideas onto paper. She's a beautiful woman. Of course her allure would translate to the canvas."

"You're right on that point. I think I can change your mind though." Marc took out his sketchbook and flipped to the middle. He placed the opened pages in my lap.

These were studies of me in a myriad of expressions. Every one was exquisite in its details right down to the tiny mole near my lips and the slight uptick of my left eyebrow. There was one difference: the woman sketched in ink was far more beautiful than my mirror's reflection.

"It's the lens," he said. "The artists' emotions for their subjects tend to influence the interpretation."

I blushed, and caressed the smooth pages. "And what are the emotions of this artist?"

He cupped my face in his hands. "That I've wanted to kiss you from the moment you bumped into me in the park."

"Then kiss me."

Fifteen

Of all the ways I had imagined my first kiss with Marc, I never had this setting in mind: surrounded by Klimt's glorious works in re-created candlelight. It was beyond perfect. His soft lips were warm, tasting like hot chocolate on a cool day: creamy, rich, and sugary. As we kissed, translucent flecks of gold leaf arose from our skin. The fragile wisps took flight, changing their shape into petals before vanishing into the ether.

When we pulled away, he whispered, "We can stay here all afternoon if you want."

"I'd love to, but don't you have other plans for us?"

"I suppose there are new places to make out."

I giggled and covered my mouth with my hand. He took my other hand in his and squeezed.

Three days, and I had fallen for him. I'd been deprived of romance all my life, and this brief taste of what my life could be like was addictive. I was whisked back to my first cliff dive in Cozumel:

the sensation of free falling and welcoming the thrilling unknown before plunging deep into the water's grip. Marc was my dive, my free fall; with him I felt all the possibilities, all the freedom, all the joy. But the dark, indifferent sea waited.

The sea could wait. Today, I would stretch my wings and fly.

We spent three hours at the Atelier des Lumières as new couples do—separated by no more than an inch.

As we exited the metro at Musée d'Orsay Station, the spring rain cascaded in steady sheets. A former train station, the nearby Musée d'Orsay was a long, rectangular, stately building with an arched glass roof. Marc had given me a choice between this destination and the Louvre. I opted for the more intimate gallery as it was already two in the afternoon.

"We can take the time to linger with your favorite pieces. The crowds are usually smaller here."

"Vincent van Gogh's portrait is here, isn't it?" I asked.

"Is that what you want to see first?"

"No, I want to see the other impressionists before we see Van Gogh's works."

I had spent years entranced by these beautiful pieces in my art history textbooks. When I was a child, Ma and Uncle Michael indulged my artistic endeavors with visits to art galleries and museums—my art history electives in college did the rest. But I never prioritized it. Never took the time and effort required to master a medium. Critiques of my work were always the same: beautiful, but without a clear point of view. Art was the ultimate expression, but I had nothing to say, so it remained a voyeuristic hobby.

We stopped at Renoir's *Bal du moulin de la Galette*.

"I love this painting," I said. "Renoir's powerful brushstrokes and his ability to capture the vividness of the moment. It's like I can hear the chatter and the music! Reminds me of a family function. The fashionable ladies are my aunties. Though I don't think they could ever be contained by any canvas."

"The more you talk about art, the less you sound like an accountant to me."

"Well, you don't sound like a . . ." I laughed. "My time is running out, and I still don't know what you do. I've narrowed it down, but not enough for a decent guess."

Marc leaned over and whispered, "Want a hint?"

My competitive nature answered for me. "I can't. It's cheating unless you do it in a way that's not a handout."

"How about two truths and one lie?" His boyish grin was infectious. I tried not to stare at his lips.

"That works. I'll play."

We stood beside one another, arms touching, and fingers intertwined. Our eyes stared forward at the large canvas.

"One: I am a professional poker player," Marc began. "Two: I waited all my life to be in this city and to work this job, but I worry the stress will kill my love for it. Three: Even after training all these years, I still don't think I'm good enough in my field to stand out."

The second statement was true: I had witnessed the stress. Marc being a professional gambler intrigued me: it seemed viable. His meticulousness with details tied in well with how the game is played. However, it didn't account for the scar on his hand, nor did it match the reputation of Paris. A gambler would be in Monaco, not the City of Light.

Why Paris? What is the city known for? Art, fashion, and food.

He denied he was an artist, and never mentioned anything about fashion.

It must be French cuisine: maybe bread or pastry related. An executive chef or sous chef could not have taken three days off. Working in the kitchen of a bakery or a restaurant would explain the scars on his hands and wrists. One more test would confirm my suspicion, but I couldn't conduct it in the museum.

A swarm of first-grade schoolchildren rushed in. They clustered around our hips like overgrown tulips in a meadow in their matching uniforms. One little Asian girl with braids tugged on Marc's sleeve. Without letting go of my hand, he leaned down. She asked him a question in French. His answer prompted an eruption of girlish giggles.

The collective, jubilant noise rippled through the gallery. Their teacher, an older woman with snowy white hair, ushered the children away. The group wandered into the next room to the sound of the educator shushing.

"What did she ask you, and what did you tell her?" I asked.

Marc smiled and pressed a finger to his lips. "It's between me and Marjorie."

"No, it was between you and sixteen other children."

"She asked if we were on a date. I said yes."

I stifled a laugh. "Nosy."

"Honest. She said she could tell by how close we stood together." He nudged me with his arm. "Are you ready to guess my career?"

"I need to conduct one last experiment. Then I'll know what you do for a living."

"And where will you conduct this experiment?" he asked.

"At a late lunch or an early dinner. Somewhere we can get something sweet."

He thought for a moment. "There's a patisserie I like down the street. They have the best choux à la crème, little golden cream puffs with a variety of delicious fillings."

"Don't tempt me into rushing through Van Gogh."

"Why don't we go see him now?" he asked. "I have a feeling you'll want to stay for hours."

Marc led me to one of the smaller rooms on the second level where the famous Dutch painter's *Starry Night over the Rhône* was displayed. Unlike *The Starry Night*, which captured the energy of the universe as seen from Van Gogh's asylum window, the work before us was more terrestrial—a night sky over the Rhône river, a scene one would see on a leisurely stroll.

"I'm guessing you've seen the other painting?" he asked.

I nodded. I had seen his other masterpiece during a visit to the Museum of Modern Art in New York over ten years ago.

"Are you disappointed?"

"No," I said. "Why would I be?"

"Everyone I've seen this with always compares it to the other one. I feel like this"—he gestured to the canvas—"never got out of the other's shadow. I can empathize."

"The other one is dazzling, while this one is quiet, but both are powerful. Sure, the universe is beautiful, but so is life here on earth." I squeezed his hand. "This is far more real. My feet are firmly on the ground. Family of accountants, remember?"

"I don't see you that way. You are an artist trapped within a candy shell of numbers."

His description was apt, contradictions meshing together into a functional person. I likened myself to a half-lit Christmas tree. Dead bulbs represented all the possibilities, paths, and relationships lost. I didn't know whether the bulbs could be replaced or if the defect was permanent.

We left the Musée d'Orsay at closing time. As promised, Marc took me to a nearby patisserie. Pink and blue morning glories and vines covered the two-story building as if nature wanted to reclaim the brick. The balcony above the entrance carried a window box bursting with pansies and daisies along its wrought iron railing. The green doors were wedged open. Inside, the furniture was painted in different colors as landscape murals covered the walls. Marc ordered a slew of sweet treats as we sipped our lemonade.

"What do you think about the two truths one lie?" he asked, stirring his drink. While he spoke, he covered the end of the straw with his index finger, lifted the straw from the cup, and then released his finger, allowing the trapped liquid to flow back into the drink. The repetitive gesture was mesmerizing.

"I think the poker player statement is your lie. The other two fit with what I know about you so far."

"Does this mean you have a guess?"

"I will after you answer my question: If you can serve me one dish you've made, which would it be? A galantine or a croquembouche?"

The galantine was pressed deboned meat encased in aspic, the other, a tower of cream puffs with strands of spun sugar as garlands. I preferred the taste of the latter. Both were notorious in their level of difficulty and considered benchmark dishes in their field.

Marc arched a dark brow and smiled. "Those are tricky to make. I've made both, but I'm better at the croquembouche."

"You're a pastry chef, aren't you?"

He laughed and then clapped. "You're brilliant. What gave it away, other than the last question?"

"Your hands. My aunties are amazing cooks, and I've seen similar marks on them. The homemade jam showed you have skill, but at the time, I wasn't sure if it was a hobby or a vocation."

"Let's have a toast then to your impressive detective skills." He raised his glass. "Well played."

I tipped my head as a substitute for a curtsy and lifted my drink. "Thank you."

The lemonade's refreshing sweetness and tang rushed onto my tongue. The enchantment of Paris and the company of this charming man almost made me forget why I was here.

Almost.

In the depths of the lemonade, a vision came to me.

Sixteen

"Are you all right?" Marc leaned over and moved my drink.

Before I could answer, the pressure of the prophecy built, coalescing in my mouth like a hard, round candy tasting of tart, unripe green mango. My jaw tensed as I clenched my teeth together. No matter how hard I fought, the prophecies always won. They were unstoppable.

"Your debts will be collected. You will be left with nothing but anger, regret, and ruin. Turn away from the game of chance before it claims both your ambition and your future."

He paled before pulling back.

The look in his brown eyes was all too familiar. Each uncomfortable truth bred the same fight-or-flight response. But it was never a choice; they always chose flight, for how could one fight a truth seared in their soul?

Before he could respond, I grabbed my purse and ran.

Our time together had been magical. My last view of him was his face, his handsome, injured face. But it was not his back as he left me alone.

As I stumbled down the street, a searing headache erupted from my right temple. I battled the nausea, lost, and threw up in an open trash can. I heaved until the jackhammer throbbing stopped. The intensity of the episode left me shaken.

Marc had shown me the city, for which I was grateful. My aunt had cautioned me that my time with Marc was fleeting. Memories of these three glorious days would need to sustain me.

Leaving had hurt, but Marc had his own problems. He was a gambler and in debt. Was he also a liar? For a few days, I'd been caught up with the thrill of seeing the city with my beautiful tour guide, but what did I know about him?

The anguish brought clarity: Paris wasn't a vacation, and had never been. Unless Aunt Evelyn could help me, I would continue to ruin lives, including my own.

I unlocked the door to the apartment and headed upstairs. Aunt Evelyn was waiting for me at the dining room table with a spread of foodie comfort: hot chocolate in dainty teacups, and an array of pastry treats: pistachio and rosewater macarons, pain au chocolat, éclairs, and four varieties of mille-feuille.

I took a seat. "I'm sure you already know what happened."

"I do. This is why I lined up early to get these from my favorite patisserie." She passed me a small dessert plate and a fork. "Romance isn't meant for us, dear. Madam Fong is right. We have no red thread, no chance at finding and keeping love."

"It's not fair."

Aunt Evelyn doled out a slice of the strawberry mille-feuille on my plate. The reds and pinks of the fruit contrasted against the golden layers of paper-thin pastry and the vanilla buttercream. I sank my fork into the treat. The scent of spun sugar hovered in the air, reminding me of Marc.

"We can see destinies. The red thread is a manifestation of one kind of destiny. I suppose it is the universe's way to maintain balance."

"It's cruel," I muttered in between bites.

"It is, but I've accepted it."

She sighed. It was a long, drawn-out sound like the exhausted hiss of a weary train pulling into the last station. The family had speculated on Aunt Evelyn's love life for years. I'd thought it had been her choice. Aunt Evelyn kept many parts of herself secret amid Auntie Faye's spy network. I envied and admired her for it.

"You will survive. No matter how hard it seems now, the hurt will fade in time. It does not, however, go away: it's like a scar. On your worst days, it will reopen, bringing all of the pain with it, but on your best days, you'll remember the good and feel grateful for the memories," she said.

"I could never get past a first date. Marc was the longest at three days and even that's gone up in flames." I reached for a bright green pistachio macaron. "We're cursed."

"This is why I warned you to enjoy it for as long as possible."

"Have you ever tried to change this? I mean, there must be something we can do."

"There isn't. The sooner you accept that reality, the easier it will be. Your efforts are better spent elsewhere."

"You mean lessons?"

"Yes. How clear are your visions?"

We shared the same ability, but with disparate skill levels.

I was cursed with predictions.

Aunt Evelyn possessed clairvoyance.

We were as similar as a bicycle with a flat is to a sports car. My aunt had honed her craft over a lifetime. I rebelled against any form of instruction. My aunt wanted the gift. There was nothing I wanted less.

"They're clear enough?"

"Are you able to pinpoint time, date, and location? Seeing a vision isn't much use if you don't have the context. What happens when you get one? Walk me through the process."

I detailed the flavors—what each signified, how I became a conduit for the prediction, and the lack of control or consent over what I was about to say. The prophecy controlled me.

"It shouldn't be a painful process," Aunt Evelyn said. "When I get a vision, I see everything as if the event were unfolding before my eyes in slow motion. I can take in whatever information I need to weave the prediction."

The stern aunt I remembered from my childhood had resurfaced: stony expression, her knitted brows, and the unforgiving line of her lips. I was six again, watching the clock for the painful lesson to end.

"I'm sorry I'm not as adept as you," my rebellious inner child replied.

She frowned.

"Sorry. Old habits die hard." I reached for her hand across the table. She returned the gesture and squeezed.

"These next few weeks will be painful," she said as her expression softened. "For both of us."

"Why can't I see more details?"

"You've been fighting against it all your life: your skill is stunted."

Of course I had fought. People treated me differently. But if I had the kind of control my aunt wielded, things would be different—I would be different.

"My own aunt, and her cousin before her, shared our abilities," she continued. "Aunt Charlotte's command was more powerful than my own. She taught both Beverly and me. From her I learned our fate with love. This is why there has never been a passing of the gift from mother to daughter: it travels along the family tree, surfacing when it finds the right recipient. Had you allowed me to teach you years ago, it wouldn't be so difficult now."

"Are you saying I brought this all on myself?"

Aunt Evelyn set down her teacup and smacked the tabletop. The china clinked in sympathy. "Stop acting like a victim, Vanessa. You have a gift. It's not a curse. If you want to continue to blame it for everything wrong in your life, you don't need to be here."

Seventeen

Ma said I was a good girl until forced to do something I didn't want to do. Aunt Evelyn had learned this when she had tried to coax me to drink tea as a child. I'd already had a habit of blurting predictions and knew what drinking tea would cause. She coaxed, cajoled, and then commanded. I defied her with every molecule of my being. I felt the same now.

Rebellion bubbled close to the surface like a simmering broth. This cursed "gift" both fed and fueled my defiance. With childish logic, I had held my aunt responsible. It was unfair then, and it was unfair now. She shouldn't have borne the brunt of my frustration years ago, nor should she be its target now.

"I'll be better with my attitude," I said.

Aunt Evelyn transferred a chocolate éclair onto my plate. "I understand it's hard for you. Right now, you don't have any control. Mastering your gift will open the possibilities."

"Did you ever see anything involving your life?" I asked.

"No. Aunt Charlotte never did either. I wish I had visions of my future. I'm like everyone else: there're a few things I'd like to change in my personal history."

I doubted she'd tell me if I asked. The disclosure of regrets was reserved for those who had earned it. I was beginning to think I might never.

She continued: "It's not possible to see our own path. Imagine how easily we could interfere and abuse our gifts. You'll learn the limitations have a specific purpose, to protect us."

"There has to be room for negotiation. There must be," I reasoned.

"Of course you'd resort to this tactic. After all, who else taught you better than your aunties?"

I couldn't help but laugh.

Bargaining was an Olympic sport among the aunties and was further divided into two subcategories: hunting and negotiating. Auntie Gloria once stalked online auctions and local flea markets for a year to find a rare starship *Enterprise* cookie jar. The haggling left the seller in tears. Auntie Gloria didn't have a cookie jar collection nor did she care about the sci-fi television series, but Auntie Ning did, and she, in turn, was holding a decommissioned Lladró figurine hostage. As far as I knew, no items had exchanged hands because the negotiations were still ongoing.

"Do you know when I discovered my gift?" my aunt asked.

I shook my head and nibbled on the éclair with the fluffy chocolate hazelnut buttercream filling.

"I was five. My piano teacher and I were having tea. I saw a vision of her getting married. Miss Hartnell was quite amused when I told her. Months later, when she did walk down the aisle, she thanked me. I still remember what she said: 'The future is the hardest creature to see. It hides and deceives with its promises of blessing and disaster. When you shared your gift with me, you gave me the clarity I needed.'

"For centuries, the women in our family used our gift to see, a line of passive observers who herald fortune and cataclysm. You must internalize the core principles of fortune-telling before you can begin to control your visions."

"And they are?" I asked.

She held up her fist and uncurled a finger with each successive tenet.

"One, all predictions are true descriptions of the future's current course.

"Two, you cannot compel a prophecy.

"Three, a fortune-teller cannot see her own future.

"Four, creating false predictions has dire consequences.

"Five, a fortune-teller does not have a red thread."

I could see the twisted logic behind the rules. If a seer could compel a prophecy regarding her own future, she could act to avoid it, which would violate the first rule. A prohibition against false predictions ensured allegiance to the truth. And the fifth rule was cosmic balance, as Aunt Evelyn had said.

"Where do we go from here?" I asked. "Are there essays I need to write or books I need to read?"

"This isn't one of your college courses. It's all practical application. Everything I know, I learned through the trials and errors of those before us. There isn't a handbook to study. What I'm going to teach you is how to listen to your gift and maximize it."

My aunt helped herself to another serving of mille-feuille and unloaded another slice on my plate.

I felt I was in Rembrandt's *The Anatomy Lesson of Dr. Nicolaes Tulpe.* Instead of muscles and bones, though, my study was prophecy. It was impossible to know how many students had passed the course, or whether I would too.

"Where do we start?" I asked.

"Practice." She paused to pour herself more tea. "Your fortune-telling is erratic. I suspect there's a backlog of prophecies you need to purge. The first step is to submit to the process."

I winced, but I had promised to comply with whatever form of torture she had in mind. After all, my aunt had been transparent about how difficult this would be.

"When you start helping me in the tea shop tomorrow, you will be responsible for sampling tea with the customers."

"The tea will compel a prophecy," I said. "Isn't that breaking the second rule?"

"In this case, no. We need to eradicate the stockpile. It's not compelling when you're running a surplus. How much of one, we'll find out."

Tomorrow, I'd be barraging strangers with predictions I didn't want to dispense and for which they hadn't asked. All the traumatic memories of my past rose to the surface: Mrs. Ferguson's accusing and horrified glare, a broken Cynthia at her wedding, the tears in Dad's eyes, and Marc's face holding an expression I could only call a cocktail of shame, shock, and betrayal.

She studied my face. "Don't look so deflated."

I forced my mouth into a toothy smile. "I'm ready to learn even if it kills me."

She laughed. "Good. You'll need that attitude."

I spoke from the heart. I was done running from my problems and resenting my helplessness. In time, and with dedication, I could be like my aunt, living a normal life, being respected by others, and making predictions with confidence.

With my aunt's help, I, too, would master my destiny.

Eighteen

My dreams had been murky, uneasy, and surreal. Whispers from faces obscured by veils of red silk spoke a language I could not understand. I awoke discombobulated, fumbling for solid ground. After a muted breakfast of eggs and toast, we made our way downstairs as Aunt Evelyn inundated me with a topical course on the intricacies of tea blends and types. One hour before the shop opened and I still couldn't stop my hands from shaking.

"Green, black, white, yellow teas are determined by the level of processing and the common leaf used: the *Camellia sinensis*. Remember, tisanes are herbal blends and are not teas. The shop sells both."

"This is for my own personal knowledge, right? I won't be talking much to the customers. I mean, I don't speak the language."

My aunt unlocked the front door of the shop. Her keys jingled on a jeweled butterfly keychain I hadn't seen before: a Menelaus blue morpho. Aunt Evelyn and Uncle Michael had taken me to the Conservatory of Flowers in San Francisco in my early teens. We walked into a beautiful crystalline greenhouse for their butterfly exhibit. As we approached the orchids, blue butterflies appeared, dancing, and surrounding my aunt as though she were a princess in a fairy tale. She had tears in her eyes that day.

My aunt's aesthetic had carried over from her Victorian in San Francisco to her tea shop in Paris, Promesse de Thé. Shades of lavender, rose, periwinkle, and sage matched the fresh floral arrangements of roses and peonies in the front windows. Clear glass jars lined the shelves behind the counter bearing labels of the hundreds of custom tea blends. The serenity of the interior's ambience reminded me of Renoir's *Two Sisters (on the Terrace).*

For years, my aunt had a tea shop in San Francisco's Chinatown. We'd visit whenever Ma had a craving for good dim sum. On a recent trip, Aunt Evelyn brought us to Qiao's Cafe, a tiny restaurant a few doors down, for the most delicious dumplings. It became popular with the cousins. Keeping a hidden gem to yourself was impossible in my family when it pertained to amazing food.

My aunt busied herself with rearranging the flowers. Before I could offer to help, she held her hand up and made a telephone gesture with the other. Seconds later, my phone rang. It was Ma. I had missed our check-in last night. Aunt Evelyn and I had decided to share a bottle of ten-year-old Loire Valley chenin blanc while rewatching *Roman Holiday*.

"I missed you," Ma said. "Are you too busy with your new boyfriend?"

I lowered my voice. "That didn't work out. He has a gambling problem."

"*Aiyah!* That isn't something you want anyway. He will break your heart and your bank account. You remember Jade's ex-boyfriend? The one that tried to pressure her to give him money because he likes to bet on sports. Not good. You need a nice boy who will cook for you. Maybe a chef? I'll ask Faye if she knows anyone."

Ma had already moved on from one prospect to another without missing a breath. I knew better than to get in the way. It was clear where my stubbornness came from. A Chinese mother's marriage intentions for her daughter were set at conception; the countdown to her betrothal commenced with her first breath. Overwhelming desire to control and to love resulted in affectionate suffocation. We children endured, only to perpetuate the process.

"No, Ma. I don't have time for that right now."

She let out a series of tsks. "You're in the city of romance with beautiful people everywhere. I'm only trying to help. How are the lessons going?"

"We start today. It's going to be hard, but I promise I will try my best."

"I have faith in you. Your father wants me to tell you that he misses you and that everything is being handled here. He said he'll wait until you come home to finish watching that horror show with you. Apparently, the new season was released."

I laughed. "Tell Dad that I miss him and I appreciate it."

"Oh!" My mother lowered her voice. "Faye found out more information about the sale of the house. She talked to Jeannie Ching, who runs a storage and moving company. Jeannie told her that a year ago, Evelyn had started downsizing, auctioning off most of her antiques, keeping her favorite pieces in storage for Paris. She had been planning to move for over a year."

I glanced over at my aunt, who hummed as she spritzed the roses and peonies. I waved and indicated that I was heading outside to take the rest of the call. With my aunt's preternatural senses, it wouldn't be a surprise if she already knew we were gossiping about her.

"Sounds like this was planned for longer than we thought," I said.

"There is something in Paris she wants. We don't know what it is yet, because why would she move there? It's so far away from the family." A note of wistfulness crept into Ma's steady voice. "Evelyn always followed her own heart. We always knew she was different, but when we're all together, it doesn't seem as obvious."

The sisterhood of aunties reeled from the loss of one of their own. The bite of betrayal slid between Ma's words: unspoken, but as palpable as the fresh gold paint on the tea shop's lettering above my head.

"She'll probably still visit. You haven't lost her."

"It's not the same." Ma sighed. "All we care about is that she's happy. Then it wouldn't be so bad that she's so far away. Do you know if she is?"

I peeked through the glass windows. Aunt Evelyn had moved on to setting a tea service display for samples. Her movements showcased a ballerina-like elegance I could never possess.

"I think she is. I haven't seen any indication otherwise."

"I better let you go. It's your first day of lessons. Listen to your auntie and try not to argue with her. I love you and I'll call you soon."

"I love you, too, Ma. Send Dad my love."

I tucked the phone into my pocket and went back inside the tea shop.

Aunt Evelyn gestured toward the tea service on the glass counter. "You'll be offering honeyed chrysanthemum tea for sampling today." She placed a notecard on the counter and tapped it. "It's all here in French so you don't need to explain."

I swallowed, and took my place behind the counter. "I'm not expected to make small talk, right? Only compel predictions and empty the surplus."

"Correct." She walked to the glass door and flipped the sign. "We have work to do."

Nineteen

A fashionable couple in their late forties came into the shop. She had copper skin and wore an ivory sweater and dark, tailored pants. Her dark hair was swept up in a colorful scarf, which complemented her gold hoop earrings and bright red clutch. Her partner sported a sharp navy suit, horn-rimmed glasses, and a trimmed beard.

I envied their easy elegance. I agonized over what to wear, but never felt my choice matched my vision. It was the same frustration I carried when I couldn't translate my ideas to paper. My ambition never quite matched the execution.

Like the couple, my aunt's sense of style appeared effortless. Aunt Evelyn had decided today's dress code: lavender blouse paired with a sage-green pencil skirt. It wasn't something I'd pick out. I tended to stay away from greens, fearing it would malign my complexion. The key was saturation: the brightness and depth of the two colors complemented my skin. The combination was beautiful and striking, and matched the overall aesthetic of the tea shop.

The pair and my aunt spoke rapid French and exchanged smiles. While my aunt offered the lady samples from three glass jars behind the counter, he walked toward me and gestured to the tea. I poured him a cup, shook my head, and pointed to the sign to indicate that I didn't speak the language.

Before he took a sip, he thanked me in accented English.

He knew English.

My heartbeat galloped against my rib cage.

I was about to assault this poor gentleman with advice I had no desire to dispense. The need to run back to the apartment and lock the door behind me took hold. From across the shop, Aunt Evelyn leveled a steady glare in my direction. Her sixth sense was equal parts unnerving and aggravating. Like an elementary school teacher writing on the chalkboard, she had eyes at the back of her head. Punished for my perceived transgression before I had a chance to conceive it.

He finished the tea and returned the teacup to the art nouveau–style silver tray. Three stray droplets clung to the bottom. They were enough. Taking a deep breath, I grasped the edge of the counter to steady myself. My stomach churned as though trapped in one of those centrifugal carnival rides.

My cousin Chester tried to force a prediction once. He was rewarded with a surprise tackle from a runaway Pyrenees that had escaped its leash. The timing was no coincidence. I had witnessed what happened to anyone who forced a prediction. I'd never been foolish enough to attempt it for myself, yet my aunt had reassured me.

I needed to trust her.

The prophecy coalesced as the taste of tangy Sinigang, a Filipino tamarind-based broth, sang on my tongue. "*In the grip of a wintry spring, your father will wander the streets of Zurich. Pneumonia will claim him.*"

Tears gathered at the corner of my eyes as I let out a sob. He froze, and looked down, avoiding my eyes.

My aunt came over and spoke in a gentle tone. Though I could not understand the words, I knew she was offering him comfort and guidance. The lady held him in her arms and escorted him from the shop.

A dull ache radiated from my right temple. For a brief instant, the lights in the tea shop shimmered blue before dimming. A network of frost spider-webbed the picture windows, then melted into droplets clinging to the glass.

"Are you all right?" Aunt Evelyn asked.

I placed the empty teacup in the sink behind the counter. The ceramic clinked against the metal sink, betraying my shaking fingers. "I got a headache from the prediction. They started before Cynthia's wedding. The worst was after I predicted Dad's best friend was going to die, and yesterday with Marc."

"Why didn't you tell me earlier?" Aunt Evelyn asked. "This is important."

"I wasn't sure they were connected. I am certain now." I rubbed my temples. "I'm thankful this one isn't as intense, but as bad as I feel, I can only imagine how much worse it is for him. I just told him his father will die."

Aunt Evelyn moved to my side and placed her hands on my shoulders. "You warned him. You did good."

"How is this good?" I asked. "He didn't come in here this morning expecting a tragedy. How many people do we have to foresee die? Should I be keeping count of how many lives I've ruined? Is there a quota you're aiming for?"

Aunt Evelyn tapped my shoulder. "Remember, you are not the message, you're only the messenger. Whatever you say, they can easily dismiss. No one is forcing them to listen."

"But," I protested.

"You're a stranger to them. Put it this way: How would you react if someone you didn't know told you about your future?"

"I would ignore them."

"No one has to listen to us, Vanessa. It's their choice. People can ignore what they've heard. Believe it or not, most people are like you—they refuse to listen to anyone who tries to tell them how to live their lives."

The grips of sorrow eased as I laughed at her pointed jab.

"Plus," she continued, "I think you've missed the point of this exercise."

"Which is?"

"You've given a prophecy and survived. You were worried about compelling them. This should ease your mind." She smiled. "You're doing fine. As for the headaches, I have a theory. I believe they're due to the surplus of predictions stored inside you. You've been fighting them all your life. This was the prophecy's way of fighting back."

I grimaced.

"The more predictions you have, the less pressure there will be. Death was the catalyst. Trust me."

I resumed my position behind the counter.

A perky twentysomething brunette and her two girlfriends swept in. Their energetic chatter and giggles were infectious. They carried tiny pastel-colored paper bags stamped with a nearby patisserie's insignia. Seeing them brought wonderful memories of going out for Hawaiian shaved ice with Cynthia.

The leader chatted with my aunt while her two friends approached. One had a blunt, blond bob while the other had swept her wavy, auburn curls into a loose bun. They both pointed to the teapot and the card.

I smiled, pouring them both a cup. The comforting scent of honey and chrysanthemums escaped from the spout. The sweetness in the air reminded me of a warm cup of milk Ma used to give me on those rare cool nights.

My aunt winked at me. The two ladies exchanged a set of giggles before tasting. I'd never had two prophecies occur in the same day.

I rolled my shoulders and willed the tension in my muscles to dissolve. The young women finished at the same time, returning their cups to the tray.

A sensation swelled in my abdomen. Instead of fighting, I succumbed as two flavors emerged, one after the other: the juiciness of medium-rare kalbi ribs on a blackened grill followed by the creamy center of a steamed egg tart. I turned to the blonde with the olive skin. *"You will be accepted into the prestigious fellowship in London. Your path to artistic success is clear."*

She raised a perfectly sculpted brow. The redhead narrowed her eyes at me. Staring into her green eyes, I delivered her prediction: *"She will reciprocate the words you long to speak. The channel will not separate you, for the heart never lies."*

The redhead blushed and mouthed the words, "How did you know?"

I smiled. The joy from their two prophecies filled me to the brim. If all predictions were as benign or as welcome, I wouldn't mind having this ability. Learning to trust in the unknown, with the knowledge that its results could be both catastrophic and beneficial, was difficult.

The resulting dull ache in my head was less than the prior one.

The peonies by the window opened wider, their petals curling, heightening their bloom and size twofold. The pure white flowers began to blush, pink spreading like the lightest of touches until the result was bicolored blossoms.

My aunt guided me toward the front window to observe the three young women as they left the shop. The redhead grasped the blonde's hands within her own. Her naked emotion needed no translation. When she finished speaking, they embraced and shared a lingering kiss. We watched them stroll out of view hand in hand.

"It's human nature to focus on the negative," my aunt said. "You believe misery weighs more than happiness. The world would be an inhospitable place if that were so." She placed the two teacups into the sink and washed them. "They are happy. Hold on to that feeling."

"It's not easy for me to forget that I foresaw a man's death earlier."

"We are the messengers of the future and can't control the kinds of prophecies we see or how people react. We aren't essential to the process of living. Events will come to pass, with or without us."

I accepted the cleaned cups from her, dried them, and placed them on the service tray. Reconciling the true nature of my abilities had never entered my thoughts. I hadn't indulged in any philosophical questions over something I considered an unwanted condition.

"The goal is to get you accustomed to seeing the future. The more you see, the more you'll learn to master it. I believe your reluctance to accept your abilities has hindered their scope."

"Once my surplus is gone, what happens next?"

"We're not close to dwindling down what you've hoarded. Let's see how many more we can get." Starlight twinkled in her brown eyes.

I had the sense Aunt Evelyn was enjoying this far more than she should.

Twenty

Paris and Palo Alto. Separated by a continent and an ocean, a language and a culture, yet the human condition—and its foibles—transcended all barriers. Each customer who bought tea also left with an unsolicited prediction. Some were minor misfortunes: a sprained ankle, a dislocated hip, appendicitis. But there were also three affairs, two marriage proposals, one inheritance, and another death.

Their faces paralleled the gamut of volatile emotions I experienced. Fortune-telling connected the fortune-teller to the people whose futures we witnessed. Death left an indelible mark, one you couldn't wash away, forget, or run from.

As each prediction escaped my lips, the familiar pressure eased like a slackening rope. The emotional energy, ever present, lingered less and faded faster. The headaches had all but disappeared. Compelling predictions had changed something inside me. Aunt Evelyn's drastic methods were working.

By noon I was exhausted and hungry. From across the shop, my aunt heard the sounds from my stomach. She giggled. "I suppose you've built up an appetite after all your hard work. There's a bakery a short walk from here known for their wonderful sandwiches."

She handed me a piece of paper and shooed me out the door.

The narrow streets of Paris retained their dominating aura of antiquity despite the encroachment of modernity. Time crawled slower across these cobblestone roads when compared to avant-garde Shanghai or Tokyo, cities that married the archaic with the contemporary, where ancient temples and glass and steel high-rises jostled to pierce the firmament. Paris had never suffered extensive damage from war. Its buildings maintained their vibrant link to its past.

How could anyone resist Paris's intoxicating, sugary perfume? Hints of brioche, baguettes, pain au chocolat, and mille-feuilles dusted the air. I could have found a bakery guided solely by smell.

A golden sign hung above the bakery my aunt had directed me to. The sans serif font spelled out *Les Trois Chats* in crisp white letters. A procession of painted cats chasing one another in an endless circuit framed the storefront window. Below, colorful daisies bloomed in a long robin's-egg-blue planter box. A beautiful brunette wearing a sunshine-yellow apron stepped out of the glass-paneled front door. She smiled at me.

"Hello! You must be Madame Evelyn's niece. She mentioned you were coming by today," she said in French-accented English. Her voice had a musical lilt. "I am Ines de Beauvoir."

"Yes, I'm Vanessa. It's a pleasure to meet you." I held out my hand.

She grasped it in a firm handshake. Her short, cropped hair and luminous brown skin glowed in the sunlight. I strove to conceal my envy.

"Come on in." Ines held the door open. "We have the best sandwiches in Saint-Germain."

Baskets bearing baguettes and various loaves and round breads faced one wall while glass-domed trays of cookies, tarts, and smaller treats lined the counters. Behind the main counter a giant chalkboard listed the menu in swirling script along with a doodle of the product, helpful for an English speaker like me.

She raised one of the domes. "You must try these. They are called langues de chat. I pulled them out of the oven five minutes ago."

A long, thin, golden cookie sparkled with its generous dusting of fine sugar. The grainy texture crumbled into a pile of buttery richness on my tongue. The citrus zest of the lemon added a bite to the creaminess of the vanilla, balancing out the sweetness.

My fingertips brushed the stray crumbs from the corners of my lips. "Oh, this would be so good when paired with my aunt's teas. Can I get a box?"

"Of course," Ines replied. She began packing them into a brown paper box with the bakery's logo. "You also want lunch, yes? I can put the order in for the croque monsieur and croque madame. Your aunt ordered them the last time she was here."

"How do you know my aunt?" I asked.

"My mother met her at the farmers' market a year ago. Evelyn mentioned that she had been to Málaga, where my mother is from. They became fast friends."

"Did she ever mention why she decided to open her tea shop here?" I asked.

Ines wrote something down on the lid, which I presumed was the name of the biscuits. Tucking her pencil behind one ear, she cupped her chin. "She said she wanted to be here for decades. That this is her chance to be happy."

I didn't understand what that meant. I'd never questioned my aunt's happiness. She appeared content or, at least, never appeared miserable. What was she missing back home that could be found here?

Ines must have noticed my confusion. She leaned against the counter. "Oh, don't worry. Old people have their personal mysteries, which they keep locked up in their chests. After all, they spent a lifetime accumulating all sorts of regrets and wishes. My grandmother once told me that my grandfather wasn't her first lover! He died without knowing the truth. I'd like to think he was happier for it."

Her raspberry lips broke into an impish smirk. I laughed.

The scent of melted Gruyere made its way from the sizzling grill in the kitchen. In my brief time in the city, I learned that the difference between the croque monsieur and the croque madame was the egg atop the croque madame. It would have been wonderful if my gorgeous former tour guide could have continued to expand my culinary and epicurean knowledge.

"How long will you be staying in the city?" she asked.

"A few weeks. I'm helping my aunt in her shop. There's something I need to deal with while I'm here."

The tiny bell above the front door rang. A handsome man with a long, dark ponytail carried a large wooden box and stepped inside. Ines tucked a stray curl behind her ear. He set the box on the counter and leaned toward her.

I didn't speak their language, but I understood their body language. His hazel eyes studied her face as if every word she spoke was precious oxygen. She watched him under a thick sweep of her curled lashes. Their hands moved with their voices in a tantalizing dance where the briefness of a touch sent sparks of gold into the air.

I moved away and pretended to browse the crispy baguettes in the baskets until the handsome stranger left.

"I'm sorry about that," Ines said.

"Are you two . . . ?"

She shook her head and giggled. "No, Luc and I aren't dating."

"Can I ask why not? You have an obvious connection. Is he married? Are you married?"

"No, it's not that. It's complicated." Her dark brows furrowed. Someone called out from the kitchen. She excused herself and returned with two takeaway boxes. "There are frites in there as well. It was a pleasure to meet you, Vanessa. Please stop by again and relay my regards to your aunt."

I waved goodbye.

As I left the bakery, a single blue morpho butterfly hovered before my face, darting in a spiral pattern. Another arrived. The pair fluttered away, came back, left, and returned, as though waiting for me. Magic was in the air. Only the jaded could ignore it. I followed the dancing couple. Soon more butterflies joined the company. They undulated in the air like a sea of cerulean petals, urging me onward.

Three days ago, I followed a flying scarf. Today, a flock of perfect blue butterflies. They led me down a side street, past a chocolaterie and an antique bookshop. I followed them through large teal wooden doors into an open white courtyard with slender trees and little round tables. The congregation stopped at a restaurant a few blocks from Ines's bakery, swirled in a tight formation, and then vanished high into the sky.

A floral garden mosaic dotted with hummingbirds graced a large wall behind the outdoor seating area. Gold letters blazed in the noon light above the stained-glass-accented glass door. I took a picture and made a note of the address. Perhaps my aunt and I could dine here tonight.

Twenty-One

My aunt and I polished off the gooey grilled sandwiches alongside glasses of her custom blend of iced honeyed chrysanthemum tea. With the shop closed for lunch, we ate in peace.

"Had you been gone longer, I'd have sent out a search party," Aunt Evelyn said as she opened the box of biscuits and peeked inside. "Ah, langues de chat."

"Ines gave me a sample. They're amazing. I think we should have a fresh box of cookies to serve with the tea samples. You can make an arrangement with Ines to figure out what will complement whatever you plan on sampling that day. Maybe she can have some of your tea to sell, or even have it available to serve, to her customers."

Aunt Evelyn beamed. "That is an excellent idea. I'll call her today and see what we can come up with."

"And I found the perfect place to have dinner tonight. Wait till you see it." I plucked two cookies from the box.

"You seem to have had a most productive outing. Where is the rebellious wayward pupil I remember?"

"She's missing," I answered with a laugh. "I am trying my best to be a good student, Auntie."

My aunt nodded, and refilled my glass with more iced tea. "Your efforts are noted."

"Are you expecting me to dispense predictions until I run out?" I asked. "I mean, is it even possible to run empty?"

"As long as there is a future, there will be predictions. Why? Are you feeling discomfort?"

The physical pain I had always experienced with prophecies, as well as the migraines, had eased with each subsequent prediction this morning. I still reeled from the content, but it stung less. My long-held reluctance regarding my ability had been reinforced by the agony I had endured.

"No, it's getting easier," I confessed. "Although I don't think I'll ever get used to giving bad news."

"Painful truths are always the hardest." Her voice had softened.

I wanted to pry. "Well-intentioned interference" ran in the family. Her misty gaze stopped me. She was a lifetime away in a place aching with regret. An invisible veil denied me entrance. I longed to help, but I didn't know where or when she had gone. My aunt kept her secrets beyond where I could go.

"Are you ready to get back to work?" she asked, coming back to me.

"As ready as I'll ever be."

The rest of the day yielded four more predictions: the taste of a flourless chocolate cake for a resolved family squabble; a hint of grilled teriyaki salmon belly for a new business opportunity; a spoonful of ginger-syrup-soaked tofu pudding showing one baby on the way; and the sharp bite of burnt kale exposing a decade-old lie.

Each brought a newfound sense of ease, as though I were riding a bicycle where my wobbling grew less the farther I pedaled. Aunt Evelyn's approving glances added to my confidence. The fear of seeing another's death always loomed over me, but I'd been spared this afternoon.

"Do you have a different lesson for me tomorrow?" I asked my aunt as I helped put the cleaned tea service into the cupboards below the counter.

"It will be the same as today. You're becoming accustomed to your gift, and there's still much room for improvement. I'm waiting for you to show you've advanced. Today, you learned physical pain doesn't have to accompany a prediction. This is an important step. In the next few days, I hope to see you expand the scope of your gifts."

Aunt Evelyn tipped her head toward the window, where an elderly couple in their seventies walked side by side. *"He will surprise her tonight with a trip to Morocco. They had their honeymoon there fifty-three years ago. She'll love the vacation, but hate the citrine earrings he picked out for her."*

From anyone else's mouth, it would have sounded like gossip or fanciful fiction from an eavesdropping writer. According to Aunt Gloria, Aunt Evelyn's foresight was unparalleled even among psychics. The aunties loved to engage in occasional tarot and spiritual readings. They had invited Aunt Evelyn a handful of times with the intention of having her perform. My clairvoyant aunt eluded them. The curious incidents left me with questions.

"Do you remember the time when the aunties asked you to tell their futures?" I asked.

"If you're referring to the year they failed to pin me down for lottery numbers, then yes."

"I doubt that was all they were after. At the time, Ma was worried about Dad's lingering carpal tunnel issues. She was wondering if the second surgery would take. I'm sure that the other aunties had similar concerns."

"Why do you think I avoided them?" she asked. "And if your answer is because I can, you're wrong."

I paused to reexamine what I assumed I had known about her and added the details I had collected during our short time together in Paris: the way she nursed a cup of lavender tea every morning; how she browsed through her curated collection of cashmere scarves and shawls every night and paired them with a vintage jeweled brooch for the next day; her love of foreign films and old Hollywood movies. These observations meant nothing. She had yet to confide anything of substance.

I knew why I would avoid the aunties, but why would she?

Twenty-Two

We are fortune-tellers, not doctors, therapists, nor hedge fund managers. The aunties were asking you to be something you're not," I replied. "I suppose it'd be different if they were seeking a friend to listen to their troubles. They should have asked you what you wanted, instead of only thinking about what they wanted from you."

Aunt Evelyn patted my hand. "You do understand."

Not everything. I kept my hand still to conceal my objection. I still didn't know what she wanted or why she had moved here. She didn't trust me, and I often feared that our brief time in Paris wouldn't be enough. She had kept so much of herself apart from the very people she considered as family. Even Uncle Michael, who was considered to be her closest friend, wasn't privy to her secrets. I knew this because he had told me once that Aunt Evelyn kept her secrets like her jar of valuable Da Hong Pao tea—sealed shut.

"I can't wait to see this new restaurant you've discovered," she said.

I remembered the butterfly garden mosaic on the eatery's wall. "I have a feeling you might already know it."

"If I've been there, I'll act surprised. Besides, I'll be going with you, and that will be a first time for me."

We closed the store, finished tidying up, and returned to the apartment to change. I chose an effervescent blue V-neck dress. My aunt picked a canary-yellow, form-fitting outfit. Her dark hair fell in perfect waves over her shoulders. I had seen her hair down only one other time, when I was six; after a long afternoon of lessons at her house, we spent the evening watching classic movies.

"Auntie, you look spectacular," I remarked. "If I didn't know better, I'd assume you had a hot date."

"Paris is the city you want to take out to dinner. Why not dress up for the occasion? Scandalous, I know. The family back home would have been divided over what was more controversial, my outfit or having my hair down."

"True." I giggled. "You do have beautiful hair."

I reached for my wristlet, but my aunt stopped me. She patted her vintage champagne-satin clutch with a rose-shaped rhinestone-studded clasp. The dispute over the bill was an ancient tradition. As was deferring to your elders. Challenging core canons of Chinese culture could wait.

Aunt Evelyn smiled. "Let's go. Let's see this restaurant you discovered."

On the short walk to our destination, my aunt drew appreciative glances from passersby. Back in the Bay Area, she possessed this aura of mystery paired with a healthy dose of intimidation. Her reputation kept intimacy distant. In Paris, however,

Aunt Evelyn was seen as a beautiful woman, not feared as a Chinese Cassandra.

I pointed to the entrance as the butterfly garden mosaic came into view. "That's the place. I'm not even going to attempt to pronounce the name of the restaurant."

"Le Papillon Bleu. The Blue Butterfly. Shall we?"

I grinned and nodded.

The male host greeted us and we were soon seated at a small table by the window. A vivid shade of turquoise splashed the walls, complementing the gilded mirrors and modern crystal chandeliers above. The table linens were a subtle rose shade, and the rounded chairs, a soft ecru. The pleasing color palette reminded me of my aunt's tastes.

I slid into my seat. "I can't wait to see what they're offering."

We were handed the menus. My aunt translated each item for me. Her fingers glided over the list, lingering on the dishes she was excited by. In the end, we decided on lobster salad, seared foie gras, sole meunière, and the daily cheese and charcuterie plate. We reached an impasse on the dessert menu. Aunt Evelyn suggested we continue that debate after we had enjoyed our courses.

"Did you know about this place already?" I asked.

The corners of her mouth tipped upward while she made a zipper gesture across her lips.

"How did you learn French?" I stacked the menus and placed them at the end of the table. "Did you take it in school?"

"I did. I took what I could. I fell in love with the city while watching *Sabrina*. I saved up and spent close to two years here after college."

I smiled at the mention of the movie I, too, adored.

When the appetizers arrived, my aunt asked for extra plates to share the dishes. The champagne-based dressing tempered the sweetness of the butter-poached lobster morsels, while the crisp, local greens added brightness to the tongue. The spiced glaze on the charred foie gras balanced its richness.

I cut the portion of the foie gras in half and transferred them on the two plates while my aunt split the salad. The best meals created the liveliest of conversations, but the tastiest meals facilitated silence: the mouth had chosen consumption over speech. My aunt and I enjoyed our food without words, reserving our praise for later.

We had finished our plates when a handsome gentleman emerged from the kitchen. He resembled Robert Redford circa *The Great Gatsby*, but with silver-streaked, raven hair. By the dark expression on his face, we had broken an unwritten law or were personae non gratae.

I reached out and placed a hand over Aunt Evelyn's forearm. She responded by covering my hand with hers. The simple gesture calmed my nerves.

The stranger pointed to the door while speaking in harsh French. I didn't need a translation. Based on his acidic tone, we weren't wanted.

Unperturbed, my aunt flashed a radiant smile.

"Hello, Girard."

Twenty-Three

Leave. You're not welcome," he said in English.

Aunt Evelyn made no move to vacate her seat. "I see you still cling to the past."

Girard placed both hands on the table. The added weight caused the dinnerware to crash together. He leaned forward, shortening the physical distance between them. "Don't you think you've caused enough damage?"

"To whom?" she asked with a calm voice. Her hand still covered mine. "If you're looking for restitution, I could be doing the same."

The entire restaurant and I watched the exchange as if it were playing on the silver screen. The tension between the stranger and my aunt rivaled that of Humphrey Bogart and Katharine Hepburn in *The African Queen*. The words left unsaid filled the room.

This man was one of my aunt's precious secrets, and I didn't need the power of clairvoyance to know.

"I moved here with my business. I'm not going anywhere," she continued.

He clenched his jaw while the table linen puckered under his curled fingers. Girard reverted to French and emitted a string of caustic expletives. His dark blue eyes were the same shade as my aunt's favorite teakettle, a rich cerulean.

His volatile emotions rolled off his crisp jacket in puffs of smoke. It smelled like woodsmoke char, the kind I loved when Dad and I went camping in Kirby Cove. The audience in the restaurant had given up all pretense of eating their meals. Every chair—every pair of eyes—was turned to our table and the pyrotechnics display.

"It's been thirty years! Why are you here?" he demanded.

She replied, "Twenty-seven years, one month, and five days."

The crystal lights from the chandeliers flickered. Everything shifted from vibrant color to a monochromatic palette of black and white. The subtle transition amped the silver tones of their skin, added shimmer to the metallic surfaces, and transformed the lamps in the room into starlight. Girard and Aunt Evelyn aged backward, a version of their younger selves. The years melted away through a hazy, cinematic filter, leaving two people reliving the memory of their past.

"Is it so hard to remember?" she asked.

"How could I forget?" He reached out to her, paused, and then pulled back.

She whispered something in French. The softness of her tone conveyed affection that was fed by years of yearning. Her gaze never left his face.

He replied in kind. Words meant only for my aunt to hear. Girard's deep voice conveyed a mixture of regret and anger—as if he longed for the very person he hated.

The tendrils of smoke around him dissipated as the lights overhead returned to their original brightness. The spell broken, the restaurant resumed its motion and color. My aunt lifted her hand from mine, picked up her clutch, pulled out two crisp bills, and placed them on the table.

"We're leaving," she said.

I bit my lower lip and followed her out of the restaurant.

An uncomfortable silence settled over us. She appeared lost in thought while I searched and failed to find the words to comfort.

"Auntie," I said, unable to bear the silence. "Are you okay?"

"Yes, of course. Why wouldn't I be?"

I held my tongue and tried a different tactic. "If you're still hungry, I'd love to be introduced to the world of French takeout."

She didn't answer. We walked along, separated by thought. The siren pull of memories could drown the strongest swimmers and the steadiest ships. Dragged down to the ocean floor, I was still waiting for her to rise and return from what appeared to be one of her most charged memories.

"I do not live my life with regrets. This is the last I'll speak of this."

True to her word, Aunt Evelyn had moved on to listing menu items from the best takeout spots within two blocks. Her refusal to confide in me stung.

We decided on a gorgonzola cream pizza with fresh herbs and caramelized onions. One of our family touchstones was to eat our feelings. As I bit into the delicate, thin crust of the steaming hot slice, I was swallowing all of the questions I wanted to ask. I could only guess what my aunt was eating, perhaps those regrets she denied having.

The rich, creamy cheese and sweet onions melted on my tongue. I sought the easy comfort that food could provide, which Paris delivered in glorious Technicolor. Aunt Evelyn had already devoured three slices and was onto her fourth when my phone buzzed. It was Auntie Faye.

"Do you mind if I take this in my room?" I asked.

"Not at all," Aunt Evelyn replied between bites.

I headed to my bedroom and closed the door. "Hi, Auntie Faye, what did you dig up?"

"Not even a 'how are you, Auntie'?" There was a pause before she erupted in laughter. "Just kidding. Here's what I discovered after talking to Chloe Lu. She took a language course with Evelyn in Paris. They roomed together as they were both Chinese Americans from California. Anyway, she was a naughty girl and took something from Evelyn."

"What?" I asked.

I didn't need to be beside her to know Auntie Faye was grinning from ear to ear. That trademark smile dripped with the smugness of knowing everyone's business. It was her own form of clairvoyance. "Chloe saved a photo that was left behind when Evelyn moved from their apartment. Evelyn had a boyfriend! Handsome man. She always had good taste. At first I thought it was a movie star, but there was something written on the back. Not in English."

"It's in French." As soon as I said it, Auntie Faye was already onto me.

"How do you know? You meet this man in Paris already? What's his name? What does he do?" Her voice climbed to a higher pitch with each additional question. "Who is he?"

A spasm of protectiveness over Aunt Evelyn sprang out of nowhere, surprising me with a streak of loyalty I didn't think I had, prompting me to scramble to outwit the Yu family's seasoned inspector. "I assumed it's French because she was in Paris. I mean, what else could it be? Dutch?"

"Ah, good point." Auntie Faye tsked. "I'll get the translation. I'm sending a photo of the picture now, maybe you can identify him for us."

"I better go before Aunt Evelyn eats all of the pizza."

"We miss you. I'll call again soon. Bye-bye."

My phone buzzed again with the promised photo. It was the same handsome man I'd seen in black and white at the restaurant.

By withholding information from Auntie Faye, I had made a conscious decision to choose a side. I had to find out what happened between Girard and Aunt Evelyn before the aunties did.

Twenty-Four

The problem with comforting someone who had a secret was resisting the urge to shake it out of them as you leaned in for an embrace. Despite my plying her with a robust local merlot later that night, Aunt Evelyn remained as tight-lipped as ever. She retreated to her bedroom humming a sad melody. The loneliness in those notes hovered in the air long after she had gone to bed.

I stayed up another hour researching Girard and his restaurant. Modern technology allowed me to bypass the language barrier and discover that Girard was a Parisian restaurateur who opened his first restaurant in the mid-nineties and had been successful for decades. Le Papillon Bleu was his oldest and most prized flagship. He headed the local business association and was a part of the city's influential circle. The Parisian gossip sites, however, reveled in his social life: he'd had an assortment of beautiful women over the years, but never married.

Maybe he still loved her.

It would explain his passionate reaction to Aunt Evelyn.

The line between love and hate was often blurred. Back in college, my cousin Chester couldn't stop complaining about an aggressive intern who worked at the same production company. He said he despised her, but by the end of summer, they were making out in the lunchroom. As Elie Wiesel had noted: "The opposite of love is not hate, but indifference."

If time was the balm to heal all wounds, their decades apart hadn't diminished the raw, unresolved emotions between them.

My aunt stressed that I throw myself in my lessons to change my own life, but she didn't tell me I couldn't also add an extracurricular activity in meddling. After all, well-intentioned meddling was encoded in the Yu genes. Dabbling in matchmaking sounded more fun than seeing the future.

The next morning was like any other ordinary day, as though the incident at the restaurant had never happened. I knew better than to ask. Denial and guilt were welcome guests in almost every home. There was a reason why Auntie Faye had a thriving business in gossip.

Aunt Evelyn smiled with more effort today, as if she performed the gesture out of habit instead of sentiment. Her dark eyes remained weary. The incandescent light inside them didn't have its usual luster.

"What are we offering as samples today?" I asked.

While humming last night's same sorrowful tune, Aunt Evelyn opened a large glass jar from the second shelf and scooped some tea leaves into a teapot. "Ginger lavender. It's known to be calming. My blend has powdered honey and a touch of clove and cinnamon."

"Wasn't honey in yesterday's sample too?"

"It was. I found a local beekeeper at the farmers' market who connected me to a collective of apiarists. I had a marvelous time trying out regional honey until I found the right one. After, I found a food chemist to work their scientific magic and transform it into powder." She reached into a locked cupboard under the counter and brought out a smaller jar of what appeared to be gold dust. She scooped a spoonful into an empty teacup, poured hot water, and stirred. "Try it."

The air bloomed with the memories of a distant meadow of wildflowers populated with busy honeybees. I took a sip and was transported to the countryside.

"To say honey is sweet," my aunt explained, "is to ignore the complexities of its origins: the nature of the bees, the colony, the flowers they frequent. Bees turns nectar into their own brand of regional wine."

"I'm guessing your honey supplier is a closely guarded secret, as is the name of your food scientist."

Aunt Evelyn nodded and winked. "When I go on these discovery trips, you should come with me. I'm planning another in six months. You'll get to see France outside of Paris."

"It would make a perfect post-graduation trip."

"Providing you pass."

"Have I given you any indication that I won't? I'm doing well, aren't I?"

My aunt tapped the counter. "So far, but we haven't done anything challenging yet."

I frowned at her choice of words.

"Finish the tea," she coaxed. "Maybe it will trigger something."

I cradled the warm cup in my hands while Aunt Evelyn prepared the tea service for sampling. The soothing drink warmed my throat. Previous premonitions had been presaged by physical symptoms. The honey tea in my cup was almost gone, and I felt nothing.

"If this doesn't work," she continued, "I'll prepare more cups for you to drink throughout the day. You should be able to narrow down location, time of day, precise details. You need the tea as a trigger, but physical prompts aren't required for predictions."

"What you're saying is that I'm still riding the prophecy bike with training wheels?"

"In a way, yes. I'm worried we won't have enough time to get you where you need to be. We may need to increase your workload."

I was hoping for some crumbs of praise at my progress. I'd done everything she'd asked of me. Aunt Evelyn's exacting standards were high, yet I believed I could meet them.

"Vanessa, it's not that I'm not pleased with what you've done, but I don't want you to become complacent or unrealistic. While you've improved, it isn't where you need to be. Your next goal is to be able to deliver prophecies without a physical trigger."

I set down my empty teacup. "I've never done that before. A first time for everything, right?"

"The tea is a crutch. The sooner you're rid of it, the more powerful your gift will become." She moved the tea service closer to the register. "You won't be doing the samples today. Instead, you'll assist me as needed. Oh, before I forget. Can you drop by Ines's bakery right now to pick up more cookies? This way, we'll have them ready, and if we run out, you can get more when you get lunch."

"Will do. I'll be back soon."

Mornings in the neighborhood were accompanied by a steady rhythm of traffic and curious tourists. I appreciated Aunt Evelyn's choice of location. Surrounded by beautiful shops, cafés, bakeries, and patisseries, the tea shop's immediate neighbors were an upscale furniture designer and an antique shop.

Antiquing was a classic aunties pastime and one of Ma's hobbies. Many weekend afternoons were spent at various rummage sales in the suburbs, out-of-the-way country stores, hole-in-the-wall spots, or posh establishments in the city. They only entered the expensive boutiques for fact-finding. Each auntie hunted for specific items, and they were helpful to one another unless it involved a long-running rivalry like that between Auntie Gloria and Auntie Ning. Auntie Faye, for example, searched for vintage costume jewelry, which sometimes overlapped with Auntie Madeline's collection of antique brooches. Auntie Suzanne brought home rare Royal Doulton teacups, while Auntie Annette and Auntie Lulu loved royal memorabilia. The twins, Bea and Belle, competed for rare editions of classic novels.

Above all, the aunties preferred the challenge of a great find at a bargain price. Bragging was done afterward at their favorite noodle shops and dim sum haunts.

As I approached the bakery, I saw Ines filling one of the baskets with brioche. Luc walked in holding a heavy crate and made his delivery. The connection between the two was apparent even from a distance. After he left, Luc took a last, lingering peek at Ines through the window.

There must be a way to get them together. Paris was the city of love, yet it seemed to need a little help.

Twenty-Five

I have madeleines for you this morning," Ines declared as I walked into her bakery. "I think they will go well with your aunt's teas."

She showed me a tray of puffy golden shell-shaped cookies with the last third painted with milk chocolate and sprinkled with crushed pistachios. From the aroma and appearance alone, I had already decided I'd be coming back for a second box at lunchtime.

She began packing them. "These have a hint of orange blossom essence. Let me know what you think after you try one."

"Has Luc been by?" I asked, admiring a display of stacked palmiers under a glass dome. The flat swirled cookies, sprinkled with sugar crystals, called to me.

A hint of a smile graced Ines's lips. "He has. There's a reason I look forward to deliveries every day."

"Why don't you ask him out?"

She shook her head. "I've been dropping hints for years. If he wants this to go beyond flirtation, he needs to make the first move."

I made a note to speak with Luc. I hoped he spoke English. His delivery schedule seemed regular enough. Speaking with him after he left the bakery wouldn't interfere with my morning cookie errand.

"Maybe he'll wake up tomorrow morning and realize what he needs to do." I paid for the package of madeleines and placed my advance order for lunch.

She jotted it down and pinned the note onto the corkboard behind the counter. "We shall see. I've known him for years. He's not one to take the first step. It's one of his more infuriating traits."

"Is he afraid to take a leap of faith? People like that tend to be the ones who are more careful with their own hearts."

"Are you sure you've never met Luc before?" Ines asked with a laugh.

"My uncle Michael was like that. I knew he wouldn't be satisfied until he found the right person who took the initiative. I introduced him to one of the bravest men I knew and they are both incredibly happy."

"Then Luc will need to find his own dose of courage to be able to do what you're asking."

A stream of customers who needed Ines's attention entered the bakery. I waved goodbye and made my way back to the tea shop.

I passed by an older man with a leather jacket and I thought of Marc. There had been no communication since we parted. It wasn't that I expected to hear from him, but I had hoped.

My phone buzzed. It was Auntie Faye. I juggled the cookie box against my hip and checked the screen. My aunt had sent a picture of the back of the photo that contained the note. The handwriting was elegant and slanted, resembling the peaks and valleys of a cardiogram.

"You have every piece of me," I read aloud. Auntie Faye sent two more massive text blocks detailing her conspiracy theories about Aunt Evelyn's mysterious beau. After filtering through the information, the aunties had latched onto the idea of hiring an overseas private investigator. The last message made me giggle: "He was pretty a long time ago, but he might be ugly old."

He wasn't. The years had been generous to both Girard and Aunt Evelyn. Unspent passion was an elixir of youth.

"Vanessa?"

I turned my head toward a familiar voice. Marc stood behind me in a black tee, brown leather jacket, and dark denim. He was close enough that I could smell the scent of sugar and coffee on him.

I searched his eyes for signs that this was an unwanted meeting.

"I didn't think I'd see you again," I said.

"I didn't think you'd want to see me after what happened." He rubbed the side of his neck and lowered his eyes. "You were right. I was getting too caught up in late-night poker games and needed to step away. Work had been stressful and I'd been using them to blow off steam. When I met you at the gardens, I had time to reassess my career, being here in Paris, and my life. You helped me figure out what I wanted."

"And what do you want?"

"You." He reached for my hand and I placed it in his. "I'm not afraid of the truth, not if it comes from you."

He was supposed to walk away. He wasn't supposed to come back. I knew the pattern. I had reconciled my lot. A lump gathered in my throat, and all of the losses I had suffered over the years overwhelmed me. A sob escaped, surprising us both. Marc gathered me into his arms and held me tight.

He whispered into my hair, "I'm here for as long as you want me to stay."

I inhaled his wonderful scent and buried my face against his leather jacket. "I missed you."

"So did I. Seeing the city through your eyes was refreshing." He held me tighter. "How did you know so much about me?"

"It's more than intuition. I have this knack for telling the future. It's embarrassing. I tend to scare everyone away."

He pulled away. "You're serious. Like you can see the future?"

"Yes, but I can't control it. I never know when I'll have a vision, or what it will be about. I'm in Paris with my aunt so I can get better at it, but what I want is to be rid of it."

"Why?"

"It's cost me so much over the years. You're the first to return."

"If they didn't stay, it's their problem. I can't be angry with you for what you saw. It was the truth."

His absolution surprised me. It was one thing for my family to forgive me; it was another for someone outside to share the same perspective.

"The truth is polarizing," he continued. "My mother taught me that when one is confronted with the truth, it's easier to lash out at others than at yourself." He lowered his gaze to his feet. "It wouldn't be fair to be upset with you. I can only imagine how difficult it must be."

"Thank you for understanding." I smiled. "I hope work has gotten better since your time off."

"It hasn't. If anything, it's worse." He groaned. "My boss is on edge. He's been wound up for the past few months, but last night . . . I wasn't in the dining room, but Colette told me he caused a scene.

After she and Henri calmed him down, the boss locked himself in his office afterwards. He was still in there when the cleaning staff left after midnight."

"Do you work at Le Papillon Bleu?"

"Yes, I'm the pastry chef. How did you know?"

"I was there last night with my aunt. He accosted us at our table. They seem to have a history together."

I shifted the cookie box in my grasp. "I don't know much about it though. Aunt Evelyn isn't the confiding type."

"Neither is Girard," he remarked. "Something changed a few months ago, and it escalated around the time I met you. He must have known when construction began on the tea shop. The timeline fits. It might be that he knew your aunt was here, but something's still off."

"If I told you I wanted to get them together, would you help me?" I asked.

He narrowed his eyes. "Why would you want to do that?"

It was a valid question. I'd be meddling in two lives I could possibly destroy with what I hoped to accomplish, but that wasn't what I was worried about. The casualties had already happened. I doubt it could get worse.

Following Auntie Faye's predilection for conspiracy theories, the narrative was simple. My aunt was miserable, maybe since she'd left France. Girard never got over her.

These two people belonged together. I knew this with the same clarity that Aunt Evelyn saw the future.

"Because this feels right. Will you help me?" I repeated.

Twenty-Six

Asking for help was easy when I wasn't asking for myself. Every fortune-teller was missing a red thread but, without a doubt, Aunt Evelyn's match was Girard. By helping them get together, I might bring some happiness back to my aunt's life. I believed she still loved him. That was all the justification I needed.

"Normally, I'd say no," Marc said. "I've seen setups go sour, but this is different. He's already miserable and making it difficult for everyone at the restaurant. It's worth a shot."

"Thank you."

"What is my assignment?" he asked.

"Find out what you can about Girard and Evelyn. Someone must know something about what happened between them."

Marc laughed. "It's not going to be easy, but I think I know who to ask. With everyone at work being on edge, there's bound to be some loose lips. When do I report back?"

"Since you're working, how about tomorrow for breakfast?" I asked.

"Tomorrow won't work. How about the day after? It gives me more time to gather info. There're a few people I need to talk to."

"Okay. The day after tomorrow."

I lingered too long, staring at his dark eyes and his lips. I missed him and his company.

He smiled and whispered, "Do you want something else?"

"Yes, a kiss."

Marc took the cookie box from my hands, and with his other arm drew me into a tight embrace. I threaded my fingers through his soft, dark hair. A playful breeze swept around us as our lips met, sweeping the tendrils of my hair upward, curling the ends into perfect waves.

The gust brought the street to a quiet standstill as a sea of pink petals wafted overhead. The breeze tickled the nearby magnolia trees, shaking loose even more petals to collect in the aerial, floral bridal train. Everyone's eyes, including ours, traveled upward to watch the petals fall. I smiled when I heard the delighted giggles of nearby children.

Marc plucked a stray petal from my hair. "I almost feel bad for the denuded magnolia trees."

"It's beautiful, isn't it?"

"You are, yes."

I made my way back to the tea shop before my aunt could send out a search party. I'd been gone too long, but I had a good excuse.

Marc.

He didn't blame me for the prediction—he wanted to see me again.

If there was hope for me, there was also hope for Aunt Evelyn and Girard. Dabbling in setups was a fun addition to my aunt's curriculum. I had a feeling today's lessons would be more challenging than yesterday's. My teacher was determined to have me do something I'd never done before.

I stepped into the tea shop, uttering a string of apologies to my aunt.

"One more minute and I would have called your phone. Then I saw the snowfall of magnolia petals." A weak smile tugged at her lips. "When will I meet Marc?"

I laughed and handed her the box of madeleines. "I'll schedule something soon."

"Enjoy every moment of it while it lasts." A somber tone entered her voice. "This city breathes fairy tales. Romance runs through its cobblestones, builds its beautiful palaces, and fuels the stone guardians overlooking the skyline. It's so easy to fall in love, but to stay in love?"

My aunt kept dropping hints of a tragic romance, but it was never enough to piece together a coherent narrative. If she hadn't said a word, I wouldn't be so tantalized with the infinite possibilities of what could have happened. The aunties back home never suspected a thing until the sale of the Victorian.

"What was your time in Paris like?" I asked. "You mentioned you stayed in the city before."

"I had studied French in college. It was only natural I visit. Spending my days in this city changed me." My aunt busied herself arranging the madeleines on a large plate. Afterward, she moved to the sink and turned the tap on full, shutting down any avenues for further discussion.

I puckered my lips into a grimace at her reticence. She accused me of being stubborn, yet her current maneuver was equivalent to the childish tactic of covering one's ears and singing to drown out all noise. I tried it once with Ma when I was five. She let me live, providing I wouldn't ever do it again.

Aunt Evelyn seemed preoccupied with washing every piece of the tea service. Twice. When she was done, she rearranged the jars behind the counter while brewing the second tea sample for the day. She poured me a cup. "Oolong. A refreshing blend of white peach and eucalyptus."

I took the tea and sipped it. The combination of the minty edge and the bright citrus of the peach was soothing. My aunt was passionate about tea, and it showed in the complex flavor profiles of her blends. She enjoyed discovering new ingredients.

"As no one else is here, you shouldn't get a prediction." She wiped an invisible crumb from the counter. "The trick today is to have one without the tea."

I responded with a cheerful smile and hoped I could do what she had asked of me. "Do you have any tips on how this is supposed to happen?"

"I can tell you how it happens for me, but I don't know if it will be the same for you." She cupped her chin and furrowed her brow. "Relax and let it come to you. It should be painless. Aunt Charlotte told me that reaching a state of serenity is ideal. You want to be the perfect conduit."

"So wait for it to come to me?"

"Yes. This is supposed to be natural. Exposure to the customers coming in today should help you. You can't see futures without the people they are tied to." Aunt Evelyn walked to the door and unlocked it. She held the sign. "Are you ready?"

I straightened the collar of my blouse as a slight tremble constricted my fingers.

Moments after my aunt unlocked the door, a young couple strolled in with their son. The father, with light brown hair, carried a backpack, which his wife rummaged through. She withdrew a small plastic container full of tiny animal crackers and shook the tub at her son. The little boy streaked around the shop with wobbly legs, giggling, and smearing his hands on every glossy surface. Judging by his unsteady gait, he must have been close to two. My cousin Farah had a toddler close to the same age. The bursts of energy from her child were in direct correlation to the dark smudges under her eyes that Korean makeup couldn't conceal.

When the boy ran to the windowsill where the flower vases were, I rushed forward to prevent one from being pulled down. His parents chastised him for the action while his bottom lip quivered. Fat tears spilled down his rounded, reddened cheeks. He pointed at the peonies. One rose above the others, its long stem stretching closer to the small, outstretched fingers.

I glanced over at my aunt and caught her slight nod. With her approval, I plucked a puffy, white blossom and offered it to him.

His unabashed squeal of delight caused us all to laugh. He buried his face in its petals and clutched the stem in his hand. Having won his prize, he took his mother's hand while snacking on the animal crackers.

I returned to my place behind the counter and tried to clear my head. Once my mind was empty, I waited for a prediction to come to me as my aunt instructed. My tongue searched inside my mouth for the elusive taste, the telltale formation of any prophecy.

Nothing.

My aunt's vague directions left me scrambling to produce a result.

So far, the only thing I could taste was failure.

By the time the family left, I resisted the urge to cover my face with my hands.

"Did you see something?" Aunt Evelyn asked.

"I didn't."

She frowned. "They were here for a while. Are you sure your mind is clear?"

"Yes. Auntie, I didn't see anything. I did what you asked, but no prediction."

She placed her hands on her hips. "Focus is hard. If you can't reach a certain level of meditation, you won't see anything."

The creeping frustration in her voice annoyed me. I was trying, but quarrelling with my aunt wouldn't help me see a prophecy. "Can't we just go back to the tea? We know that works."

"That isn't an option. You can't rely on that, Vanessa."

I exhaled and kept my breathing steady. Aunt Evelyn walked to my side and placed her hand on my arm. "You will have plenty of opportunity to try again today. Focus and I'm certain that by the end of the day, you'll get this."

As if on cue, a busload of German tourists entered the shop. I assisted my aunt with their orders, taking down the specific glass jars she needed and helping pack purchases into printed lavender paper bags. All the while, I kept myself open and clear for any predictions to come to me. I searched for one around every tooth in my mouth, hoping it was hiding and all it needed was a gentle prod.

Nothing.

Despite her preoccupation with the customers, Aunt Evelyn

managed to sneak in a quizzical look in my direction. Her glances increased with every ring of the cash register, as did the tempo of her elegant pumps tapping the wood floor. Clairvoyance wasn't required to sense her growing impatience.

When the group cleared out, she leveled her gaze at me. "There were twelve people that passed through here. Surely you saw something."

"I tried, Auntie." I rubbed my temples. "This is new territory for me. I don't know if this is possible."

"Of course it's possible. Many women before you have done this—for hundreds of years." She paused, and closed her eyes. "I don't understand why your gift behaves the way it does." She started pacing parallel to the counter. The click of her brisk steps echoed in the empty store. Aunt Evelyn was taking in my failure as her own.

"I'm kind of behind. Think of me as the mature student," I said with a nervous laugh.

"There's nothing amusing about this. You haven't gotten a vision. I'm worried you won't. You should have seen something. It didn't have to be specific or important. I'd accept a weather report at this point."

"But it's not like I've lost my power. I can do it if you let me have the tea."

"You said you wanted control. You're not in control if your predictions are at the whim of what you drink. You can't have control if you refuse to change. Predictions are a part of you. You are clairvoyant. We're special."

I kept silent. I didn't want to tell her that I didn't see it the way she did. I wanted control, but not as an investment in becoming a better fortune-teller.

"If only you saw something. It would mean we're on the right path in your education."

I made the decision then. I wanted to ease her fears and to show that there was still hope.

"I mean, I might have seen something," I lied.

A hanging light fixture fell from overhead, striking my shoulder before shattering on the floor. It happened so fast that I almost didn't feel it. I stared at the spot where the glass fell, unsure of what had happened, when my brain registered the pain. My hand pressed against the growing soreness. The sound of a crash echoed in my ears alongside the phantom noise of squealing tires.

"Vanessa!" My aunt rushed to my side and checked my shoulder. "Are you all right?"

Bits of glass and fragments glittered in the sunlight streaming through the shop windows. The pattern of particles traced out skid marks from tire treads, down to the grooves and ruts running in parallel.

She finished her examination. "Nothing's broken. You will get a bruise later though. You're lucky it missed your head. If you had been standing an inch in the wrong direction, it could have been catastrophic."

"Auntie, I'm sorry. I lied."

I had broken one of the cardinal rules of fortune-telling. My shoulder throbbed.

Twenty-Seven

Aunt Evelyn kept the shop closed. I asked her to reopen, but she refused.

"Family above all else," she said.

As we cleaned up the mess, I justified why I had lied. Aunt Evelyn poured the shattered glass pieces into the trash.

"This is serious," she explained. "As much as I appreciate you wanting to make me feel better, this wasn't a good choice."

My cheeks reddened.

She frowned. "I don't want you to be injured or, worse, in some freak accident. It's clear this was a side effect. I want you to promise me that you won't do it again."

"I promise." I consoled myself by stealing three madeleines and nervously nibbling on them.

"You had a setback today." She massaged her left temple in a slow circle. "Aunt Charlotte was strict, but she got results. I felt her methods wouldn't work with you, so I've been trying a different approach."

"You think you've been too easy on me?" I retorted.

"Yes, I believe I have been."

I was incredulous. I had done everything she asked, trying my best. To imply she'd been too lenient wasn't fair. I pursed my lips. "You're asking me to do something I've never done before. You expected results as if I'm a savant, but I'm far from it."

She began pacing. With how hard her feet struck the floor, I was certain she'd break the heels of her shoes.

"If your motivations are clear, then you should be progressing. Aunt Charlotte taught that appreciation for what we do and what we provide for others is important. Tell me again why you want to learn now."

"I've told you already." The thread of exasperation wound itself around my voice. "I need to control this. I'm tired of hurting people."

"You don't appreciate your gift. For you, it's a curse. Without appreciation, you're blocked from receiving a vision without a crutch." She paused in her pacing as her eyes focused on me. "It's important to value your ability, Vanessa."

"Have you thought that maybe all these rules aren't as infallible as you think?" I asked.

"They are there for a reason. You're in no position to question them."

Marc had come back. That proved there was room for doubt, at least for me. "One of your rules is that we have no red thread, yet Marc came back to me."

"We have no red thread. What you have with him will not last." Aunt Evelyn resumed her pacing. "The sooner you understand, the better."

"How can you be so sure it won't work out after I leave the city?"

"Because whatever spell this city holds, it dissipates over the ocean. It's better to resign yourself to accepting heartbreak if you think you can change that." Her hands balled into fists. "I tried once. It's not meant to be."

I lost my temper.

"You're talking about the guy at the restaurant. Why is it so hard to say who he is?"

Aunt Evelyn stopped midstep and turned. "What happened between me and him is none of your business." Her voice was crisp. Each word warned against further discussion.

"Why not? It's not terrible to want love, Auntie. We all deserve to be loved."

"You speak of these things as if you know more than I do. I've been living with this burden all my life. You had the luxury of ignoring it until it became too uncomfortable." She crossed her arms. "You don't know what losses I suffered. What I had to give up to live with this gift."

"Of course I don't know. You won't tell me!" My inner six-year-old emerged in all its rebellious fury.

She sighed as though I were a misbehaving puppy who had chewed a pillow. "I know you're angry. I'm frustrated too. But as I said, family means everything."

"You chose family over him, didn't you?" I demanded.

"Yes, I did."

With that rare admission, the anger I'd been holding on to evaporated. It explained everything. Her dark eyes met mine: they mirrored my regrets. The pain behind them was as palpable as my own.

I realized the truth.

Her silence was born from anguish. Her need for intense privacy was a shield from the people she chose over him. She had given enough to the family and had moved here for herself. After decades apart, my beautiful, brave aunt showed up for a reunion with Girard, dressed in her emotions and intentions. He didn't want anything to do with her. The missing red thread poured lemon juice into a wound that had never healed.

My aunt moved behind the counter and poured glasses of cold-pressed strawberry juice from a small fridge for us. We both took long drinks. The cool liquid doused the flames of our argument.

Leaning against the cold quartz, I said in a soft voice, "Have you ever seen anyone exhibit the same peculiarities as me?"

She took a deep breath. The pain and vulnerability I'd witnessed vanished beneath her usual calm exterior. "No. You are an oddity. The gift has presented itself in the same way for over a thousand years. The classic signs are so remarkable: it is easy to identify a child with the talent. You presented the right way. It's how we knew. Everything afterward was unusual."

"I can't be the only one," I said, half as a joke.

"You're the only one I've heard of, but I can consult my peers."

I almost spit my drink out. "Are you saying there's a secret society of fortune-tellers?"

"There is." She pressed a finger to her lips. "You would have learned about them after your initiation. I'm telling you now because we need their help."

"It's kind of cool that you have a secret club."

My aunt laughed. "I never thought of them that way. These women are my sisters and my aunties. If there is a precedent, they will know. They have the records and diaries of every fortune-teller who's been born."

"Can I read yours?" I asked.

She gave me a hard look. "No. They are available after a seer dies, and you have to be a member to access them. And, before you ask, you aren't qualified. You must demonstrate detailed, reliable, and accurate predictions for consideration. The criteria they'll use to judge you will be more difficult."

I scrunched my face.

Twenty-Eight

Aunt Evelyn vowed to reopen the shop after lunch and a quick trip to Ines's bakery for another box of madeleines. We walked together to a nearby quiet Vietnamese restaurant.

The translucent wrap of the cold rolls transformed their contents into an impressionistic painting of greens and oranges alongside grilled sugarcane sticks carrying fried shrimp paste as tasty appetizers. Thin cuts of lemongrass-spiced pork chops, barbecued to perfection, were paired with colorful Vietnamese fried rice. Over a spread of gỏi cuốn, chạo tôm, grilled pork chops, and cơm chiên, we discussed the origins of Auntie Gloria and Auntie Ning's feud. A bit of family gossip helped ease the tension between us.

"Those two have such a rivalry because they have similar tastes," Aunt Evelyn explained.

When we were young, the cousins and I were shuttled around to various practices. Donna Summer blared from both aunties' minivans. They enjoyed collecting ceramics and watching soap operas, and both volunteered at the local women's shelter. With so many overlapping interests, they should have been best friends.

"I can see that, but they don't really hang out."

"Ning and Gloria will insult each other to us, but if anyone outside of the family ever insults the other, she'll defend them to the death. It's the family way."

"When did this start?"

"High school. They both tried winning Donna Summer concert tickets on the radio. Ning won. Gloria insisted that Ning cheated, but she couldn't prove anything. It was the same year they both had a crush on Tom Lau, the quarterback, which didn't help matters. Gloria won that battle. Years later, we found out both had cheated, and how they did it."

I let out a scandalized gasp.

"I think at this point, the two quarrel out of habit, or for appearance's sake. There's a lot of love there, and we all know it." She paused to pluck another piece of salad roll from her plate. "I do miss them. All of them. When you go back home, it'll be more lonely than what I had imagined."

"Don't you have friends here?"

"Ines's family, and some shopkeepers at the farmers' market I'm friendly with."

Aunt Evelyn made friends easily, but always withheld a part of herself. She had effortless charm, and a grace that disarmed everyone. Getting to know her, however, proved to be a challenge. Auntie Faye said Aunt Evelyn's admirers called her "the Dream" because she was too beautiful to be real and impossible to attain.

"Then it won't be as bad. Of course, you'll miss the weekly gatherings and various occasions, but you'll be back for the major holidays, right?"

"Yes, Christmas, Thanksgiving, and a week or so in the summer. I'll be available after I've hired help for the shop."

I helped myself to more of the fried rice. "Since you know Ines's family, what do you know about her and Luc?"

"Their relationship is complicated."

"Why? They look like they genuinely care for each other."

"His parents have chosen a girl for him to marry. It's a merging of families—his family owns a small chain of grocery stores, while the bride-to-be's are wealthy organic farmers. Ines's family are bakers: they tend to only marry other bakers."

"I'm sure there's a way. They belong together."

"Don't interfere, Vanessa." My aunt's warning tone mirrored Ma's. "You can't toy with people's lives. We are fortune-tellers—our role is to observe."

I held my tongue and noted that she didn't approve of my matchmaking plans. No need to keep her updated then. After all, she was an expert on secrets: it would be hypocritical for her to ask me to divulge mine.

I switched the topic. "What was Great-Aunt Charlotte like?"

"You two would have gotten along well," my aunt laughed. "You both have much in common. She, too, rebelled against our lack of a red thread. Spent her life trying to deny it. She never married, and the few, short relationships she did have ended poorly."

Great-Auntie "Char" was a notorious eccentric who died before I was born. She drove a 1970 lime-green Plymouth Barracuda with hot-pink leather seats and racked up a mile-long paper trail of speeding tickets. She was a powerful clairvoyant, and her visions helped the fortunes of the Yu family.

"She didn't die, like, in a strange way, did she?"

"She died in her sleep at eighty-nine with a bottle of Macallan on her nightstand. She was known to take a shot before bed. Fortune-tellers in our family live long lives."

"How many fortune-tellers are out there?"

Aunt Evelyn cut her pork chop into bite-size strips. "It's two per family, and three on rare occasions."

"But you were the only one left after Aunt Charlotte and Aunt Beverly died," I protested.

"Yes." Aunt Evelyn smiled. "And then you were born."

We finished up lunch and headed to Ines's bakery side by side. Ahead of us, Luc had parked his white Peugeot van on a side street and was gathering his delivery for Ines.

"Go in without me," I said. "There's something I saw back there that I have to take a picture of for Auntie Gloria."

"Gloria doesn't need more knickknacks." My aunt made a dismissive gesture with her hand. "Don't take too long."

I headed down the street and pretended to admire a stained glass lamp in a store window. When she entered the bakery, I hustled to Luc's van. The rear double doors swung open. He was holding a worn wooden crate in his arms, full of bags of flour and blocks of butter.

"Hi. I hope you speak English." I smiled and waved.

"I do. I recognize you from the bakery. Can I help you?"

"Actually, I wanted to help you."

And with those words, I set my matchmaking machinations into play.

Twenty-Nine

My parents are marrying me off to Liselle Goulet. I've been going to dinners at their house since I was a child. The business arrangement is set." He lifted the crate onto his shoulder. "I can't disappoint my parents."

"Do you love this Liselle?"

He hesitated, then blurted out, "It doesn't matter if I do."

"That doesn't sound like true love to me. After all those mandatory dinners, I'm sure you see her more as a sister than a wife." My comment prompted a long sigh. Had I been in his situation, I'd be rebelling against the whole notion of a business merger through an arranged marriage. "Allow me to put it this way: If Ines was getting married tomorrow—and it's not to you—how would you feel?"

A deep flush of red traveled from his cheeks, past his short beard, and down his throat to the neckline of his shirt. "Miserable. I love her, but I can't go against the desires of my family."

"You've decided to be miserable then. A woman like Ines isn't going to wait forever. If you want her, you need to choose her."

He looked away and didn't answer.

I turned and headed into to the bakery, Luc following three steps behind.

As we entered, Aunt Evelyn frowned. I was sure she suspected what I had done. I blushed and joined her near the counter while Luc made his delivery. He spoke little before making a hasty exit. I hoped what I'd said had made him think about what he wanted.

My aunt muttered under her breath, "Interfering with lives is a dangerous game."

"I'm helping them. Unless you've seen something that says I should stop." I glanced at her. She remained silent. "No? Good, then I'm going to continue what I think is right."

Her dark eyes creased at the corners. If she were one of her teakettles, she'd be boiling now. "You have to think about what can go wrong."

"And what about what could go right? It's not too late for them."

Before she could respond, Ines took a folded piece of paper from her pocket and handed it to my aunt. "Do you know about this?"

Aunt Evelyn read the flyer. Twice. A wispy ring of smoke rose above her head. Her internal temperature resembled a red copper pot left on the stove overnight. She said something in French and, judging by its inflection, cussed.

"What are you planning to do?" Ines asked. "How can I help?"

I reached out and touched my aunt's arm. "What's going on?"

"Girard is plotting a boycott of my business. He claims my teas are inferior and imported. He's appealing to French pride, to patronize only true Parisian businesses."

I rolled my eyes. "That's racism disguised as nationalism."

Ines snorted in agreement and crossed her arms.

"If this gains traction, though, it'll ruin the tea shop." Aunt Evelyn folded the bulletin in half and ripped it—an abrupt, satisfying sound of paper carnage. "Do you know how far these were distributed?"

"A few neighborhoods, including the cafés and hotels. Though I'd think most of your allies are there. I worry about Madame Hebert and Monsieur Chirac. They're close friends and admirers of Monsieur Renaud." Ines picked up the discarded paper and tossed it in the trash behind the counter.

"I know them."

Since I couldn't contribute to the discussion, I listened, and gathered as much information as possible. This boycott made me more determined to mend the rift between Girard and my aunt. He longed for her still. Only the hurt caused by unconsummated passion could lead the man to take such lengths to rid himself of her.

"Auntie?" I asked, interrupting the discussion by the counter. "I'm guessing he wasn't like this before?"

"Combative? Unreasonable? Extreme?" Aunt Evelyn offered.

"Bigoted."

Both women pressed their lips into thin lines. The grooves at the corners of their mouths deepened.

"I mean," I continued, "let's call this boycott what it is. We know you use locally sourced ingredients: lavender from Provence, honey from local hives, etc. France doesn't grow tea leaves. All tea is imported. To accuse you of this is to accuse every other tea peddler in the country. I bet he wasn't like this when you dated. I can't see you associating with this kind of crap behavior."

"You were involved? Oh my," Ines said, her mouth agape as she cupped her cheeks in her hands. "That would explain much. Up to this point, Monsieur Renaud has had a sterling reputation in the city. This is very vindictive."

"No, he wasn't like this."

"Why don't I look into this?" I asked.

Aunt Evelyn looked at me with a raised eyebrow. "How?"

"Marc works for Girard as a pastry chef. He would know more about this."

"Marc Santos?" Ines smiled. "Oh, he's quite handsome. You and Evelyn have good taste in men."

My aunt and I both thanked her at the same time, prompting a giggle from Ines. She finished packing up the madeleines. "I will do my part and keep an eye on the business owners on this street. I'll make sure the lies don't spread."

"Thank you, Ines. Give my love to your mother and father." Aunt Evelyn leaned in and they exchanged a set of cheek air-kisses.

I carried the box of cookies as we left the bakery.

The moment we stepped outside, my aunt uncorked her pent-up rage. "Of all the things he could do. The man's determined to drive me off the continent."

"Have you considered that this might not have come from him?"

"It had his name on it. Girard is very careful about how his name is used. He would never allow something like this to be circulated without his endorsement."

My eyes didn't deceive me that night at the restaurant. He still loved her, had always loved her. They belonged together. Even if they themselves questioned it, I didn't. With my life littered with uncertainties, there were few things I was sure of, but this was one of them. I was as certain of this as I was that my favorite color was pink. It wasn't logical, but it was true.

Our walk back to the tea shop had given Aunt Evelyn time to work herself into a froth. She stormed to the sink and began to scour her hands. Drying them, she threw the used towel against the backsplash, and then broke two madeleines in transferring them from the box to the plate. I rescued the rest by volunteering to take over the task.

"It's going to be all right, Auntie." I placed the final cookie on the plate.

"Why? Because you've had a vision?"

She parroted my words back to me. Instead of being irritated, I laughed. "No, because we can do more than observe."

Thirty

After the frustrating morning, late afternoon proved no better. Aunt Evelyn, disappointed, allowed me to cheat and use tea to ensure I could still produce a vision. I predicted an unexpected visit from a grandfather from Manila, which tasted like a cinnamon-sugar-dusted churro fresh from the fryer. I hadn't made any progress since yesterday, to my aunt's annoyance.

Aunt Evelyn busied herself with phone calls all evening. With my lessons suspended for the night, she focused on saving her business and seeking aid from the fortune-teller society. While she rallied her contacts, I finalized my breakfast date with Marc, caught up with the cousins' group chat, messaged the aunties, and called Ma.

The cousins were envious of my sudden Parisian trip. Auntie Faye and the others had pooled their resources and hired a private investigator. Auntie Ning let it slip that it was standard procedure for anyone marrying into the family. In Girard's case, it acted as a protective measure. Ma updated me on what was happening at the firm, and I spoke with Dad. I missed them both.

I deflected the questions concerning my lessons. Being so far away, they couldn't do anything to help. I treated my sense of helplessness as a potent, communicable disease, which I kept to myself. No need to worry those I loved back home.

I went to sleep with a single selfish worry: Would Aunt Evelyn's focus on stopping Girard's boycott distract her from teaching me?

Marc and I had agreed to meet at our usual spot. Seeing him waiting for me near the top of the stairs, leaning against the metro sign, banished the chaos swirling in my life. He wore his leather jacket with another dark tee underneath and distressed jeans. His dark hair appeared still wet from an early morning shower. As my thoughts traveled in that direction, I tugged on my blouse's collar to let out a small swell of steam from the heat growing inside me.

Marc noticed and grinned. "The forecast for today is supposed to be cool."

I stepped into his open arms and stood on my toes to kiss his cheek, but he turned his head, our lips meeting in a deep, passionate kiss. The breeze swept in, enveloping us in its embrace like a translucent veil. It dissipated once the kiss ended.

I reached up and ruffled Marc's now-dry hair. "Better than any blow-dryer."

He laughed. "Agreed. How are your lessons going? Doing well I hope."

"I'm tanking. Aunt Evelyn says I'm an odd case, and now she's preoccupied with the store. Hopefully she won't forget why I'm here."

We took the metro to an Australian eatery Marc said was known for its pancakes. It was packed with tourists, so we squeaked into a cherry-red vinyl booth. I selected a stack with seasonal fruits, chocolate, and crushed hazelnuts for us to share. He insisted the portions were generous.

Marc handed me a sheet of paper from his messenger bag. "Have you seen this?"

"The boycott notice, yes. My aunt is furious, with just cause."

He creased his brow. "I'm disappointed in him. This isn't the man who offered me a position in his kitchen. This is coded, racist language from someone I consider a mentor. So I did a little digging."

"I hope you found something."

"I did. This garbage," he said, tapping the paper, "wasn't written by him. This came from the desk of Claude Chirac. Claude is a xenophobic kiss ass who hangs around my boss. Vivianne, the kitchen manager, told me she overheard them talking. This might be a case of Claude trying to gain Monsieur Renaud's favor."

"When I asked my aunt, she said that this didn't sound like the man she once knew. She's rallying her supporters to counteract the boycott. Did you find out anything about their past relationship?"

Marc shook his head. "No one in the restaurant has been there longer than fifteen years."

"Auntie Faye found a picture of him from an old roommate. He looked like how I saw him at the restaurant." I showed the picture on my phone to Marc.

He whistled. "That looks like a photo she took of him."

"What do you mean?" I asked.

"You know the saying, about a picture having a multitude of meanings? It was probably taken by her. It's in the way he's looking at the lens, that this is for her, that he's giving a piece of himself, that he loves her."

He pulled his phone from his pocket, tapped, swiped, and then placed it on the table for me to see, a photo of me laughing while holding a pistachio ice cream cone in Montmartre.

"I look at this and remind myself that there's so much more to look forward to," he whispered.

I bit my lower lip. "That's not fair. I don't have one of you."

"That can be easily remedied," he said, grinning.

Before we could take a picture together, the pancakes arrived with their decadent aroma of butter, syrup, and sugar. They were drenched in maple syrup, and crushed hazelnuts mingled with spears of tart strawberries and slices of bananas at the top of the stack. The hotcakes themselves were liquid gold captured in suspended animation and pressed into fluffy disks. My fork sank into them as though they were marshmallows.

"These are so good," I declared in between bites. "Like unreal good."

He lifted a piece with his fork. "After Guill brought me here to eat, I keep coming back trying to figure out how they're made. It's the baking powder and shortening ratio, and some sort of secret ingredient the chef is adding. The air pockets resemble sponge. I also haven't ruled out the flipping technique—that can also make a difference."

The way he spoke about pancakes reflected his passion and innate curiosity. The more time I spent with him, the more I realized how much I needed to find a way to outwit destiny's desire.

Thirty-One

Marc and I scheduled a late-night dinner at the apartment for him to meet Aunt Evelyn. He told me he'd need to request half a night off from work, but that it shouldn't be an issue.

I walked into the shop humming a happy tune. Aunt Evelyn was at the counter arranging round sablés on a plate. The sugar crystals on the cookies glittered in the light. I made plans to sneak one into my mouth later.

"I hope you had a lovely breakfast," she said.

"I did. Marc took me to a pancake place. You'd love it. He'll be coming over for a late dinner sometime this week. As for the boycott, he doesn't think his boss wrote that notice. He's looking into who is responsible."

"It doesn't matter who wrote it. Girard's name is still there." Aunt Evelyn folded the empty bakery box and tucked it below the counter. "His sphere of influence is more than mine. He can—and will—ruin me if given the chance. I'm dealing with more forms. More red tape."

She walked to the door, stopped, and surveyed her shop. Even in the empty store, she commanded the room. Her posture was that of a dancer: confident, powerful, and in full control. Not one tendril of hair slipped from her tidy updo. My aunt was indomitable, a resolute force.

Aunt Evelyn opened the store doors and ventured outside to draw people in. I took my place behind the sampling tray of tea. She concentrated on bringing in a small stream of patrons.

When my aunt was not attending to customers, her hand wandered to her pocket, where she kept her keys and the blue butterfly keychain. Independent of one another, they had clung to the same symbol of their shared past: Girard made it the emblem of his restaurant, she carried it with her. They wore their affections in public and in private.

No one seemed to see this but me.

It was the middle of the afternoon, and Aunt Evelyn had only issued commands related to the tea shop. She stayed on her phone when not canvassing passersby. I wanted to be supportive and offered to join her, but she declined with a smile.

"I appreciate your desire to help, but you do not speak French," she said. "Anyway, it's lunchtime. Stay here. I need to run a few errands and shore up more support. I'll pick up lunch and more treats from the bakery."

Annoyed, I swallowed my protest.

Under the impromptu house arrest, I took the opportunity to text Auntie Faye for an update. It was past midnight back home, but I figured she'd answer me when she woke. Three seconds later my phone rang. She did prefer voice to texts.

"I'm so sorry to bother you. It's really late. Why are you still up?" I asked.

"It's mahjong night. We have no curfew," she declared on speakerphone. The background was filled with the noise of clacking tiles, laughter, and clinking glasses. "We have a list of exes."

Auntie Gloria took over. "One is a movie star, and there are three models."

"Not a movie star, a director!" Auntie Ning corrected her. "There's a difference."

An argument ensued, but Auntie Faye took control and possession of the phone. "Your mother says hi and she'll call you soon, but she's busy refereeing right now."

I laughed. "You found his dating history, so you know who he is?"

"Girard Renaud. Restaurateur and philanthropist. No family left. Only brother died seven years ago. No marriage! Not even engagements."

"Maybe he still loves Aunt Evelyn."

Auntie Faye clicked her tongue. "Could be. Oh, and he still looks good. Not ugly old at all. Ning and several others have a crush. And he's rich. Not as rich as your uncle Jimmy, but he has enough."

Uncle James "Jimmy" Yu started in the family tea business but made his money in the stock market. His uncanny instincts were often mistaken for clairvoyance. He and Aunt Evelyn were close, and it had long been suspected that she had a tidy nest egg because of their association.

"Girard owns restaurants here," I said. "The food is great."

"Is Evelyn still interested?"

I wanted to answer yes, but that would leave Aunt Evelyn exposed. I refused to allow my current annoyance with her to create a mess I'd need to clean up later. Aunt Gloria once hired a singing zebra to help woo her son's crush by crashing their romantic picnic date. If the aunties back home detected a hint of reciprocation, their heavy-handed version of meddling would ruin the tenuous situation here.

"I'm not sure. I'll have to get back to you on that. You know what she's like."

"Keeps everything hidden like she's ashamed of her feelings." Auntie Ning took the phone and held it close to her mouth. "She needs to stop being tragic and grab that beautiful man with both arms."

"And both legs. Climb that French tree," Auntie Gloria yelled from the background. Her emphatic statement was received with raucous laughter.

The women were clearly enjoying their wine. Mahjong nights with the aunties lasted until the morning, a quarterly event of competition, gossip, food, and drink. They went all out with theming, choice of catering, and venue. They handed out prizes for the tournament: spa packages and designer and luxury goods. The grand prize was a tiara and a sash. Ma won a few times and pranced around the house for weeks like she was Miss World.

"Keep an eye on her and take care of her. After you leave, she's all alone over there." Auntie Faye sighed. "I have to go. We love you."

"Love you all too."

When I left, my aunt wouldn't be alone. She would be with Girard living their happily ever after. She deserved happiness and so did he.

Aunt Evelyn returned and, without a word, placed a wrapped sandwich before me, entered the storage room, and locked the door behind her.

Thirty-Two

Auntie?" I knocked on the door. "Are you okay?"

The lock on the door clicked and she ventured out. Her creased brow and half-eaten sandwich betrayed her waning appetite. She hummed the same sad tune I recognized from that night at Le Papillon Bleu. The notes hovered in the air and reverberated within the shop like a somber chorus.

"What happened?" I asked.

"The posters are everywhere. Every person I tried to enlist to my cause had that damnable paper taped to their door or window: Jerome the butcher, and Miette, whose shoe shop I loved going into. I thought they were my friends or, at least, neutral. How can I combat this wave of prejudice?"

There wasn't anything I could say to help. Hate was fueled by emotions; it couldn't be reasoned with. The micro-aggressions I faced did not compare with the coordinated campaign of discrimination directed toward my aunt. She was a foreigner and was outnumbered. Our family, a source of strength through numbers and kinship, was an ocean away.

Her phone buzzed, interrupting our lost thoughts. She withdrew it from her pocket and scanned the screen, her thumb dragging across the glass. Her dark eyes looked at me, her pupils pinpricks. "That was from the fortune-teller society. They have no answers. I'm to document and keep them informed."

"So I'm their guinea pig now?"

"Yes, it seems so. They did, however, agree with my assessment that this is due to you rejecting your early training. All of this is supposed to be second nature. I find it difficult to teach you when you're not where you should be."

I took a deep breath. "I can't go back to the past and change things. It's not helpful. We need a plan to accommodate and accelerate what I can do."

"And what can you do at this point? Right now you can't even dispense the vaguest fortune without tea. I find it hard to praise mediocrity."

The insult stung. My pinched lips begged to release the temper I was trying to keep in check. I could understand her frustration with the boycott, but not her decision to direct it at me.

"At your age," she continued without pausing, "I could predict events to within thirty minutes. You can't consistently narrow down the timelines of your visions. I could see specific details. You have unclear impressions."

My anger escaped, breaking free in a hiss. "Maybe the problem is with the instructor and not the student."

"Yes, because taking responsibility for your ability now absolves you of the consequences of avoiding it all these years." Aunt Evelyn crossed her arms. "You choose to reject a remarkable life for an unremarkable one. You want *their* lives."

She wasn't wrong. I wanted nothing more than to be like my cousins, with their bubbles of normalcy. If wishing for the ordinary was a crime, I was already convicted.

"You might be happy watching life happen to other people, but I don't want this. We deserve to be more than passive observers."

"We?" Her dark brows shot up. "I paid the price. I adhered to the code and sacrificed. There's always a cost to everything and you haven't—"

"Yes, I have! I don't have friends that aren't relatives. The longest relationship I've had is with Marc, and that's not even a week. And before you tell me that I'm supposed to accept this, I won't. It's not what I want!"

She placed her hands on her hips. "You were given a gift, and you don't seem to understand that. You are a fortune-teller. The sooner you accept the realities that imposes, the better."

I shook with impotent rage. My fingers curled and uncurled into fists while the air around them vibrated with heat. She wasn't hearing me. How could I *accept* the stupid rules if doing so meant relinquishing all control of my life?

"Before you tried to teach me, you never even considered breaking a rule. You didn't have the courage to. You accept every tragedy like a gift because you believe it's the price you have to pay to have clairvoyance.

"If this is how it really is, that you're relegated to observing life without the chance to live it, then you're choosing to be miserable. I told you from the beginning that I never wanted this. You do. That's your choice. I'm not you, Auntie. I don't want to end up miserable and alone."

My aunt's beautiful face reddened as though I had slapped her. Her eyes brimmed with tears. She turned her back to me.

I didn't mean to hurt her, but in my anger the truth spilled from my soul. I grabbed my purse and left the shop before the first teardrop fell. My aunt didn't follow.

I unlocked the apartment door upstairs. After I packed up my suitcase, I booked myself a room at a nearby hotel. Once settled in, I would call Ma and tell her what happened.

This was what I'd feared when coming here, that the differences between me and my aunt were too great to overcome. The same argument at six repeated itself again at twenty-seven. We were too far apart on this one subject and it poisoned everything else. Any hope I had of truly connecting with my aunt during this trip was destroyed.

I jotted down a quick note telling her that I needed space and where to find me. The urge to apologize for what I had said crept in, swaying my pen to write out those two words. I refused. They needed to be said face-to-face, and that wouldn't be anytime soon.

Every corner of this beautiful apartment reflected my aunt: the striking colors, the fresh flowers, the antiques, the elegance. I'd miss it and, yes, I'd miss her, but to stay here a moment longer would be untenable and improper. If I were my aunt, I wouldn't want to be under the same roof as my ungrateful niece.

My trip to Paris had been a bust.

This venture with my aunt had not panned out as planned. Instead of a triumphant return as a transformed woman, I would return a failure. Back to the same job. Back to the same devastating predictions. Back to a life I could no longer bear.

The only positive outcome from Paris was my friendship with Marc. We still had time to enjoy one another's company and explore more of what this city had to offer. I wanted our remaining time together to strengthen our bond and keep us connected after I returned home. For the first time in my life, I had someone to call my own. Red thread or not, I didn't want to lose what I had with Marc.

I pulled out my phone and sent a text to Marc, relaying the reasons behind my impromptu move with a promise to send another message when I was at the hotel, and left the hasty note for my aunt on the kitchen table before rolling my overstuffed luggage down the stairs. The hotel was on boulevard Saint-Germain, the much wider street that needed three crossings due to how it intersected with the other roads. I yanked the handle along and, after looking both ways thrice, crossed the first and second intersections without incident.

Heading east across Saint-Germain was the trickiest—it was the busiest and widest road. The rolling luggage emitted a creaky squeal. It had been groaning from being over capacity from the extra clothes—the new wardrobe Aunt Evelyn generously gave me.

The secret society of fortune-tellers didn't know what was wrong with me. The person who was supposed to help me couldn't help herself.

I let out a long sigh dripping with regret.

We got along well except for this. I loved her and I knew she loved me. Perhaps after a few days of cooling off, we could still meet together for that dinner with Marc. This wasn't how I wanted it to be between us. I enjoyed spending time with her outside of the mandated lessons.

A crackling sound interrupted my thoughts as the wobbly left wheel gave way. The lopsided luggage swayed, careening to the left as I stumbled off balance amid a cacophony of noise. I looked up to see a black delivery van upon me.

Thirty-Three

My phone dropped from my hand. Fine lines branched out across the screen, turning it into the cracked surface of a thawing, shallow lake. My eyes focused on the approaching headlights of the van, two bright suns I couldn't tear myself away from.

The low rumble of the engine reverberated through my ears, changing pitch as it neared, accompanied by the spinning tires chewing on specks of gravel.

My distorted reflection in the chrome grille increased in clarity as a hollowness of silence flooded my ears, drowning out everything but the percussion line of my heart.

The driver was staring ahead, his dark eyes looking through me.

He wasn't slowing down.

The rhythm of my heart accelerated to what felt like the speed of the delivery vehicle bearing down on me. The paralysis of sound transferred into me as I became an observer of my own circumstance instead of an active participant.

No more family, no more aunties, no more cousins.

No Aunt Evelyn. No Uncle Michael. No Ma or Dad. No Marc.

Twenty-seven years alive and I'd finally found love. I had hoped being here would change my life.

No time left.

Here and now, in this beautiful city, I was destined to die.

Fate had decreed it.

Thirty-Four

No.

I'd never been one to follow directions. I wasn't going to start now.

Defiance marked my presence in this world: it would guide me now.

I wasn't dying today.

With a heave, I kicked my broken baggage forward. The front of the van hit the hard shell of the suitcase as I was thrown to the curb, landing heavy on my hip and arms. My luggage burst open, scattering my clothes everywhere, a palette of colors fluttering in the wind before settling across the crosswalk in a swirling pattern.

Throbbing pain radiated from my bruised and bloodied hip and forearms as my heartbeat drummed against my rib cage. I pushed myself into a sitting position. All around me, strangers' mouths moved, but I couldn't comprehend them. There was only a high-pitched ringing.

Everything was out of focus, as though reality had motion blur applied, no discernible shapes, only blobs of color overlapping one another like dollops of paint on a wooden palette. The smearing, shifting pigments churned my stomach.

With a shaking hand, I picked up my phone with its cracked screen, found my aunt's contact information, and handed the damaged device to a woman in white. As she took the phone from me, I burst into tears, my chest heaving from the trauma and of what could have been.

The American Hospital of Paris felt the same as a hospital back home in Palo Alto. There was comfort in the familiar aesthetic even though everyone spoke French. I was kept overnight for observation.

Aunt Evelyn had hovered by my bedside last night but said little. Curled in an uncomfortable vinyl chair beside me in the semi-private room with knees drawn to her chest, she still slumbered. Her breathing was soft and steady. My sleep had been restless, and I had the luxury of a bed.

"Auntie?" I called out.

She stirred. Wisps of dark hair escaped her elegant updo. Her complexion was pale. She sat up, straightened her blouse and hair, and crossed her legs at the ankles. Only my aunt could look elegant in a hospital room.

"How are you feeling?" she asked.

My skin stung from the cuts, and my left hip ached. "Grateful to be alive."

"The doctor says you have a bruised hip flexor. One to four weeks to heal." She pointed to a wicked curved scar near my right elbow.

"The stitches are dissolvable so you don't need to come back to have them removed. It will leave a mark though. Considering the alternative, I imagine it's something you can live with."

I touched the bubbling, pink skin and ran my fingertip alongside its three-inch length. A new gruesome story for my nieces and nephews. They'd eat it up.

"They gave me a prescription for the ointments to help you heal. And, fortunately, no concussion. The doctor mentioned you'll be discharged today," my aunt added. "Depending on your level of soreness, you may need a cane for a while." An aqua-blue cane leaned near the door—it looked like a question mark with a small, stable base. Subdued, but probably the most fashionable option available.

"Thank you, Auntie."

Despite our differences we were family. No disagreement could divide us. With what had transpired, with how close it had come to ending, clinging to a grudge felt childish. "Auntie, I'm sorry for what I said. I was angry. I don't want to argue anymore."

She reached over and held my hand. "Apology accepted. I'm sorry too. I don't like fighting with you either. Sometimes I wonder if we squabble because we're so different or because we're so alike."

"Maybe it's a little of both."

"After you left, I thought about what you said. I've never known anyone who so soundly rejected our gift. I found my calling when my training began, and expected the same for you."

"I know you're disappointed. I understand there are benefits, not everything we see is bad, but it's never been something I *wanted*, Auntie. I desire neither the power nor the burden."

She nodded. "I can't force you to make my choices. However, I'm not sure where that leaves you."

"Do you remember seeing the tire tracks the shattered glass

made after I lied? Was it a prediction about this? What does this mean?"

"I'm not sure, but we can deal with that after you come home with me. That is, if you want to."

Her uncertainty touched me. She gave me an out. I could decline and ask for more time to myself, but I didn't want to be alone.

"Of course I'm coming home with you. I love you, Auntie."

Aunt Evelyn kissed my forehead. "I love you too."

"Now that it's settled, can you get me out of here?"

"I'll go get the doctor and see to getting you discharged," she replied with a laugh.

Thirty-Five

It was afternoon by the time we arrived at the tea shop. Aunt Evelyn chose not to reopen with only three hours left in the day. She sent all the dirty clothes to a dry cleaner and salvaged the unblemished ones, running a full load in the washing machine at the apartment.

"Have you told Ma yet?" I asked over a cup of honey ginger tea at the kitchen table.

Aunt Evelyn bit her lower lip. "I haven't. I know I should have, but knowing Linda, she would have taken the next flight out. After I found out that you had minor injuries, I decided not to. I didn't want to worry her. We have it handled and we can tell her later. Besides, it's their special mahjong tournament. I don't want to interrupt that."

"Have you ever gone to one? Ma always raves about how much fun she has."

"They always invite me, but I always decline."

I decided to use my almost-died card to my advantage and pried. "Why?"

Aunt Evelyn blushed. She left the table to refill the empty ceramic teapot. "At first I thought it would be too noisy and busy, but as the years went by, it was too late to say yes."

"Then go next year. I'm sure they'd love to have you. I mean, they continue to invite you anyway. They love you."

She poured hot water from the kettle on the stove into the teapot. "I know. I love them, too, but I can only take them in doses."

"Do you mean in time or in number?"

"Both."

We laughed.

"You do raise a good point about the tournament. I should visit during the next one. I'm starting to welcome the prospect that a visit is my idea. I do love gathering for special occasions like weddings, milestone birthdays, and such." She paused and smiled. "I did tell one person about your mishap yesterday. Why don't you get the door?"

A knock arrived two seconds later. Judging by her expression, she already knew who the visitor was.

I made my way to the entrance and opened the door.

Uncle Michael stood at the threshold toting a small carry-on. He opened his arms to hug me and stopped when he saw the bandages on my arms. "Evelyn called and told me what happened. I took the next available flight from Munich to surprise you both."

"It's great to see you, Michael," Aunt Evelyn called from the kitchen.

"She expected me, didn't she?" he asked.

"Right down to the knock." I leaned against him, bypassing the hug, and gave him a kiss on the cheek. "I missed you."

After taking off his shoes, he threw his arm around me and walked me over to the table where Aunt Evelyn had placed an impressive charcuterie plate. Slices of thin-cut, cured jambon sec, viande de grison, and saucisson decorated a wooden board along with a small bowl of grainy, stone-ground mustard. A basket held two baguettes with an accompaniment of Bordier butter. Two generous wedges of brie aux truffes and clusters of Burgundy and Champagne grapes occupied the cheese plate. A spoon handle stuck out from her jar of homemade fig jam beside a small bowl of crunchy cornichons. The last component of the meal was a pâté de campagne that Ines's mother made as a gift for my aunt.

Uncle Michael whistled. "This looks incredible. I should drop in more often."

"There's much to celebrate." My aunt brought out three flutes from the cupboards and a bottle of champagne from the fridge. "Our niece cheated death."

I took a seat and helped myself to the baguettes. "That I did. I don't really want to confront my mortality until I'm old, you know?"

My uncle and aunt exchanged glances.

"What?"

He pried the bread knife from my trembling hand, revealing a mangled baguette. "Maybe you should let us handle the pointy implements," he said. "Physically you got off with minor injuries. Mentally, however, you're still processing all of this. It will take time."

"Don't stress. You will be fine. You're a fighter." Aunt Evelyn patted my upper arm. "We still don't know what the aftereffects are, if any."

She placed three buttered slices of baguette in front of me. "Wishful thinking. I don't think anything has changed."

"It could," Michael countered. "Near-death experiences are rare and, from what I've heard, they change you. Jack told me how his dad rolled a car in his late teens. He survived it and it ended his reckless streak permanently. When the old man talks about his teenage years, you'd think he was a different person. He still runs his ginseng farm in Vermont and insists that he'll retire when he's dead. At eighty-one, he's healthier than most men my age." He heaped papery, coral slices of jambon sec and portions of the pâté onto my plate. "This might change you or it might not. Only time will tell."

My aunt cut herself some of the pâté. "We have two weeks until you go back home. It'll be good to take the time for yourself and figure out what you want."

"What I want?" I asked.

"Before you left, Linda mentioned something to me. She's noticed that you're not really happy at work anymore. You do your job well, but she's concerned about your happiness. She knows you'll never tell her, so she asked me to speak to you."

I stared at my aunt as heat bloomed in my cheeks. Had I been so transparent about my lack of purpose? My performance reviews had always been exceptional. My clients trusted me, and my desk groaned with baskets of various chocolates, wines, fruits, and cheeses every Christmas.

As if she read my mind, Aunt Evelyn smiled. "You wanted to please your parents and the family, and you've done that. They want you to be happy. Clearly, you're not. You talk about food with more passion than you do about your quarterly reports or spreadsheets."

"She has you there. You don't talk about work outside of work." Uncle Michael sipped his champagne. "It's not a reflection of how much you care about your job, only that it is a job versus a career to you. Have you thought about what you want to do? Most Yus are in tea or accounting, but we do have family that do other things."

There were chefs, artists, and entrepreneurs like Auntie Faye. "When did this conversation turn into career counseling?"

"It's not," both of them answered at the same time.

Ma told them. She knew that if it came from her, I would deny, derail, and dismiss. My loyalty to the family was unquestionable, and to have a career crisis at the Yu accounting firm was tantamount to treason.

"I don't dislike working in accounting. I mean, I'm good at it."

My uncle laughed. "Yes, that's what HR wants to hear when they're interviewing prospective candidates."

"It's something to think about," my aunt said. "Maybe by the time you leave, you'll know."

I reached for the fig jam. "All I know for now is that I want Marc to be a part of my future."

My uncle grinned. "This I need to hear."

Thirty-Six

"Will I get a chance to meet him?" Uncle Michael asked while placing the leftovers in the fridge.

I stacked the clean plates on the counter. "There's a meal tomorrow night, a late-night dinner. He's planning on cooking."

"By the way, I had your phone checked. Only the screen was broken." Aunt Evelyn retrieved my phone from her purse and handed it to me.

A radial spiderweb of fine white lines marred the screen. My finger caught on the edges of the damaged glass. It wasn't pretty, but at least I didn't lose it. There were messages from the cousins, but nothing from Marc. I brushed away my disappointment. He might have had a long night and hadn't checked his phone yet.

Aunt Evelyn prepared a fresh pot of oolong tea while I finished putting away the dishes and cutlery. My uncle packed up all the food while peppering me with questions about my favorite pastry chef. I chose not to mention Girard, for Aunt Evelyn's sake. She and I received the gift of a new beginning, and I didn't want to ruin it by disclosing her secret. It was one thing to question her in private but another to do so in public.

"How are lessons going?" my uncle asked.

I cleared my throat and waited for my aunt to answer.

The ghost of the explosive argument between us hung in the air—complete with invisible scorch marks. Words were spoken that could never be unsaid. The truce we shared, while needed, didn't change the lack of resolution to my prediction predicament.

"Her headaches are gone, but it's our only victory. In the end, I'm unable to help her. I've enlisted aid, yet we have no answers," Aunt Evelyn replied. "The fault is mine. I promised to help you, and I failed. I don't know how to proceed."

I placed my hand on her arm. "Together, we'll figure it out somehow."

She smiled, though not as confident as that evening in my apartment, and covered my hand with hers. "Yes, we will."

Squeezing her arm for comfort, I turned to my uncle. "How is Jack doing?"

"He and I are meeting up in Monaco in a week. He has a job there shooting very beautiful and important people." His phone buzzed and he picked it up. Judging by the smile on his face, it could only be the man he loved calling. A glowing red thread snaked out of the phone, traveled down his arm, and connected to the left side of his chest.

Uncle Michael excused himself to take the call.

"Did you see that?" I asked.

She tilted her head. "See what?"

"The red thread on Uncle Michael. When Jack called, it popped out and connected to him."

Aunt Evelyn pursed her lips. "Clairvoyants cannot see red threads."

"I know, but I did see one. It connected to his heart. How is it that I could see it?"

Her fingers gripped the top rail of the chair. "I don't know. Everything about your situation is unprecedented. I'm questioning what I thought I believed to be immutable."

My aunt, one of the steadiest people I knew, held on to the chair as if it were a lifeline. While I craved change and rebelled against anything contrary to my desires, Aunt Evelyn revered tradition and devoted herself to her clairvoyance. Seeing her doubt was unsettling. What was she thinking? In her place, I would wonder if I had made the right choices, if my beliefs had barred the possibilities presenting themselves to those bold enough to grasp them.

Uncle Michael returned from his call with Jack. With the phone tucked away, I couldn't see the thread anymore. "He's settled in and suggested we stop by after Monaco. He's been in Paris numerous times, but he'd like to see you two again."

My aunt recovered and mustered a smile. "It'll be good to see Jack. I'm sure he'll want to see the tea shop."

"He's offered to take promotional photos for your website or future advertisements."

She narrowed her eyes. "It is supposed to be a nice visit, not work."

Uncle Michael held his palms up. "It was his suggestion. Of course, if you give him a tin or two of his beloved tea, he wouldn't object."

"He's just as bad as you are." Aunt Evelyn shook her head. "You found a good one, Michael."

"It was actually Vanessa who did. She introduced me to Jack. Thought we'd be perfect for each other."

I preened at the compliment. "You are—I was right."

"You're lucky it worked out," my aunt said.

For her, love was sacred and yet unattainable. Before Marc had returned, I believed it too. Now I was convinced that my instincts were right: she and Girard belonged together. No one should be alone unless they desired it. But she moved to Paris for Girard, and for herself. I would text Marc tonight for an update and to tell him what happened yesterday.

"With risk comes reward, Auntie. As an entrepreneur, you know this well," I said.

She sighed. "Yes and, lately, too well."

"What is happening with the tea shop?" Uncle Michael asked.

I listened as my aunt informed him about the boycott and a few other challenges she neglected to tell me: nasty rumors defaming her character, some of her suppliers dropping her, extra repairs, delayed shipments, and miscommunication and errors with the ads she purchased in local papers. I felt like a child watching two adults speak.

My uncle frowned. "Does this boycott have traction?"

"I find myself standing outside my shop more often, trying to draw customers in. The foot traffic in the market is there, but they're not coming in. They visit everyone else." My aunt sounded worried, more worried than she had ever revealed to me. "I was closed again today. With the current climate, I can see people getting behind the boycott. I could lose my suppliers. No customers and no stock means no business."

"Evelyn," he said, embracing her. "I don't want you to fail, but the family back home will be there if you need to return."

She lowered head. "I can't. Even if the business collapses, I'm staying here. There's nothing for me in California."

"You thought all this through, haven't you?"

"Yes." Aunt Evelyn straightened her posture. "I've made my decision. There's no room for anything but success. I'm not going back, Michael. I'll still visit, but Paris is my home now. I already started the immigration process."

Another bombshell that I should have expected since she declared her move to be permanent. My aunt's trust in my uncle was a testament to the strength of their friendship. They were best friends, but I doubted he knew about Girard.

"I was hoping your stay here was only temporary. A few years to experiment since you're such a Francophile. As long as you're happy, Evelyn, I'll support you."

I stood beside my aunt and placed my hand in the crook of her arm. "Don't worry, she is."

She might not be now, but she would be by the time I left.

Thirty-Seven

Happiness is a state of mind; however, just declaring yourself happy did not, in itself, persuade others, nor did it fool you. No one but you would know the lie, if you told it. Aunt Evelyn wanted to be happy. It was the reason she moved to Paris and chose this neighborhood. I had to help her.

I searched for an opening to speak with my uncle in private about my plans to reunite Aunt Evelyn with Girard. When my aunt excused herself to take a call from Ines's mother, I took advantage of the situation and asked Uncle Michael to go for a short walk. He balked at the suggestion, but I convinced him that we wouldn't cross any intersections and that fresh air was conducive to recovery. Besides, I needed to test out the cane and learn how to navigate with it.

"I don't think Evelyn will be pleased." He closed the apartment door behind us.

"She's busy. As long as I'm being chaperoned, I don't think she'll mind." I linked my arm with his. "Her whole life is in that store and she's doing her best to save it."

At six thirty in the evening, most of the shops were preparing to close. We went into an antique store, perusing antiques, furniture, and artwork. I took care maneuvering around the breakables with the curved handle of the cane. I was grateful for the extra stability that helped take the pressure off my sore hip.

"I warned her. Opening a shop is difficult even with support; then you add in a different culture, on a new continent, in a competitive city." Uncle Michael picked up an old framed black-and-white photograph of an apothecary storefront. "It helps that she knows the language, but she's all by herself here."

"She has friends. She'll be fine." I set down a painted ceramic bird I had been examining.

"I have to admit, I had been concerned about how well you two would get along."

Years ago, during one of my failed clairvoyance lessons, Uncle Michael had picked me up from Aunt Evelyn's. He gathered a sobbing six-year-old and drove to our favorite gelato shop, where he listened to my biased version of how the lesson went.

"It was as bad as you expect. She's a strict teacher; I'm a terrible student. I'm not like any seer she's seen before. We argued, but when we weren't bickering, we enjoyed one another's company and ate the best food. We don't see fortune-telling the same way, but I think it's okay now. We've reached a truce, and all I had to do was almost die."

I picked up the bird again and, on a whim, decided to buy it for Ma. It fit in the palm of my hand and was painted with a robin's-egg-blue crackle finish. It would look perfect on the fireplace mantel next to the white ceramic stag she had bought from a local gallery. My uncle offered to carry it for me.

His manicured hand clutched the small bird. "I can't imagine what you've been through."

"I emerged relatively unscathed. Sure, my left hip is sore and I have this awesome scar, but I'll take that over the alternative." A married couple in their early thirties entered the antique store, a baby in the man's arms. A red thread linked them both, heart to heart. Even when they wandered apart, they remained tied. Threads were everywhere. "I see red threads connecting couples now. I couldn't do that before."

Uncle Michael squinted at the people around him. "Well, that's certainly new. When did it start?"

"When Jack called your phone. That couple with the baby has it too."

"You seem sanguine about this new ability, unlike earlier. Is this something you want?"

"Yes."

The answer came so naturally, I almost thought I hadn't responded. I rejected fortune-telling because of the burden, embarrassment, and shame that came with it. Knowing the future held no appeal to me; however, my new aptitude didn't terrify me. I wanted to learn more, what it meant and its scope.

"Given your history, that's not at all how I expected you to answer." He headed toward the cash register with the bird and the photograph.

"It hasn't made anyone run screaming from me. It's nice seeing their connection. Speaking of which, you probably won't approve, but know I'm going forward anyway."

My uncle seldom used his warning tone, but a rebellious child knew the inflection—whether from family or a stranger. "Vanessa."

"Aunt Evelyn is in love and I'm certain he feels the same way. It's someone she was involved with when she was in Paris in her twenties. Recently, they saw each other for the first time in decades at his restaurant. There are unresolved feelings."

"Did your aunties back home put you up to this?" he asked.

I shook my head. "They didn't. This is my idea. They are busy meddling in their own way: they hired a private investigator."

My uncle covered his face with his free hand and uttered a curse in Mandarin. "I expected this from them, but not you."

"I want her to be happy. I think she will be with him, and vice versa. It's a gut feeling I have, but it's the same one that told me Jack and you belong together."

We reached the counter, and my uncle stopped me from taking out my wallet. He paid for both the bird and the photograph.

"This old boyfriend of hers, what does he look like?" he asked as we entered the next store.

"A French version of Robert Redford. Quite dashing. The aunties were impressed."

Rococo oil paintings, in their gilded frames, stood out against the deep red walls. Bronze sculptures populated the shelves. My fingers itched to reach out and touch them.

"Evelyn is one of those rare souls who is open to others but also guards the most private parts of herself," Uncle Michael continued. "She knows the name of every family member, is generous at every occasion, and attends every function. Yet, how many do you think she's invited into her home? Me—and you."

I had never realized how alone Aunt Evelyn was.

Red threads were everywhere. Sparkling ruby garlands wove

through people like a moving spiderweb. If I could fly overhead, I could see the patterns of constellations representing the bridges of humanity. For someone who never had one of her own, seeing them brought me joy. This was what I'd been missing all my life.

And my aunt didn't have one.

It was a steep price to pay for her clairvoyance.

It wasn't fair.

Thirty-Eight

The next morning, I woke up breathless. My heartbeat hovered near the edge of my throat as my skin hummed with an electric energy that popped the sheets and blankets around me. It was as if my body was reminding me that I was alive.

The experience had left me reassessing what kind of life I was resuming. I failed at controlling my predictions, but gained the power to see red threads. Where did that leave me? Did I want to go back to my office at the accounting firm? Spend countless weekends alone while surrounded by family?

I wanted to bring Marc home to meet them, but after that? Despite a rebellious streak, I had ended up working at the family firm like a good, respectable Yu.

Now, I wanted more, from love, from life, from everything. Ma knew this.

I was no longer cursed.

There wasn't anything now stopping me from what I wanted.

I didn't know what would come next, but I wasn't scared.

After dressing in a pair of dark jeans and an off-the-shoulder cashmere sweater and checking my phone (still nothing from Marc), I made my way to the kitchen. Midmorning sunlight streamed through the windows. I must have slept in. Prophecy lessons were canceled. I was a carefree tourist again.

My aunt had left a note on the kitchen table.

Dear Vanessa,

No need to come into the shop during the day. However, if you feel well enough and can manage, I would appreciate you dropping by Ines's bakery and picking up some treats. The few customers coming in appreciate the tea and biscuit pairing.

Love,
Aunt Evelyn

The boycott and gossip were denting her profits, and with my accident she had lost another day. Her conversation with my uncle last night uncovered a direr picture than what she had presented to me. Failure wasn't an option. My aunt had too much pride to move back. While I didn't know yet what I wanted to do with my life, Aunt Evelyn had gambled everything she owned for her heart's desire.

Reuniting her with Girard would save her business. My schedule was now clear and, with a little over a week left, I could focus on this task. I checked my phone again, but Marc hadn't responded to my messages. My coconspirator was missing in action, and I was worried that his boss might be responsible.

I needed to recruit another to my cause. I needed Ines's help. She considered my aunt family. Aunt Evelyn's support system was small, and Ines's family was its core. I headed to my favorite bakery with the cats painted on the front windows.

There was no sign of Luc when I arrived at the bakery. The glorious aroma of butter, sugar, vanilla bean, and cacao hovered in the air. When I eventually left Paris, I'd miss the luxury of bakeries within walking distance. Ines lounged at the counter. Her short, pixie hair cut exposed a sharpened pencil tucked behind her ear.

"Oh my, Vanessa! Are you all right?" She rushed to greet me from behind the counter.

"I'm fine. I had a minor accident." I tapped my cane. "This is temporary. I have a sore hip and it's helping me. This scar, however, is permanent."

She examined my right elbow. "It looks like it's healing well though."

"No delivery from a certain someone today?" I asked.

She sighed and resumed her position behind the counter. "Someone else is doing the delivery now. I'm not sure if it was his or his parents' idea to change his shift. Knowing Luc, he wouldn't dare stand up to his parents."

"Has he always been that way?"

"He's a good son." She lifted a glass dome and handed me a thin, round waffle cookie. "Galettes. You will love these."

I ran a fingertip across the tiny square indentations. The toasted cookie was crisp and delicious, and left tiny crumbs at the corners of my mouth. This reminded me of the crunchy bits of batter left at the sides of the waffle iron, which were always my favorite.

"They will go well with whatever tea your aunt is sampling," she said, stacking the galettes into a small box before placing them in a paper bag with handles. "How is she? I heard the shop was closed yesterday. My parents talked to the other shopkeepers; they are disappointed in them. We don't understand how they can spread these lies to their customers and to tourists. It's cruel."

"It is."

She handed me the bag and leaned in closer. "If only their romance hadn't soured."

"It's not hopeless though. I have a plan."

Ines's dark brown eyes widened and her poppy-red lips gaped open. "You're going to set them up?"

"Why not? They loved each other once."

"They would make a striking couple." Ines jotted down the order on a slip. I reached for my purse, but she waved me away. She pointed to tins of my aunt's teas on a nearby shelf. "Don't worry about payment. We have an arrangement in place."

I took this as an opening to recruit her to my cause. "Will you help me?"

"This is going to be a difficult mission. Monsieur Renaud is a hard man to get a hold of. He's very busy and very inaccessible. He keeps a tight counsel and is notorious about his privacy."

"Does this mean you're not going to help me?" I asked.

"Oh, I'm going to help. But you must know what we're up against." Tearing a sheet from her order pad, she wrote down her phone number before reaching below the counter to reveal a small envelope. "And this is for you."

"Me?"

Ines winked. "A handsome pastry chef dropped it off early this morning."

Marc.

He hadn't forgotten about me.

Thirty-Nine

I tore open the packet outside the bakery.

The letter smelled of chocolate; the instant I unfolded it, a slight breeze carried the scent upward, enveloping me in the sweetest of embraces.

Inside was an ink illustration of a heart-shaped croissant. The intricate strokes rendering the pastry's layers illuminated his attention to detail. He signed it, "You have my heart, Marc."

I pressed the paper against my chest.

All was well. Ines had agreed to help. If I could determine Girard's schedule, it would be easier to "run into" him and plead my case. But how could I convince him that he and my aunt belonged together?

My only evidence was an old photograph, his intense feelings for her frozen for eternity. I sent a short email to Auntie Faye, asking her to overnight the photo to me. It was midnight there, so it would probably arrive here tomorrow or the day after. The time difference wasn't conducive to coordinated conspiracy.

A familiar face emerged from a nearby bistro: Luc. He walked to his delivery van. I had to find out why he was avoiding Ines. Hobbling toward him, my hip screaming in protest, I called out.

"Luc, please wait. Can I talk to you?"

Dark shadows crept under his hazel eyes. He loaded two empty crates onto the rear of the vehicle. "Did Ines send you?"

"No, should she have? Why are you avoiding her?"

"My parents have set a date for the proposal." Luc slammed the doors shut. "Why continue to see her and torment myself with the unattainable?"

"Because you love her and you don't want to get married. You want to be with Ines."

He flinched. The truth stung. It hurt, more so when it was already known but never spoken.

"I understand family is important. I get it," I continued. "But what about your happiness?" Luc's dilemma mirrored my aunt's from all those years ago. She had chosen her family and paid the price in years of loneliness.

"I can't go against my parents." His deep voice dropped to a whisper.

All I could think about was Ines. She loved him—was waiting for him to choose her. As tortured as he seemed, his decision was clear.

I frowned. "At least tell her what you've decided instead of avoiding her like a coward."

"I can't." His chest caved, turning inward.

"Then you don't deserve her."

My aunt stood outside the tea shop. Her once straightened shoulders slumped. An errant strand escaped her upswept hair. People were walking the street, yet no one was going inside.

It wasn't as if they ignored the shop; instead, they paused, whispered among themselves, then proceeded onwards. I'd seen this behavior before: in the hallways at high school, around the water cooler at work, even by the buffet table at family gatherings.

A walking tour guide passed by with his group and my aunt confronted him. I couldn't follow the conversation, but I didn't need to. Their body language communicated much more than words. Aunt Evelyn advocated for her shop; the guide wasn't receptive. His group scattered into the nearby stores.

My aunt walked away fuming.

Stopping this required the man responsible to set things right before the rumors become a sentient entity of their own; otherwise, it would be impossible to control the narrative.

I entered the store and handed the cookies to my aunt. She opened the box, then closed it.

"Thank you for picking these up. I'm afraid there aren't many customers to give them to. I went out there and tried, but no one comes inside. That tour guide is like the others: they repeat the horrible, false information about me and my business. Nothing I can say clears my name." She slouched against the clean countertop. "I'm the newcomer. They're not going to listen to me. Ines's family is doing their best to talk to them. I expected resistance in some form, but I thought I had the luxury of a few months to get established."

"It shouldn't be this way. Girard isn't playing fair."

"No, he isn't." Aunt Evelyn sighed and moved to the tea service behind the counter and poured me a cup. "This is my dragon tea. Try it. No one else has."

I took the warm teacup in my hands and inhaled. Spices teased my nostrils: cardamom, ginger, and cloves, along with a promise of an earthy base.

"This smells delicious." I drank deeply.

She flashed a weak smile. "I'm glad you approve." Her eyes never left me.

"Are you worried I wouldn't like it?"

"No. I stand by the quality of my tea."

I sat the teacup down and reached for a galette, taking a bite of the waffle cookie.

She tilted her head toward a young hipster stroking his beard outside by the window. He was reading the tea listing posted behind the counter. Her eyes, however, never looked away from me.

"What?" I asked.

"You drank tea, Vanessa."

A lingering taste of oolong filled my mouth. Nothing pressed against my lips. No intrusion compelled me to speak. My eyes widened and I began to cry.

Forty

Aunt Evelyn placed a hand on my arm to steady me. "It's what you've always wanted."

Had I known it would take almost dying to cure me, I might have jaywalked earlier. It was like a part of me, the part I could never tame, died on that Paris street corner.

Wiping my eyes, I refilled my teacup before stepping outside to observe a crowd of people pass. All the while, I sipped my tea, without pain, and without worry. My aunt followed me out, smiling as she watched me finish the cup.

"Do you want to walk around town drinking tea to make sure?" she asked.

"I'm tempted to," I laughed. A sound straight from my soul, loud, joyful.

For the first time in my life, I truly felt free.

Red threads were everywhere, connecting people near and far—a tapestry of silk strings sewing souls together. In the ocean of couplings, two people, though, were unconnected: my aunt and me. My excitement contrasted with her growing dimness.

I came to Paris and got more than what I desired, yet my aunt had not.

"Why didn't you tell me you were struggling, Auntie?"

"Because I chose this." She waved her arm to encompass the whole neighborhood. "I went in with eyes open. I took the risk, and thought I could do it. Now, I'm not so sure."

Her voice broke. Without any hesitation, I hugged her. She rested her head against mine, leaning in for support. I loved her and wanted nothing more than to see her happy.

"Don't worry, I'm going to help you," I said, squeezing her close. "By the time I leave Paris, everything will turn around."

"If only I had your confidence. I was so sure this would be my time, that I earned the right to choose what I wanted." A joyless laugh escaped her lips. "I'd been foolish in thinking there was still a chance, but it's too late. Sometimes, dreams are meant to stay outside the realm of reality. Yearning for the stars won't bring them to your fingertips."

She had given up, but I refused to allow her dream to die.

Though I wasn't needed at the store, I stayed and kept her company. The tension in our relationship was gone. No longer instructor and pupil, we were now just aunt and niece. However, tension had given way to a lingering sadness, which plagued my aunt. My tasting her teas brought her momentary joy, but she soon returned to her morose state.

I yearned to see the confident, strong woman I'd admired that fateful night at the restaurant. She had been resplendent then, challenging her old love with her presence and her words. Now, the fight had abandoned her, leaving exhaustion and resignation in its wake. Gone were the glorious golds: she now wore muted grays.

It wasn't fair; I had what I wanted, she didn't. We fell into an odd waltz: I dampened my happiness, she masked her sorrow.

The prospect of meeting Marc for dinner raised her spirits a little. I still hadn't heard from him, aside from the drawing I carried in my purse. I missed him.

When the shop closed and Uncle Michael returned from his meetings, I retreated to my room upstairs in relief. My failed stint as a cheerleader left the bitter taste of disappointment on my tongue. I dialed Auntie Faye's number.

"Hi, Auntie, did you send the picture?"

My aunt was in her salon. The ambient noise filled the background, making it hard for me to hear her. "Yes, it should arrive tomorrow morning. What's the rush?"

I ignored the question. It would lead to too many follow-up demands. "Did you find anything else out?"

"Mr. Renaud has many admirers. So many desperate women. The worst is his close friend's sister, Leticia Chirac. She has been after him for years. One time, she bribed the concierge of a hotel he was staying at in Zurich to get into his room. It caused a scandal. She was waiting for him on his bed, naked. Allegedly. One of the maids found her when he called to have someone check if he had left his briefcase in the room. Everyone involved was fired. He travels with his assistant now."

"Creepy." I shuddered. "Does this mean he has a bodyguard then?"

"You mean his driver and assistant. Mr. Leo Lieu. Ex-marine. Ninth-degree red belt in jujitsu. He's a distant relative of Ning's husband. I asked George, and he said they met once at a family reunion in upstate New York."

I might be able to use this. Uncle George had always doted on me, and dropping his name on the bodyguard might give me access to Girard. Enlisting him in my matchmaking scheme was a stretch, but at minimum, I hoped that the vague family connection could grant me an audience before he put me in a chokehold.

"Linda wants to know when you're calling. You know you don't want to keep your mother waiting. Call her after you get off the phone with me."

"I will. I promise."

"How is Evelyn doing?"

Miserable and defeated. "She's with Uncle Michael now. He's visiting from Munich," I said instead. "We're going to have dinner soon."

"Good. We're worried about her."

"You sound like you miss her."

"I do. We all do. She's one of us, even she can't deny that." There was a pause and a sigh. "Go call your mother."

"Yes, Auntie. Thank you again."

I hung up.

Before I could call Ma, I needed to figure out how to downplay the accident. She would worry regardless, yet I had to mitigate the damage as much as possible. The best-case scenario happened: I was alive and free of the curse. And I had a romantic prospect. If I could get her to focus on the latter, maybe she'd gloss over the former.

I dialed Ma's number and crossed my fingers that she was in a meeting and I could leave a voice message.

No luck. My mother picked up. "Vanessa, why haven't you called? Are you avoiding me?"

"It's been busy here. I need you to do me a favor: please don't freak out." I then detailed what happened in a gush of words, an inundation of trivial facts in a shower of syllables. It was the preferred tactic of a guilty child caught in the act. "And I'm about to have dinner now with Uncle Michael and Aunt Evelyn. They're going to meet Marc."

Ma created a series of exasperated noises that made me thankful I was 5,571 miles away. "You almost died and you didn't even call your mother!" Her scream made me pull the phone away from my face.

"I am okay. Only minor scrapes. My suitcase took the brunt of it. I'm fine, Ma, really."

"That's not the point. I'm also upset with Evelyn, but that's between me and her."

I didn't want to be privy to that conversation, nor the current one, where my dear mother needed to be placated like an angry deity. "She didn't want to alarm you. She talked to the doctor and knew I was fine. Calling you would have freaked you out when the situation was handled. She probably asked them to keep me overnight, and I was discharged the next day." The last part was a lie, but my aunt needed all the points with my mother that I could give her.

"Still." The decibels decreased as her outrage subsided. "You both should have told me sooner."

A message flashed across the screen. It was an incoming call from Marc.

"I have to go. It's Marc. I have to take this."

"Fine. We'll talk later."

As I hung up and switched to the other line, I felt a foreboding sense of dread, not from any kind of preternatural ability, but born from the repeated experience of being stood up.

Forty-One

I'm sorry. I couldn't call earlier. The boss has me working long hours and is making me come in during my time off to help out. It's worse then ever, if you can imagine that. I miss you."

"I miss you too." The sound of his deep voice was soothing. "Did you get my earlier message?"

"About the hotel. Yeah, I'm sorry I didn't get a chance to respond."

"Marc, I almost died the other day. I was going to the hotel. A van almost ran me over."

"Oh God, are you all right? I should come over. I'm so sorry. I should have been there . . ."

"It's okay. I was a bit shaken up, but my suitcase bore the brunt of the impact. My aunt helped me and I decided to stay with her."

There was a pause, and then he sighed.

"You're not coming tonight, are you?" I asked.

"I was set to come, but then, a few minutes ago, he called me back in. I swear, he's sabotaging my life. It feels like forever since we shared pancakes."

I pushed down my disappointment. The slight bothered me, but I didn't want to make a fuss: I understood the pressure he was under, but I wanted him to make time for us.

"As bad as my problems are, I'm sure they're minor compared to your aunt. How is she doing?" he asked.

"Not well. Few people are going in. The boycott and setbacks are killing her business, and her hopes. Everything she has, she poured into the store. Did you find out anything?"

"Claude's sister, Leticia, is responsible for the flyer. She's been in love with the boss for years. She eats dinner at the restaurant every night just to see him. Beautiful woman, but obsessive and territorial."

"Leticia Chirac?"

"You've heard of her? There are some scandalous stories. I haven't found out anything else. I hardly have time to get home, sleep, and take a shower before I'm back in the kitchen." He paused. "Have I told you I miss you?"

"You have, but it doesn't hurt to hear it again." I smiled.

"Can you send my apologies to your family?"

"I will. My aunt and uncle will be disappointed, but I know you can't afford to lose your job."

"When do you leave?"

"A little less than two weeks. We have plenty of time." I opted for false bravado to help alleviate his guilt. If circumstances were ideal, we'd spend every minute together, and begin to figure out what would happen after Paris. I wanted this to continue, despite the challenges of a long-distance relationship. The future was murky, but at least I had a future—one I embraced.

"Did you get my drawing?"

"Yes, I didn't know your heart was made of delicious butter and carbs."

He laughed. I could picture his gorgeous brown eyes crinkling at the corners. "If I get too busy, I'll leave you something with Ines. Hey, I . . ." His voice became faint, followed by the sound of shattering glass. The call disconnected.

Great. Now his phone was also broken. As if we needed more obstacles. I braced myself before heading out to give my aunt and uncle the bad news.

A family dinner to meet the boyfriend was compulsory. It was an event I always wanted. I yearned for the stress, the aggravation, and the interrogation that I'd seen with my cousins when bringing their significant others. Despite all my recent changes, I was still denied for another day.

My parents notwithstanding, Uncle Michael and Aunt Evelyn would have made the perfect introduction to the Yu family. My uncle was disappointed, my aunt more so. We ordered from my aunt's favorite Italian restaurant. She pushed her rotini arrabbiata around the plate, and ignored her glass of cabernet sauvignon. My uncle gave me worrying glances throughout the meal as he attempted to engage her in light discussion. After dinner, she retreated to her room, humming her now-familiar melancholy melody.

"I hate seeing her like this," Uncle Michael said. "The business is her life. If it fails, I don't see her recovering easily. Have you made any progress in reaching Girard?"

"His bodyguard is a distant relative. I'm hoping he'll let me speak to his boss."

He folded an empty takeaway box. "Wouldn't he be violating some occupational code by allowing you to do so?"

I groaned and slumped into my chair. "You're right. What do you suggest?"

"If you're going to use subterfuge, don't use family connections. At least, not that way." He withdrew a card from his pocket. "Here's Jack's business card. Say you're his assistant and you're scouting locations. The restaurant is beautiful, right? Totally plausible."

I held the card to my chest. "Uncle Michael, what will Jack say?"

"He loves me." My uncle blushed. "He'll forgive this. I think. Call to set up an appointment. Use an alias—a name similar to someone you knew from college. It'll be easier to stick to the details."

"Are you sure you're a designer and not a spy from some secret organization?" I teased.

He winked, and pressed a finger to his lips. "Call now. The restaurant should still be open and, providing he's available, you can get an appointment for tomorrow morning during the off-hours."

"I should have just asked you to plan this whole thing."

"I leave tomorrow, and I prefer to go knowing that you and Evelyn are better off than when I arrived." He lifted my chin up. "She needs our help, but she won't ask for it: she's too stubborn. You have that in common. If there was an official test for obstinacy, you both would exceed the recommended level."

My uncle was correct: Aunt Evelyn wouldn't dare ask for help. It went against her nature and her infamous streak of independence. Why had it taken me this long to realize that she and I weren't that different?

"She deserves to have what she came here for," I declared.

Love. All my aunt wanted was the love she had denied herself due to her commitment to the family.

With Uncle Michael's coaching, I arranged an appointment with Girard for the next morning at eleven. He also had a precise wardrobe: ponytail, dark denim, white blouse, and flats. Annie, Jack's assistant, dressed in a similar fashion. My uncle's natural aptitude for subterfuge amused me.

Tomorrow, I would talk to the man who held my aunt's heart in his grasp.

Forty-Two

Before I donned my disguise, I had my morning errand of fetching a set of biscuits from Ines's bakery. As I walked out the apartment door, a courier arrived delivering the photograph from Auntie Faye.

I ripped the cardboard envelope open. The picture of a much younger Girard fell into my hands. I turned the five-by-seven-inch photo over and traced my hand across the inscription on the back before sliding it back into the safety of the cardboard jacket.

As I stepped out onto the sidewalk, red threads surrounded me. An elaborate embroidery undulated as the crowd flowed around me.

I took a different route to the bakery—less direct—as there was a place that I needed to return.

Boulevard Saint-Germain and rue du Bac.

Nothing was different. No errant piece of luggage. No stray garment. No physical trace of what happened two days ago. But my body remembered: the trembling of my hands, the scar on my arm, the ache in my hip, the blue cane I now used.

And a new fear of crossing streets.

I tightened my grip on the cane, dampening the tremors in my right hand while I pressed my left hand against my thigh. Avoiding this would make everything worse in the future. My erratic fortune-telling had held me hostage for too long. I couldn't allow this to do the same.

A small group of people waited with me on the corner, oblivious to my fear. I listened for the voice of the pedestrian lights, which I couldn't understand, and waited for the chime and the green walk sign.

The crowd surged forward.

People pushed past me as I remained rooted to the sidewalk.

My heart was racing, my breath ragged.

The lights changed. A new group formed.

I can't do this. It was a mistake to come this way.

Beginning to turn back, I noticed the red threads. Some were thin, but bursting with energy, while others were heavy and soft with sporadic knots. No strand seemed the same. They wrapped me in their cocoon.

My heart rate slowed. The lights turned green. The cat's cradle moved forward. I stepped off the curb and into the road.

Each thread willed me forward. My steps became steadier as I focused on them.

On the other side, they untied themselves as the couples dispersed down the street.

I exhaled. I had made it unscathed. I was going to be fine.

Lost in thought, I rounded the corner and gasped when I spotted Luc's van parked by the bakery. Curiosity spurred my feet forward despite my still-sore hip. I stopped short; I didn't want to interrupt whatever was happening inside. Pressing myself close to the edge of the window frame, I attempted to blend in with painted cats on the glass.

Luc and Ines stood across from each other. A poppy-red thread glowed and wound its way between them, linking both of their hearts. I didn't need to know what they were saying—sparkling gold dust blazed in the air with their every touch. Ines reached across the counter, tugging on Luc's collar, and pulled him tight for an intimate kiss.

I looked away and started to cry. Ines achieved her romance without compromising on the terms of her happiness. I shared in their joy. Just as I knew Ines and Luc belonged together, I was convinced that Aunt Evelyn and Girard also did.

Luc emerged from the bakery light of step, a whistle teasing his lips. He noticed my presence after loading his van.

"You were right," he said. He sounded like a man freed from a heavy burden. Luc's thread floated in the air, still connected to Ines inside. "I spoke with my parents. They aren't pleased, but that is my problem to fix."

"What made you decide to choose Ines?"

"When I realized my parents had put their needs over mine. They didn't care about what I wanted. They never asked me." He leaned against the side panel. "This is my life. I had to make a choice."

"Then you are happy?" I asked.

He smiled, elation bathing his face. "The happiest I've ever been. I love her. Today was the first day I said it aloud, to myself, to my parents, to her, and to the world."

"If you had waited longer, you would have lost her."

He gave a rueful nod before hopping into the driver's seat.

Luc's happiness banished my concerns. He reminded me that the rewards were far greater than I could hope for. Though his situation differed from Girard's, the goal remained the same. There could be no greater comfort or reward than reciprocated love.

I waved goodbye and headed inside.

Ines stood by the counter refilling a glass platter of wafer cookies. A not-so-secret smile stretched across her lips. She handed me one. "Tuiles aux amandes."

The warm, paper-thin, curved golden cookie was decorated with slivers of almonds. The shape reminded me of a can of stackable potato chips from back home. "I saw Luc drop by."

"He did." Her smile dripped with smugness and satisfaction. "He declared his love and chose me. And not a moment too soon."

I laughed before biting into the sweet treat. The combination of almonds and sugar along with the crisp texture made them irresistible, and the smell was intoxicating. If I could bottle the aromas of Ines's bakery and bring them back home with me, I would.

She began packing the wafers into a box. "How is your aunt doing? Maman wanted me to ask. She's quite worried about her. Fighting the boycott isn't going well. All this could be cleared with one word from Monsieur Renaud, but he won't unless compelled."

"And that's what I'm planning to do." I resisted the urge to beg for another delicious cookie. "I have a meeting with him in an hour."

"How did you manage that?" Ines asked. "My bartender friend mentioned that Monsieur Renaud was making himself unavailable to local businesses. He hasn't done that before. For years, he ran a mentorship program for fledgling entrepreneurs. My parents attended. The more I think about it, the more puzzled I get. He is known to be a decent man, yet this boycott is such an indecent act."

"Do you think he might not know it's happening? Is this possible?"

"Anything is possible." Ines handed me the sealed box of tuiles aux amandes in a paper bag and another envelope from Marc.

"I guess I should ask him."

Forty-Three

My aunt was cleaning a teapot when I walked in. Her wardrobe was, again, dark gray. Gone were the romantic and cheery pastels she had been known for all my life. A severe, high-necked dress was paired with a charcoal shawl. With her upswept hair, she appeared like a character in a gothic novel, the stern heroine standing against an isolated rain-soaked English country house.

"Good morning, Auntie. I brought almond wafer cookies that look like potato chips." I set the bag on the counter. "How are you?"

"Fine, I'm fine." Her reply convinced no one. The weariness in her voice implied another night of restless sleep. "What are you up to today?"

"Oh, seeing more of the city. There's still so much I haven't explored or eaten. I intend to come home with enough memories to sustain me until I visit you again."

She nodded her head, but I doubted that she heard me. Her dark eyes gazed into the distance as if she were lost in a waking dream. The haunting melody returned, settling in as a low hum from her lips.

"Call me if you need anything," I said. "I'll be back later this afternoon." Hopefully, with good news.

"Have a good time, dearest," she replied as I walked out the door.

I walked to the courtyard doors, punched in the code, and climbed the stairs. My aunt's unhappiness had encroached upon mine, such that I decided to leave Marc's envelope sealed. He wasn't going anywhere, and I needed to focus on the task before me.

As I made my way toward Le Papillon Bleu, I rehearsed what I needed to say to Monsieur Renaud. While I didn't fear being flustered, I was concerned with the structure of my argument, that reminding Girard of his past love for my aunt might not be enough. I had no other avenues or angles. If I was unable to convince him of my aunt's affections, she would be worse off. Her feelings would be exposed to the man who could do the most damage.

Personal history was a tricky, mercurial narrative. Two people might be present at the same event, but their recollection differed based on emotions, biases, and attention to specific details. Family gatherings were often a forum to demonstrate and debate how past events had unfolded. There was never an impartial judge or a shortage of opinions.

I tapped the cardboard sleeve with the photo inside. If only I could speak with the man from the picture. That man's love for my aunt was unquestionable.

Le Papillon Bleu was empty when I arrived, ten minutes before the designated time. Punctuality was a dominant Yu trait that even my bad-boy cousin Johnny couldn't escape. No one in the family was ever late—except for Cynthia.

The hostess, a pretty redhead, greeted and escorted me to the bar to wait. The art nouveau decor spilled into the space in its gilt and flowing plant-influenced sculptural details. Liquor bottles glowed like jewels against a glittering, golden mosaic backsplash. The vibrancy of the color palette brought a smile to my face.

Ten minutes later, she returned and said in heavily accented English, "Monsieur Renaud will you see you in his office now, Miss Chu."

I picked up my structured navy vegan-leather tote from the stool beside me and followed.

The path to his office was through a series of hallways, none of which passed the kitchen. I had hoped to catch a glimpse of Marc. My guide led me to a door with a gold plaque bearing the proprietor's name. She gave me a tight smile and left.

I took a series of deep breaths and opened the door.

Oil paintings and framed watercolors of Montmartre graced the far wall while the others had photographs with noteworthy people, press events, and newspaper clippings. With a round stained glass window depicting peonies behind him, Girard Renaud sat at his desk in a high-backed, tufted leather chair. A small stack of folders lay in a rectangular, wooden tray in the top left corner. The rest of the desk surface remained free of clutter.

Two Queen Anne–style chairs were stationed for guests. I recognized the style as the same as one of the beautiful, comfortable chairs Aunt Evelyn had kept in the parlor of her Victorian.

He stood up and gestured to one of the chairs. "Please have a seat, Miss Chu."

There was no look of recognition in his blue eyes—I almost

sighed out loud from relief. He only saw my aunt that night. I sat down and placed the tote on my lap.

"Jack McCrae is a talented photographer. I'm an admirer and flattered that he wants to use the restaurant for one of his shoots." Girard returned to his seat. "I'm especially drawn to his personal collections. I have a piece hanging in my house from his Prague architectural series."

I remembered this collection. It was the exhibition in San Francisco where I had introduced Uncle Michael to Jack. There were buyers from all over the world. My uncle was ecstatic with his purchase.

"Which one?" I asked.

"The exterior shot of the House of the Black Madonna."

"Ah, the cubist building. One of my favorites. Black and white or color?"

"Black and white." A smile teased the corner of his lips. "I should have known that his assistant would know all of his pieces."

I nodded. That particular collection had a significant memory attached to it. I hoped he wouldn't quiz me about the rest.

Before the conversation continued, I opened my tote, withdrew the cardboard envelope containing his photograph, and slid it across to him facedown.

He picked it up and pulled out the photo. A kaleidoscope of emotions—surprise, shock, regret, fury—shifted across his face. He closed his eyes as his fingertips brushed against the edge of the paper. His other hand held the edge of the desk, knuckles white from the tight grip, his breath ragged. After a stretch of silence, he asked, "Where did you get this?"

"This was you, when you were in love with my aunt." My reply was quiet, but firm. "You loved her then."

"Did this come from her? Did she hold on to this?"

"No. She doesn't know I have it. I came here to show you this and to ask you to call off the boycott and to help dispel the rumors about her."

His handsome face was implacable.

All traces of his earlier emotions had vanished. "What happens to her business is no concern of mine."

"But this is a bigoted attack on her character! The language in that flyer is inflammatory and racist. You're supposed to be a man of integrity. Everyone will assume you share the same hateful view."

His spine straightened as his jawline tensed. "I wasn't aware of what had been disseminated." Every word was precise. "I assure you that I will put a stop to it at once."

"And what about my aunt? She loves you. She moved here for you. She's risked everything she owns to make a new life here."

"And she told you all this? She's made her affections clear?"

"Not in so many words, no."

"If she feels this way, why isn't she here? Instead, you're here. Her family is always interfering and she allows them to. She cares more about them than she ever did about me. She made her choice and she's made it clear."

"Yes, she loves her family, but she also loves you. It's not—"

"You weren't there," he interrupted, "when I waited that day at the airport, or the next when I sobbed in the apartment we found together, or the years I spent hoping she would return because I had made my restaurant a reality."

"But she left us all behind. She sold her house in California, and put everything she owns into her business here, to be with you. Isn't that enough? What more proof do you need to convince you that she still loves you?"

"Proof? You have no proof. You have a faded photograph from a previous life. You lied to see me. How do I know you're not lying about everything?" He leaned across the desk. "She could have seen me at any time. She chose not to."

"She is your match," I protested.

"Do you know why I named my restaurant Le Papillon Bleu? We were walking through Luxembourg Gardens. The flowers were in bloom and I told her I loved her. All around us, blue butterflies appeared, dancing in clusters. Blue butterflies followed us whenever we were together.

"I told her my dream for this restaurant, and I have made it a reality. I was here, waiting for her. I named the restaurant after our butterfly so she could find me. For years, I waited. She never came."

"She is here now," I replied. "She came back for you."

"I don't believe you, and if you were me, would you?"

He handed me back the photo and I tucked it into its envelope.

"I'm sorry to have bothered you," I apologized, and walked out of his office. The door made a solid snap behind me.

He had been waiting for her all these years, and he was still waiting.

Whether she never knew—or had always known—I had to find out.

Forty-Four

I returned to the empty tea shop heartbroken. I closed the door and locked it behind me. My aunt entered from the back room.

"What's wrong, Vanessa?" she asked.

I pulled out Girard's photograph and set it on the counter.

She cradled the picture in her hands. "Where did you get this?"

I didn't answer.

"I haven't seen this in years. I thought I had lost it in Paris." Her fingers traced his face. "I always suspected my roommate stole it. Whenever Chloe thought I wasn't looking, I would find her admiring him. How did you get it?"

"Auntie Faye got it from her. You were right. She did steal it, but she told Auntie Faye you left it behind by accident."

Bursts of color bloomed in her cheeks. "Wait. Faye found her. They're investigating me?"

"They wanted to help. When you moved away, you didn't tell anyone. They were worried about you being all alone here."

"I should have known you'd be complicit in their demands. I trusted you," Aunt Evelyn hissed. "And you betrayed me, to them."

"They are our family. Their methods might be questionable, but we look out for one another. Everyone is worried about how you don't have anyone here. You push people away when they want to help you."

"Yes, because unsolicited help is the solution. Interference, subterfuge, gossip, and outright manipulation. That's what my family is good at. Why did you think I wanted to get away?"

"That's unfair, Auntie. We love you and are trying to help. We think you'd be happy with—"

"With Girard? 'We think,' because I'm too stupid to figure it out myself and you all know what's best. Is that it?"

I took a deep breath to collect myself. She was too busy being angry to listen. "You've done all the work to get here. You made the big move, started your business, you just need to reach out to him. That's it. That's the last step, Auntie. He loves you so much and is waiting for you to tell him that you feel the same."

"And how do you know? Your aunties or the private inspector they hired told you?" She crossed her arms. Her gaze hardened.

"I talked to him myself. He told me everything, about the blue butterfly, his goal of opening his own restaurant, and how long he waited for you. You just have to go to him. Tell him."

"How dare you, Vanessa. You had no right. This is my life."

Her anger chilled the room. Frost spread across the glass surfaces in the shop, fogging and obscuring. I shivered, and hugged my bare arms as the temperature dropped. Goose bumps appeared on my skin.

"Why won't you talk to him?" I asked through my chattering teeth.

"That's none of your business."

"Did you know he's been waiting for you all these years?"

"Of course I knew! He never married, although he's dated his fair share of women. The restaurant was exactly where he said he would build it. I chose the location of the tea shop because of it. I did all of this"—the fury in her voice broke—"so we could be together." She stepped back and collapsed against the counter. "For years I've kept track of what he was doing and what he's accomplished. I've always known."

"Then why won't you talk to him?"

"I can't. It's not meant for me. Leave me be."

"You keep pushing people away, Auntie. People who love you." I took a step toward her. She waved me away. "Auntie, please."

Tears of frustration and sorrow ran down my cheeks. I cried because she wouldn't. Her crippling fear was keeping her from her own happiness. She accepted she was destined to be alone, so she was alone, a self-fulfilling prophecy.

I escaped the confines of the wintry shop and made my way back to the apartment. I had given it my best shot. There was nothing left that I, or the aunties, could do. Aunt Evelyn was the master of her own fate and she chose not to act. I was more invested in helping her than she was.

In need of comfort, I sought out Marc's envelope in my purse. My fingertips ripped the edge clean to reveal another drawing inside. I laughed at the subject: a forlorn, shattered phone in the shape of a heart. The scattered pieces formed the pattern of tiny arrows. There was a short note on the other side of the paper.

The phone is dead. Will need to get a new one. I miss you.

I don't know when I'll be able to see you. Boss has bumped up my hours. I'm even busier now. I'm so stressed out and the boys have offered to cheer me up in the little time we have free after midnight. I'd much prefer seeing you.

The writing was sloppy. There was no attempt to coordinate another meeting, which worried me. This situation was untenable, and we were running out of time. When I met him, he was agitated and overextended, but this was worse.

Outside the window, the cityscape of Paris called out to me in tantalizing whispers: the Champs-Élysées, the Eiffel Tower, and all of the galleries and museums I'd yet to visit. I had planned to explore more neighborhoods, but it wasn't as appealing without my gorgeous tour guide. I didn't want to be out alone.

I flopped down on the bed and sighed.

The two Yu women on this side of the Atlantic were in rough shape. Nothing was going according to plan. My settled routine had been upended, and I spun like a compass needle searching for north. I had arrived in Paris with so much baggage, had tried so hard, only to have fate intervene. The woman who woke in the hospital was free, but freedom meant nothing without purpose. All my life, my peculiar propensity for predictions had defined me, had circumscribed the possible and narrowed my world. Without it, who was I? I had hated it, but it made me unique: I was now ordinary, but what did that even mean?

I stood up and began rearranging the decorative pillows on the bed, agitated.

Ines and Luc had been my project; they were happy, but how could I claim any credit? They had known each other for years. He would have made the right choice, eventually. It was a false sense of confidence: I tried with Girard and Aunt Evelyn and failed, taking a complicated situation and making it worse. And Marc and I were in limbo, a couple in name only.

I hadn't helped anyone. This must be how my aunt felt when she was unable to help me. The disappointment spread into the other aspects of my life until I, too, was dissatisfied.

What was I supposed to do? The uncertainty shook me.

I did what I had always done when I felt this way: I sought out my mother. It was early morning back home. Ma would be cradling her cup of coffee and clicking through her celebrity gossip blogs.

"Ma?"

"What's wrong?" My mother picked up on my mood despite being thousands of miles away.

I detailed the meeting with Girard and the situation with Marc. I yearned for guidance and her wisdom.

"For Evelyn, there isn't anything left for you to do." There was a pause and the sound of sipping coffee. "As for your boyfriend, Vanessa, you know what to do. Why are you really calling?"

Forty-Five

Ma's powers of perception overshadowed my own when it came to my emotions. She already knew. I'd ask if she had clairvoyance, but her insight only pertained to me. A form of foresight forged by maternal love.

"I can't hide much from you, can I?" I asked her over the phone.

"I love you and, of course, I pay attention because I care. I only made you and no replacements." My mother often used that phrase to denote my lack of siblings.

"I feel lost, Ma. I don't know what to do with my life, or even where to look for answers."

"Your life changed recently. It would be unusual to not be introspective, but you're young still, you can take the time to figure it out. I don't know what you'll become, but I know the moment you get an inkling, your feet won't be able to run fast enough to get you there." She chuckled.

"I hope it's soon. You know how impatient I am."

"I do. And you'll make this work with Marc. As for Evelyn, we'll have to wait and see. I have never seen her upset. She is one of those rare types who keep their emotions to themselves. As upset as she is, though, I don't see her holding on to grudges for long. That's Ning's specialty. Evelyn is strong. She is a Yu, whether she admits it or not."

"I love you, Ma."

"I love you too. Try and enjoy your stay there. You're coming home soon and it hasn't been much of a restful vacation."

I made a face and laughed. "I'll call you soon. Send Dad my love."

"I'll tell him you called."

Energized by my conversation with my mother, I decided to surprise my aunt with dinner, and began foraging for takeout ideas while waiting for her to close the store for the day.

One way to show love was through food: the act of preparation, feeding, and eating. For weekend get-togethers, my aunties spent between a night and several days making their signature dishes. Each ingredient and seasoning was picked with meticulous care. The recipes they used were their own creations, or else passed down through their direct ancestors. Tradition guided their hands.

Feeding was more than an act of nourishment. The call of an auntie to eat during a visit was equivalent to a demonstration of affection. To coax a relative toward the ladened dinner table was an unspoken inquiry into their well-being, creating an endless paradox of constant offerings of food and unwanted observations of expanding waistlines.

Communal eating fostered and strengthened our family. Food was the official reason why we gathered, yet the comfort of each other's company remained the underlying cause. My cousin Chester once likened our parties to a biblical locust swarm: no trace of food was left in the aftermath.

Aunt Evelyn needed support. She wouldn't accept any comfort from me through words or an embrace, but she wouldn't turn down the offer of dinner. There was a sushi restaurant I had spotted a block from the apartment. No language barrier could prevent a Yu from ordering an assortment of maki and sashimi.

The shop closed at six in the evening, and Aunt Evelyn made her way upstairs. I had laid out the giant platter of sushi, maki, and sashimi. Rainbow, unagi, and dragon rolls clustered around each other like colorful mosaic tiles in a mural medallion. Strips of raw, marbled salmon, crimson tuna belly, bicolored surf clam, fine slices of avocado, and creamy snapper rested on waves of spiralized daikon radish and pink roses made of pickled ginger. The bounty on the table was more than enough for four people, let alone two. Like the women in my family, I intended to smother my aunt with edible affection.

Aunt Evelyn put away her shawl and almost bypassed the feast waiting for her.

"I thought you'd be hungry." I pulled out a chair.

Her tight smile betrayed effort. She took her seat and gave the food a cursory survey. I knew her appetite was waning. "This is too much food, Vanessa." She picked up the takeout chopsticks, pulled them apart, and rubbed them together to remove any stray splinters.

I joined her at the table and performed the same ritual with the chopsticks. "How was your day at the shop?"

"I had three customers. Ines's mother, Fatima, along with her two sisters, came to show their support and bought a few tins. While I appreciate the gesture, it's not sustainable." Aunt Evelyn plucked a toro sushi and two pieces of matching sashimi off the platter. "It's not right for my friends to shoulder the burden."

Without a word, I added three more pieces of red tuna to her plate. "What is your plan to counteract the boycott?"

"I don't think there is anything I can do anymore. I contacted the business associations in the area, but ran into interference. The grand opening was supposed to be modest, steady, and sustainable. That didn't last beyond the first few days. How could I anticipate a boycott? I'm insured against natural disasters and fire, not bigotry. Unless something changes, I'll need to contact my realtor and sell."

I opened my mouth to make a suggestion about alternative financing, but I doubted she'd be receptive. The fight had gone out of her; my aunt was the portrait of resignation.

"I want to help."

She winced and looked through me, her eyes bloodshot and glassy.

I had hurt her, again.

Before, my barbs were born of frustration with my situation, like a toddler throwing a tantrum. Today, however, I had the unearned confidence of a teen, sure of my cause without regard to the consequences, and created a wake of drama, another mess for the adults to clean up.

"I know I've screwed up," I said. "I've made it worse for your business and between you and Girard. It's my fault. You don't deserve any of this." She raised her hand and parted her lips to speak, but I continued, halting her objection. "Before you say anything, I want you to know how sorry I am for what I have done."

"I'm not angry with you, Vanessa, just hurt." She put her food down, and rested her cheek on the back of her right hand, elbow on the table. "You had good intentions. You thought you were helping and, even though I had warned you against interfering in people's lives, you did so anyway, and mucked it up. Hopefully you've grown and learned that, sometimes, things don't work out the way we intended, planned, or hoped."

Nothing I could say could take back the pain I had caused, so in true Yu fashion, I filled her plate with her favorites and hoped it was enough for now. Forgiveness could not be asked for, it must be earned, and it took time. We ate in silence, swallowing the words we dared not say aloud.

Forty-Six

My aunt found me in the kitchen making jasmine tea at sunrise. I bucked the trend of sleeping in to provide support for my heartbroken aunt. She still moved with grace, yet an underlying weariness tainted every gesture. Dark smudges settled under her eyes.

"We have leftover sushi. Do you want that for breakfast?" I asked.

She pulled the chair out. The legs dragged on the hardwood floor from the effort, an uncomfortable sound that echoed through the apartment. "It has to be eaten."

I took the food from the fridge and grabbed the plates and cutlery. "You will get through this. Not because you've foreseen it, but because you are one of the strongest women I know."

She met my eyes, searching for a sign that I had said my words in jest and, when she found none, reached for my hand across the table. I squeezed her hand in mine. Aunt Evelyn drew in a deep breath as if to collect herself.

"You will survive this," I repeated with a smile. "Uncle Michael mentioned you are as stubborn as I am."

"More so. I had more years of practice." Aunt Evelyn straightened her shoulders. "Today, I'll open up the shop. It's another day that I can fight. Come to work with me. You can pretend to be a customer."

I laughed. "If you want me there, I'll be there."

"I'd really appreciate the company."

In her shop Aunt Evelyn seemed more like herself.

She wasn't as hopeful or as cheerful as I'd seen her, but her smiles were more frequent. For the first time in days, my worries about her welfare subsided. There was a quiet strength underneath the immaculate facade. This beautiful woman, whom I was proud to call my aunt, survived the most devastating of heartbreaks.

She would be fine.

I would be fine.

The bell above the door tinkled.

Ines entered carrying two small boxes in her arms with her bakery's logo. The gold bangles on her wrist jingled, matching her dangling gold earrings. The smile on her ruby lips rivaled the sunshine outside. "Good morning, ladies."

Aunt Evelyn and Ines exchanged three sets of cheek air kisses.

"How are you and Luc?" I asked.

"We are quite happy." She blushed. "Our parents met for dinner and it went better than expected. It didn't occur to Luc's parents until now that having their in-laws as bakers could be beneficial to their grocer business. They've been so fixated on organic farming that they failed to see other possibilities. There will be a formal meeting of families in two weeks at his grandparents' chateau in Toulouse. We're both optimistic, and terrified."

Aunt Evelyn's eyes crinkled at the corners. "I'm happy for you, Ines. I know how long you waited."

"You're looking better." Ines unloaded the boxes on the counter and examined my aunt's face. "Maman was worried about you."

"Fatima is sweet." My aunt reached for my hand and drew me to her side. "I had a chat with my niece this morning. She adjusted my perspective."

"You are going to fight then?" Ines asked.

"Yes. I'll find a way to get around this ridiculous boycott."

I let go of my aunt's hand to investigate the wonderful aromas coming from the boxes Ines delivered. One contained a variant of the lacy egg roll cookies I was used to back home. Unlike the round cylindrical shape of the egg rolls, these were rolled flat, a deeper golden color, and as small as my pinkie finger. Half of the stack was chocolate dipped and the rest were plain.

"Those are crêpes dentelles," Ines explained to me. "They're very crispy and one of your aunt's favorites. Aren't they?"

My aunt didn't answer.

Her gaze was fixated on one of the windows, where a lone blue morpho butterfly clung to the glass.

Forty-Seven

I waved my hand in front of her face. "Auntie?"

Aunt Evelyn didn't budge. Her dark eyes never wavered from their point of focus.

Ines followed our gaze. "Is that a butterfly? Oh, how beautiful."

We all fell silent. A figure appeared outside the window, accompanied by a cluster of dancing blue morphos. Girard. He wore a tailored dark navy suit. The serious expression on his handsome face contrasted with his whimsical, fluttering entourage.

Ines stood on one side of my aunt while I took my place on the other. We flanked her for protection and support.

"What do you think he wants?" Ines asked in a low whisper.

I frowned. "I have no idea, but if he wants a fight, I'm not leaving my aunt's side."

Girard stood near the door. He seemed to be rifling through a small stack of papers in his hands. After a few seconds of reading, he tucked the pile under his arm and opened the door.

Aunt Evelyn didn't move. Her posture remained stiff, and her unwavering dark eyes were fixed forward, toward the exit. Her hand shook in mine, tiny tremors that I steadied with a firm squeeze.

Girard stepped inside. The butterflies hovered by the windows, dancing to an invisible melody in a cascading holding pattern, a curtain of undulating blue petals.

"Monsieur Renaud, may I ask what your business is here? I can't imagine you've dropped by to purchase tea." My aunt's tone was brusque and professional.

"May I speak with you in private, Evelyn?" he asked in English.

Ines and I refused to move. I didn't need to look over to confer. We were waiting for my aunt's word.

"What you can say to me, you can say to them." My aunt stood firm. "This isn't negotiable."

"Please, Evelyn." His deep voice broke into a whisper. "But, if you insist. Why did you come to Paris? I need to hear this from you."

"Isn't it obvious?" She let go of our hands and stepped forward. "I came here so we could be together."

Ines and I moved behind the counter. It was too late to give them privacy without being obvious: the interior of the shop was small, and Girard blocked the only exit.

She and Girard moved closer until there were only a few steps separating them. A soft mist gathered at their feet, spreading outward, coalescing into fluffy clouds that reached us behind the counter. It was unexpectedly warm, and its color thickened into the opaqueness of whipped marshmallows.

"Years ago, you told me how important your family was to you, that we couldn't be together. You chose your family." His blue eyes focused on her. Girard and my aunt might as well have been the only ones in the room. "What changed?"

"I chose myself. I didn't have the courage until now."

"I waited for you." Girard lowered his head. "I knew you were moving here. I watched the renovations from afar. When you showed up at the restaurant, I was angry. Seeing you brought back too many painful memories. You're as beautiful as our first day together, but what I saw that night was a woman whose confidence intimidated me. I thought you returned to show me you had moved on."

Aunt Evelyn remained silent. She clasped her hands together, I suspect, to keep them from trembling.

"I questioned what we had. I told myself that you never loved me, that my memories were nothing but beautiful lies. Everything I had done with the restaurant was to fulfill a promise and show you the man I became. I was angry and acted inappropriately."

She narrowed her eyes.

"The boycott and the rumors to target your suppliers weren't my idea, but I claim responsibility. I did nothing to stop or discourage it. Leticia and Claude orchestrated the campaign. I don't expect you to forgive me." He paused to fidget with the papers in his hands. "I called all of my contacts to clear this up. I also made arrangements with journalists to have a few pieces written about the tea shop in the papers. It's only a start. I need to do more."

"If you only came here to apologize . . ."

"I did, but also because of these." He handed her one of the yellowed envelopes from his stack.

Aunt Evelyn examined the envelope and gasped, holding a free hand up to cover her mouth. "How did you get these?"

"I received them yesterday. They were addressed to my old family home, but we haven't lived there for decades. The current residents forwarded them to the restaurant." He pressed the rest of the stack against his chest. "You loved me. You wanted to be with me as much as I did."

"But I never sent them. I tucked them away in a box in the attic and forgot about them."

The envelope in her hand looked familiar: the handwriting, the address, the paper. I had found them in the mailbox when I arrived, and had mailed them. At the time, I assumed someone must be waiting for them, and someone was—Girard.

"Lost things find their way to where they need to be, Evelyn. I know the whispers of your heart echo mine." He walked over to her, dropping the letters onto the floor, where the thick fog covered them.

Girard took her trembling hands in his, steadying them with a firm squeeze before he reached up to cup her cheek. His hand hovered an inch away, as if to ask for her permission. She reached up and pressed his hand against her skin, tilting her head to lean into the caress.

The intimate gesture made me blush, and a quick glance toward Ines suggested she felt the same.

"I love you, Evelyn. I never stopped. You have always had every piece of me." He kissed her fingertips. "I don't know if you still feel the same way. After what I've done, I can't expect you to."

She touched his lips. "Are you asking if I still love you?"

"Yes. Do you still love me?"

Forty-Eight

Ines and I leaned forward behind the counter. My aunt's happiness hinged on her answer. She wanted Girard to come to her, and now he had. It didn't matter that she didn't have a red thread: love in its simplest form was standing before her.

I didn't dare glance at Ines. She probably had her heart hovering in her throat like I did.

Aunt Evelyn fought for family, for her business, and for me, but when it came to love, she hadn't.

I had no right to interfere with my aunt's decision-making process; however, the temptation to bring them both together like the dolls I pretended to marry as a child was great. The aunties back home would never have had the discretion, self-control, or patience to stand by the sidelines.

With every passing heartbeat, my doubts grew.

In times like these, the right choice was clear to everyone but the person burdened with it.

The earthbound clouds shifted in color. Shades of pink from the softest blush to sparkling coral to the deepest fuchsia. The intensity of the hue changed with every microsecond.

Please, Aunt Evelyn.

Make the right choice.

This is your chance to be happy—to be loved.

It's your time.

"Yes."

Ines and I exhaled as Girard cupped my aunt's face in his hands and kissed her. She wrapped her arms around him, burying her fingers in his hair as he drew her closer against him. A red thread, sparkling and new, wound its way around the couple. The magnificent sparks flew from the string, strengthening, transforming into a braid.

The kiss between them rivaled Klimt's painting. Decades of longing matched the intensity and duration. After a while, I turned away; Ines continued to watch.

She purred. "Those two have endurance for their age."

I choked from swallowing my laughter.

"I mean, I'd want that for me and Luc, as I'm sure you'd want the same for you and Marc." Ines scrunched her nose and grinned. "I hope Marc will follow you back to America after he finishes his stint at the restaurant."

I did my best to hide my sadness.

The warmth near my feet vanished, and the floor returned to normal. Aunt Evelyn and Girard stood side by side, skin touching, holding hands as if they couldn't be physically parted. A soft blush settled on my aunt's cheeks. The red thread linked their hearts, dangling with the slack of a pocket watch chain.

"As you can see, we've settled our differences," he said.

Aunt Evelyn laughed. "We certainly did."

"Auntie, you have a red thread," I declared.

She pressed her hand against her chest. The thread wrapped itself around her fingers. "How?"

"I don't know, but you didn't need me to tell you. You feel it, don't you?"

My aunt nodded.

Ines checked her watch. "I have to get back to the bakery. Don't worry, I will tell my mother how everything worked out. Maman will relish all the details." She giggled and made her exit with a bouncy skip to her step.

"I hope she'll leave out the more intimate specifics," Aunt Evelyn said to me.

Girard bent down and carefully gathered the fallen envelopes.

"So what now? What are you two going to do?" I asked her.

"I'm not sure yet, but whatever it is, it will be together. There's much to talk about," she confessed.

"I'll let you do that then." I excused myself and gave them their first moment of true privacy.

The blue butterflies clustered around the window as if they, too, wanted to shield the lovers from prying eyes.

There was no question I was happy for Aunt Evelyn, but I also missed Marc. There was room to feel both without invalidating either emotion. My aunt told me there was no cure for heartbreak if I didn't want to let him go.

Seeing the city on my own seemed daunting and exhausting. I had planned on spending the day with my aunt, but that was no longer an option.

I sighed.

"Vanessa?"

I turned toward the voice. Girard stood beside me. "I wanted to thank you."

"For what?"

He showed me one of the envelopes. "Evelyn and I figured you were responsible for mailing these."

At the time, I didn't think much of them because I'd been guided by an innate sense of duty. "I found them in the mailbox. I didn't know they were written by my aunt or that they were meant for you."

"I'd like to think that you were more involved than that." He tucked the envelopes under his arm. "Evelyn and I reunited not because of fate, but from human intervention."

"You don't believe in destiny?"

"I do. Evelyn is my soul mate and my destiny, but regarding this, no. Our ability to control our fates is what makes life interesting. If everything had been predetermined, don't you find the lack of free will disturbing?"

Girard's philosophical side was in line with how Aunt Evelyn's mind worked. I could imagine them having conversations stretching from dusk till dawn. Marc and I, instead, would be at the night market, eating our way through every stall.

"I don't know if my aunt told you. I've never been one to listen to what I'm told unless I agree with it. I believe that we have the ability to shape our own lives."

"To me," he continued, "you are responsible for our happiness. You approached me at my office to advocate for your aunt. Combined with the letters, I see you as a most brilliant matchmaker." He kissed the back of my hand. "Come to dinner at the restaurant tomorrow night with Evelyn. You are the first member of her family I have met. There's much to talk about."

I smiled. "I'd be delighted."

Forty-Nine

With my aunt receiving her happy ending, I was more determined to get my own. Aunt Evelyn and Girard had left the shop together with my aunt telling me, "I have an important late engagement and will not be back until morning." The giddiness she exhibited was infectious and made me excited about my own romantic future.

Tonight, I intended to see Marc after work.

I glanced at the antique French ormolu clock on the mantel. There was time for a decent nap before I went to see Marc at the restaurant. I wanted to see him and, according to his notes, he felt the same. Yet I shared Girard's predicament, the need to see the proof of love for myself.

It wasn't that I doubted Marc's love; it was more that I wanted to see where this new relationship would lead. My aunt found her happily ever after. Why couldn't I get mine too?

Hours later, after a languid nap, I left the apartment and headed for the restaurant. The time apart had increased my anticipation of seeing him. Under the streetlamps, I stood before the blue butterfly mosaic mural and waited. Girard's love letter to my aunt, made of tile, brick, and mortar.

The restaurant was closed but I could still see the light from the kitchen through the dim windows. They must still be finishing up. I pulled out my phone and killed time until, at last, the lights turned off.

I lingered by the mural and peeked around the corner for anyone exiting the building. The pretty redhead who had escorted me to Girard's office exited the front door, toting a heavy satchel. She was locking up. No one was with her.

Hoping she might remember me, I emerged from my hiding place and waved. "Hi, I'm looking for Marc."

A flicker of recognition flashed in her eyes. "He is heading out the back. You can catch him around the corner. I think he's going out with the boys from the kitchen."

After a quick thank-you, I heeded her instructions and caught a group of men walking down a side street.

"Vanessa!" Marc said as he waved me over. "What are you doing here?"

"I came to see you."

He put his arm around my shoulders and introduced me to Jacques the sous chef, and Kristoff and Pierre, two of the five sommeliers on staff. Each gave me a polite smile in return. Pierre said something to Marc before he took off with the others in a different direction. Marc called out to them. They paused to wave and continued on their way.

"You look good." Marc smiled and drew me into his arms. "I've missed you."

I pressed my cheek against his leather jacket. "I missed you too."

As my fingers found the hem, I saw a subtle glow. I stepped back.

Sprouting from my chest, thin as embroidery floss, a fragile, wispy, red thread sparkled in a brilliant shade of poppy. I reached out to grasp it, felt nothing, yet the thread moved, reacting to my gesture.

I believed, for years, that I couldn't be loved. My path had been set with the unfinished tea Ma had left twenty-four years ago. Failed relationships and broken hearts. A life devoid of hope, stripped tea leaf by tea leaf.

Now, on this Parisian street corner, my deepest desire had been gifted to me. The thread wound its way among our clothes, binding us closer.

Lasting romance was within my reach. I wouldn't allow it to be taken from me. Not now, not after all this time. I would have my happy ending.

Ines and Luc. Girard and my aunt. Marc and me.

Everything was possible.

"I'm really happy to see you," I said, wiping my eyes.

Marc kissed the tip of my nose. "Come on, there's a place I want you to see. It's not far from here." He tugged on my hand and we started walking.

My piqued curiosity dreamed of a hole-in-the-wall bistro, or maybe a late-night art exhibit. Something intimate, low key, and memorable—perhaps a spontaneous pop-up. The spots he had picked in the past were delightful. I didn't want to ruin the surprise by guessing. We chatted about the accident for two short blocks until he declared that we had arrived. I had not noticed the neighborhood's changing atmosphere.

"This is it." He gestured to a seedy bar.

Discarded cigarette filters littered the pavement as a thick veil of smoke wrapped around the entrance like folded hands with fingers intertwined. A few broken light bulbs gave the cheap sign a gap-toothed quality. Goose bumps prickled my skin.

I held my breath as we ducked inside. Two billiard tables flanked a long, noisy bar with a handful of circular tables in the back. Jon Bon Jovi blared on the tinny speakers. I would have thought this a joke if I weren't on a date with my boyfriend. Marc guided us to one of the tables in the back.

I recognized the players at the table: the men from the restaurant. Marc pulled up a stool for me.

This wasn't what I wanted.

My fingers gripped my sequined black clutch. The tiny discs dug into my palms.

Marc settled in and was dealt his hand. The others barely acknowledged my presence—they were too engaged in the game. Marc exchanged a few words with his friends and laughed.

I might as well not be here.

I drew my arms in, hugging myself. The worn stool under me wobbled from its age and uneven legs. I compensated by balancing myself on the balls of my feet. Tendrils of smoke thickened like a chalky fog. My throat was scratchy from the haze of cigarette smoke. I coughed in response and made no effort to minimize the gesture.

Instead of asking me if I was all right, Marc flashed me a smile before starting the next round.

I forced an awkward smile in return. He never noticed. His attention was centered on the cards in front of him.

I placed my hand on his arm in an effort to draw his interest. Without turning his head, he covered my hand with his and squeezed, treating my gesture as a form of encouragement.

Outing his gambling habit had caused a temporary rift between us. Marc told me he had cut it out of his life, yet he was here, lured by a pastime that could easily trip into something worse.

One of my clients at the firm owned an office supply business that couldn't feed his gambling addiction fast enough. It poisoned everything, from his personal and business finances to his marriage and family life. I didn't know how to handle it and had to escalate it to one of the managing partners.

I didn't need my aunt to read my tea leaves to know where Marc and I could be headed.

He laughed, flashing his straight, white teeth when he won, revealing his cards.

It would be so easy to take him home after this trip and introduce him to the family. The aunties would love his charm and his good looks. They didn't need to know about the gambling habit. I could bury it. It wasn't so hard to see what I didn't want to see.

I had everything I had wanted: my predictions gone, a relationship with a man I cared about.

It should be enough.

But starting a serious relationship with coping mechanisms in place was never something I wanted, no matter the man. I could not be content to live with this shadow looming over us, to be so grateful that I'd been given this gift of romance that I'd overlook any flaw, to care about love more than I cared about myself.

The smoky air thickened, constricting my throat.

"Can we talk?" I asked, tapping him on the arm and glancing toward the exit.

I risked losing everything I had always hoped for.

Marc nodded. He left the table and we made our way to the exit, but not before his hand found mine and clasped it. I welcomed the cool night air as we found a spot under a nearby streetlamp. Before I could say a word, he cradled my face in his hands and kissed me. I leaned into his warm lips and his embrace, reaching up to thread my fingers through his thick hair. His strong hands traveled down to the small of my back. The heat of his touch burned through the jersey fabric of my dress. Any coherent thought in my mind burst like golden bubbles in champagne.

A soft breeze sent wisps of my hair into the air as the clouds overhead parted, revealing a field of sparkling stars whose light rivaled the city's lights. We broke apart long enough to crane our necks to the sky and admire its impromptu brilliance.

Marc brushed his thumb against my lower lip. "As you can tell, I've missed you."

"The feeling is mutual." I cupped his cheek where a two-day stubble grew.

"I know I've been working too much—"

I placed a finger to his lips. "You know we don't have much time together. And don't try to kiss me again. I'll forget what I need to say."

He nodded and kept silent. His beautiful brown eyes focused on me.

If I said nothing, I would resent myself and, in time, my resentment would transfer to him.

The weight of what I needed to say caused me to pause before proceeding. I chose each word with care, as if they would be tattooed on my skin.

"I hoped for this all of my life. For the longest time, I wanted to be in love and to be loved. And to fall in love in here, I couldn't have asked for a better fairy tale." I placed my hand on his chest. "I understand your job is stressful and your need for an outlet is justified, but I can't compete with that, nor do I want to."

"What are you saying?"

"I love you, Marc, but that"—I gestured toward the poker tables—"can't be more important than us." I tiptoed and kissed his cheek. "I'm sorry."

He didn't try to stop me.

Our red thread snapped like a taut rubber band and vanished as my heart constricted from the loss.

I walked away and headed toward the apartment, hearing the rumbles of thunder overhead. The colorful awnings of the shops and cafés turned into a smeared pigmented blur through my clouding peripheral vision. The weight of what I had given up caused a deluge of sobs and tears as the sky wept with me.

Fifty

There was only one heartbroken Yu woman in the apartment the next morning. I had stayed up all night; my aunt returned after sunrise. She was the exact opposite of how I felt: jubilant and glowing from a night with her true love.

"You look terrible," Aunt Evelyn remarked, taking the teacup I offered.

Since I crumpled the note I had left last night explaining my absence, I told her between sips what had happened.

"I'm sorry, Vanessa. I had hoped you would continue your relationship."

"I had the choice to not say anything," I whispered into my tea. "I could have lived with it."

"That would be a disservice to you and your needs. He also lied to you by saying that he wasn't going anymore. You deserve better. You made the right decision."

"But it hurts, Auntie. He was such a great guy."

The tears fell again, big droplets trickling down from my cheeks. The sobs soon followed. The logical part of me protested, saying I didn't know him long enough or well enough. The justifications of why I shouldn't have fallen in love couldn't mitigate my anguish. Not even close.

Last night, I chose myself over what I wanted most. Ma once told me, "When you love someone, their love should always be more than yours, even if it's only by a spoonful. Treat love as the most precious of gifts. Never take advantage of it. To love someone blindly is only good if that person thinks of you first, and won't allow you to fumble in the dark."

When my aunt's arms wrapped around me, I cried harder and, for the longest of moments, my tears were hers. My aunt understood my anguish. Heartache didn't discriminate nor did it decrease in intensity. The only cure was time, and knowing that my aunt had been nursing hers for years, and hadn't recovered until now, brought me no comfort.

"Your first love leaves an imprint on your soul. You have to want to forget and, even then, you're haunted by the memories," my aunt whispered against my cheek. "I thought of him when I should have moved on. The autonomy of the heart and its wishes contradicts even the most obvious logic."

"Did you foresee this with me and Marc?"

"Yes, I saw this, and I mentioned it. There was no point in dissuading you: we both know you wouldn't have listened. Besides, why would I rob you of the experience?" She opened the cupboards to search for a particular tin to brew a fresh pot of tea. "Falling in love, regardless of whether it works out, is something everyone should experience once. Do you regret it all?"

Every moment I spent with Marc, until the end, was a joy. "No."

"Are you going to give up on romance?"

The memories would sustain me until I learned to love again. And I would love again. I owed it to myself and my red thread. "No. I'm too stubborn to give up now."

"Yes, you're certainly that." Aunt Evelyn kissed my cheek. "Choosing yourself was admirable."

"I agree, but I wish it didn't hurt so much."

"There's always a measure of pain involved in difficult decisions. One would be a fool to believe otherwise."

The wound in my heart was undeniable.

Helping my aunt get ready for a date lifted my spirits more than I could imagine. She showed me her impressive collection of jewelry and debated between which pieces to wear before deciding on a bold poppy-red, fishtail midi dress.

"The pendant or the chandelier?" She raised a diamond to her left ear, examined her reflection, then picked up a larger, gold chandelier earring accented with diamonds. "Is this too much?"

If she wore a garbage bag with a plastic bag hat, Girard would still say she looked beautiful. Seeing Aunt Evelyn happy diminished some of my heartache. "Unless you're changing your shoes, I'd go with the diamond pendant."

"Then you wear the gold. It goes with your dress." She placed the earrings in my hand.

I decided to wear a gathered crêpe de chine gown in a shade of lilac so light it was almost white. A high slit on my left side showed off the gold sandals. "Thank you for letting me borrow."

"Tonight will be a wonderful meal. We're going to have the chance to eat dessert this time."

"You've foreseen it?" I asked. "No major disasters? Getting kicked out of a restaurant is an experience I don't want to repeat."

My aunt laughed. "Yes, this will be a beautiful night. Don't worry, and enjoy yourself."

"I never understood why you loved your gift, but now that I'm rid of it, I think I understand: it's your means of helping people, isn't it?"

"That's exactly it. I have helped many people over the years." She finished putting on the pendant earrings and moved toward the gown laid out on the bed. "That reminds me, do you remember the gentleman to whom you gave a prediction about his father?"

"How could I forget?" I had foreseen the father's sickness and eventual death.

"He came back to the tea shop and asked me to pass along his gratitude. His father now has someone checking in on him, and spare keys were given to the neighbors as a precaution." My aunt slid into her gown and presented her back to me to help with the zipper. "You saved him."

I puffed out my cheeks and let out a sound of relief. It was a pleasant surprise that this incident worked out, but the burden of seeing the future was one I was glad to be rid of. My aunt was born to wield this kind of power. I admired her for it.

I pulled the slider to the top stops and smoothed out the tiny bump along the seams. "If you had to give up your gift for love, would you?"

"No, I want both. I'd like to think I've made enough sacrifices in my life to be spared this choice." She adjusted the tail of her gown. "There isn't a rule written down that we can't make the most-selfish decisions for ourselves. I'm sad it took this long for me to realize that."

When I got here, my only goal was to return to California in control. Instead, I gained a new ability and rid myself of my curse. I found love in Paris and lost it along with my sense of purpose. If I had my wish, I'd want to bring Marc home with me.

"You're thinking about him, aren't you?" Aunt Evelyn asked.

"I am. I wish I could stop, but I can't."

"Love will find a way. If Girard and I can be together now, there's hope."

I checked my scarlet lipstick in the vanity mirror. "Did you ever see both of you getting together again?"

"No. If I had, I would have done this years ago. I'm content not seeing my own future. It would make life boring otherwise. It was, however, quite helpful seeing yours. Still, I don't know how to explain what's happened to you, why your clairvoyance vanished after your accident and why you gained this new ability. And why do I have a red thread?"

All of my aunt's concerns were valid, yet I didn't want answers. My problems were solved; the details weren't important. I'd spent too much time, thought, and misery over how much my predictions affected me. I wanted to move on to the next phase in my life even if I didn't know where it would take me.

"The red thread is a good thing," I replied. "Why wonder where it came from or what caused it?"

Aunt Evelyn arched a brow and smiled. "That is the difference between you and me. I will consult the society. This is a set of mysteries that's irresistible to any auntie. Curiosity is a powerful motivator, and you know we are a nosy bunch."

"Does this mean you've forgiven them?"

"I have, but I haven't told *them* that. Give me another day." Aunt Evelyn shut her jewelry box and held the door open for me. "We don't want to be late for dinner."

"Because you have a hot date," I teased.

"That I do." She gave me a playful smack on the arm.

Fifty-One

Girard's restaurant was like I remembered, and having him greet us as we walked in, a welcome surprise. He wore a sleek suit in charcoal with a peacock-blue silk dress shirt. Their red thread linked them together and matched the hue of Aunt Evelyn's gown. Now that I could see the physical manifestations of two people bound together, wedding rings seemed a formality.

He lifted Aunt Evelyn's fingers to his lips and kissed them and then whispered something in French in her ear. She giggled. A lone blue morpho danced over their heads.

"You both look beautiful," he said, offering an arm to me while my aunt took the other.

I placed my arm in his. "Thank you."

We stepped inside and were escorted to one of the private rooms. The opulence of the main dining room was a fraction of what I was led into. Girard explained that there were three private rooms styled after three of his favorite art nouveau artists: Alphonse Mucha, René Lalique, and Gustav Klimt.

After having seen Klimt's exhibit, I imagined that room to be full of golds and bursts of jewel tones. René Lalique, the master of glass, was a familiar name because the aunties collected and coveted his pieces. His room must showcase Girard's personal collection.

We entered the Alphonse Mucha–inspired room and were surrounded by murals of ethereal fairy women in flowing robes. Their soft, ageless faces contrasted with the heavy line work of flowers and vines. About a decade ago, I'd seen an exhibit featuring advertisement art and saw one of Mucha's works.

"Oh, Girard." My aunt placed a hand against her chest. "You remembered."

He turned to me. "Evelyn and I took a train to Prague and saw his work there. She and I have fond memories of the city."

The focal point was an exquisite bronze bust in the corner of the room, encased in a glass box. "This is a replica of Mucha's bust of Nature. A version in white and gold is housed in the Virginia Museum of Fine Arts." He smiled. "There are variations out there, but I've always been partial to this version, which was shown in Brussels."

The sculpture was highlighted by two iridescent green earrings and an accented headpiece. He pointed to the gemstone. "The original is malachite. As you can see, I've asked them to use jade."

"It's an excellent choice," I said.

He moved to pull out a gilded chair for me. I thanked him and took my seat. My aunt followed suit.

The table setting was exquisite. The plates, golden cutlery, and crystal all bore swirling, organic fluidity that was associated with the art movement. These differed from the less ornate silver set in the main dining room.

It was opulent for an intimate family dinner, yet for this momentous occasion, it was worth it. Girard and Aunt Evelyn never broke physical contact. Even now, their fingertips touched on the tabletop.

A server walked in and spoke with Girard and, moments later, reappeared with an enormous silver platter ladened with crushed ice and seventy-five oysters on the half shell and a small tray of accompanying mignonettes: traditional, sweet, and spicy. The silence between my aunt and me expressed our shared reverence for this particular mollusk.

Girard chuckled. "I see you're like your aunt. I could give a tour of where they are from, but I think it'll be more beneficial if you ask me questions after you've tasted them."

My aunt and I shared a wink and toasted each other with shells.

If I could eat only one thing in the world every day, it would be oysters. The unusual texture polarized diners. The lucky ones, who weren't repelled, became addicts. To enjoy this delicacy was to love the taste of the ocean; nothing else brought the intensity of the brine, or the power of those vast waves. They come in two shapes: cupped, from deep ocean waters, and flat, native to Europe.

The key to eating oysters was to savor the meat and drink the flavored water in the shell. Each had a subtle, distinct taste. My favorite—Kumamoto—was buttery and rich.

Before adding any extra condiments, I preferred to taste them naked and raw. I picked up a flat oyster. The moniker deceived: it was, in fact, rounder and smaller. The oyster slid through my lips, carrying a hint of citrus along with the signature saltiness.

I raised the rough, rounded shell toward Girard. "Which one is this?"

"Arcachon from the Brittany region. A lovely note of citrus, yes?" He pointed to a shell on the third tier. "Try that one."

The oyster carried a slight greenish tinge. The flavor was bold and decadent with a memorable finish. I loved it so much that I grabbed two more.

"Those are Marennes-Oleron, and they are my favorites of the breeds found in France." Girard smiled and plucked a few of them off the tray.

My foray into French oysters was a lesson I wouldn't soon forget. Girard turned out to be a fellow connoisseur as he explained which region each breed came from. Soon, we stacked the empty shells, clinking them together. They mimicked the sound of pieces of ceramic.

My aunt let out a contented sigh. "This was lavish. Merci, Girard. What a wonderful start to a meal."

"You're most welcome." He turned to me. "Thank you again, Vanessa. You've given me what my heart most desired, Evelyn back in my life."

I blushed. "It's really not my doing. I mean, you and Aunt Evelyn could have gotten together on your own. Eventually."

My aunt laughed. "It would have taken much longer, perhaps even years, without your help. You are quite good at this."

The situation between her and Girard had been tenuous. If I hadn't chosen to intervene, we wouldn't be having dinner together now.

"Evelyn tells me we're not the first couple you've matched," he said.

Three couples: Uncle Michael and Jack, Ines and Luc, and Aunt Evelyn and Girard. Setting them up was instinctive to me in the same way certain people correct a tilted picture frame on the wall when entering a room. When I saw two people who were meant to be together, I didn't question it. It was like I could see their red threads without seeing red threads.

Aunt Evelyn creased her brow. "I've been thinking about your accident. There are so many unanswered questions. I'll need to confirm with my sources, but now, I think, I can make sense of all this."

"What?"

"A part of you died that day," she replied.

Fifty-Two

"What?" I replied, choking on my champagne.

Aunt Evelyn took a sip from her glass. "It makes sense. You were born with two destinies. Clairvoyance and matchmaking." She laughed at my confused expression. "You existed with two gifts, with clairvoyance being the dominant one. You fought predictions with every fiber of your being, while the other gift remained passive. The constant struggle wasn't tenable."

"And that's why I was terrible at it?" I asked.

"Yes. The headaches and the death prediction manifested, signaling how precarious the balance was between the warring forces inside you. It explains why your predictions disappeared after the accident. Your gift died then to make room for what you were really meant to do. Seeing red threads is the mark of a matchmaker, Vanessa. You are a matchmaker, and you were always meant to be one."

The only matchmaker I had met was Madam Fong. She commanded the room and was a force. At best, I was a hapless dilettante.

"You can learn, you know. Maybe you'll take to those lessons better than the ones I gave you." Aunt Evelyn smiled as if reading my thoughts. "It's not too late."

"How are you so sure that this is what I am?"

She grinned smugly. *"You will spend the next year in Shanghai. Frustrating at first, but after a period of persistence, you will thrive and impress your instructor."*

Only a fool would question a prediction from my aunt.

"Is that something you want to do?" Girard asked me.

As I imagined a future assisting those seeking love, the whole picture slid into place like a puzzle game. An expanding web of silken red fibers flowing out from around me as I sewed a cloth of romance. It was a prediction I was happy to embrace.

"I want to do it." I turned to Aunt Evelyn. "Will I be the first matchmaker in the family?"

"Yes, but I can check our genealogy records to confirm, if you want me to."

Girard refilled my glass with more champagne. "I have friends and connections in Shanghai. If you are looking for apartments, I can help."

"Thank you. I'll take you up on your offer." I took a sip. "Ma and Dad will support my decision—I think the whole family will. I wish I wasn't going alone."

"If you're referring to Marc, I'm afraid he doesn't work in my kitchen anymore."

I almost dropped the flute in my hand. "What happened?"

Aunt Evelyn exchanged a look with Girard. He gave her a slight shake of his head. "He quit and, before you ask, I don't know where he's gone or what his plans are. His work visa isn't due to expire until fall."

My hands shook as I set down my glass. Aunt Evelyn watched me from across the table. Her dark eyes softened. The wounds from my heartbreak were still fresh. Marc.

"He'll be fine," Girard said. "You don't need to worry. He's very capable. Marc is curious and a gifted, intuitive chef. I offered to be his reference. If it provides you any comfort, I have no doubt he will succeed."

I wasn't worried about his career as much as I was about his gambling. Stress seemed to be a trigger, and if he found another inhospitable work environment, it might not end well, but he had made his choice, as had I. Marc was free to live his life as he saw fit. I wouldn't dwell on what could have been, or wish for what might be. If he wanted to be with me, he would have made it clear. The chair beside me wouldn't have been empty.

"Vanessa." Aunt Evelyn called my name, snapping my attention back to the table. "In any other case, I would say life is unfair, that every crumb of happiness is hard won. However, if there's anything that you've taught me, it's that anything is possible and, sometimes, you get what you wish for."

I cracked a weak smile.

Girard and my aunt exchanged another look. I didn't want pity from them, but I was willing to accept empathy.

"Enough about me." I downed my champagne flute and refilled my glass. "What are you two planning to do after I leave?"

"I need to focus on the tea shop. There needs to be a proper grand opening. It'll be challenging, but once I reach sustainable profits, I can hire someone." She squeezed Girard's hand.

He smiled at her. "And that's when we'll go on holiday together. We want to see Prague again. In the meantime, I hope Evelyn will be able join me at the restaurant for dinner once a week, or however often her schedule allows."

Their red thread glowed, sparkling in the light as it wound its way from their hearts to their joined hands. Love was such a miraculous gift. In time, I would learn to bring more people together and maybe find it again for myself.

The second course appeared: three kinds of hors d'oeuvres on dark slate slabs. The first were bite-size golden puffs with a cheese filling, judging by their distinct aroma. The second were an elaborate, decorated piece of pastry. Swirls and flourishes trimmed the edges, while perfect concentric circles accentuated the top. I suspected a delicious and wonderful surprise inside. Tiny, round meat tarts that appeared deceptively simple in composition and appearance completed the trio.

Aunt Evelyn pointed at the puffs. "Those are gougères." She moved on to the impressive pastry. "That is duck pâté en croûte, and the last are pissaladières."

Girard offered me the plate of puffs first. I helped myself to three gougères and three tarts. The gougères were golden, airy, and cheesy. I had assumed they were filled with cheese, but in this case, the cheese was infused into the dough. The combination was addictive. If unguarded, I would have filled up on these alone.

Aunt Evelyn brandished her knife and cut into the fancy pastry. The crust gave way to an interior that matched its elaborate crust. Inside the pattern was a replica of Klimt's *The Kiss*, using a palette of pâté, black trumpet mushrooms, various vegetables, and gelatin.

The memory of the dim gallery, the golds, projected paintings, and the man I kissed flooded back to me.

My aunt touched my arm. "Sometimes, what you wish for isn't impossible after all."

I glanced at the doorway and dropped my fork.

Marc.

Fifty-Three

Marc stood in the open doorway dressed in his white chef's jacket with the restaurant's insignia, gorgeous, competent, and in his element. My aunt and Girard rose to their feet, excused themselves, and exited the room, leaving me with him.

"I didn't think I'd see you again." I shifted in my seat. "You're as talented as I imagined you to be."

He took the seat beside me. "I asked your aunt and Girard to help me arrange this. Please don't blame them. They were only trying to help."

I laughed. My own excuse, now used on me.

"Do you still work here?" I asked.

"I put in my notice. Tonight's my last night." He lowered his eyes. "I called my parents. I talked to them about the gambling. My mother wasn't impressed. She gave me a rundown of my options, and I enrolled in an online support group. She did praise me for recognizing the issue early, but I gave you full credit for that."

Hope fluttered inside me, yet there was no red thread between us. I didn't want to rely on a physical sign, but without it, I couldn't trust where this conversation was leading. Marc had shown he was committed to dealing with his gambling habit, yet I'd still had yet to hear what would become of us—if there was still an us.

"It's great that you're doing that."

"I did it for me. I don't want this to define who I am, or who I want to be." He took a deep breath as if to center himself. Marc clasped his hands before him. The sight of his long brown tapered fingers linking together brought back memories of when we held hands.

I asked, "So what will you do now?"

"It depends."

"Depends on what?"

"You." He reached across the table for me, brushing my fingertips. "I'm afraid to hope. I know I'm not worthy, at least, not yet. I'm working on it."

My heart constricted. Was this how Aunt Evelyn felt when Girard came back to her? They had decades apart; Marc and I had days. The uncertainty of not knowing if love remained defied the boundaries of time: seconds or years, the gnawing anxiety was the same.

"What do you want?" he asked.

This was what I wanted. My aunt's words echoed in my mind. She saw my future or helped orchestrate this with Girard. It didn't matter which, the result was the same. I wanted nothing more than to say yes, but I had to make sure that he knew where I planned to go.

"I'm going to Shanghai to train to be a matchmaker."

Marc pulled back. "This is a recent development."

"Yes. I figured out what I want to do with my life." I told him about Aunt Evelyn's theories, and the resulting changes. Marc, to his credit, listened and didn't interrupt.

After I finished, he asked, "So you're set to leave for Shanghai after Paris?"

"Yes, with a brief stop in Palo Alto to talk to my parents and the rest of the family." I bit my lower lip.

"I guess I'll need to brush up on my Mandarin then."

"Wait, you want to come with me?"

"I was thinking of leaving Paris, but I didn't know where to go. Now I do."

I sobbed. Tears streamed down my cheeks as I covered my face. He wanted me. He would move thousands of miles to follow me—to be with me. The years of rejection had built a reservoir of deep despair, which, now crumbling, poured from me in heavy tears.

"I didn't mean to upset you." He knelt beside me. "If you don't want me to come along, I can—"

"I love you, Marc." I wiped away the last of my tears.

"I love you too."

I grabbed his gorgeous face with both hands and kissed him. He tasted like sugar and coffee. The warmth of his lips and the heat of his kisses sent shivers down my spine. His strong arms lifted me from my seat as his fingertips danced across the exposed skin of my back. I pressed my hands against the front of his jacket, feeling the strength of his solid chest underneath.

We moved together, re-created *The Kiss* in the flesh. Nothing else in the world mattered more.

After the kisses, I apologized to Aunt Evelyn and Girard for the delay in their meal, and Marc joined us for the rest of dinner. He took his place beside me and held my hand on the table.

"I take it you'll be going with her to Shanghai?" Girard asked him.

"Yes, I think I can find work there."

"You have my reference and I can provide you with the names of some of the restaurateurs I know. I have no doubt you'll have interviews after you land." Girard's expression softened. "I didn't make it easy on you after I found out Evelyn was moving back to Paris. I acted inappropriately and placed undue pressure on you and the staff. I'm sorry. You will all receive an added bonus with your paycheck. It's the least I can do."

"Apology accepted. No one takes heartbreak well. I know I don't, and luckily, this time I don't have to." Marc squeezed my hand under the table.

"My niece chose well," Aunt Evelyn said. She had a playful smile and gleam in her eye. "You're as handsome as Vanessa described."

I giggled when I saw him blush.

"If you're also accompanying her to Palo Alto," she continued, "you need to be prepared. The family is quite challenging. You'll need to be coached. Vanessa's parents are wonderful, but her aunties are the ones you need to watch out for."

"Auntie Evelyn!" I protested.

She shushed me and leaned closer to Marc. "They are sweet on the outside, but inside they are like a Molotov cocktail. The moment your plane ticket is printed, they've already done a background check, so don't even think about glossing over any details. Being truthful and vocal about your commitment to Vanessa will be your saving grace. If you play your cards right, you might even be treated to the first taste of Gloria's famous rice-stuffed chicken."

Marc and Girard listened in as my aunt pointed out the obvious landmines in etiquette and conversation. I couldn't tell if the two men were horrified, fascinated, or a mixture of both. My aunt spared no details and, as much as I wanted to interrupt or protest, she told no lies.

"Are they expecting a marriage proposal?" Marc asked.

"Vanessa has never gone on a second date before you. Of course they are. No matter what you do, just tell them, firmly, that it's between you and her."

"I mean, I'm not ruling it out in the future, but we need more time." He turned to me and grinned. "It'll be nice to spend more time together."

I poked his shoulder. "In Shanghai, if you survive my family."

A red thread appeared, winding its way from his heart to mine. It glowed and shimmered, matching the brightness of the one between Aunt Evelyn and Girard. My thread was thin in comparison to theirs, the width of one of Auntie Ning's chunky yarns for her crochet projects. It didn't matter how it looked, I only cared that it was there.

I loved this man and he loved me. For the girl who grew up devouring romance novels, I finally had a chance to write my own.

Destiny was mine to shape. Love was the only business I wanted to be in. There was no greater cause than giving people the joy of finding their soul mates.

Epilogue

One year later, in Paris

Le Papillon Bleu was busier than I remembered. Marc and I walked up to the mosaic mural of the blue butterflies hand in hand. We landed in Paris the night before, and settled into a nearby hotel. The jet lag wasn't as horrible as the last time I landed in the city.

I leaned my head against his shoulder. "Do you ever want to come back and work here?"

"It depends on where you'll be after you graduate." He kissed the top of my head and pulled me closer.

"If I pass. Madam Fong is hard to read, but said I have at least another six months left, if I work hard. We've been away from family for too long." I turned my head and gave him a peck on the cheek. "I'm glad we squeezed in the visit to Montreal to see your family."

"I can't believe Dad asked you for tax and investment advice."

Marc sighed. "I told him you're not doing that anymore, but he always needs more opinions. He collects them like basketball jerseys."

"I don't mind. I talk to Ma and the aunties often enough to get a gist of what the general trends are investment-wise. I don't miss being glued to my desk though." We stopped at the entrance of the restaurant.

I adjusted the collar of his charcoal sports jacket and gave the hem a little tug while Marc tucked a stray strand of auburn-brown hair behind my ear. I smoothed down the short silk charmeuse skirt of my scarlet strapless gown. My aunt had established the dress code when she sent the invitation. The meal she and Girard promised would be spectacular to mark the occasion.

"Shall we go?" I asked.

He offered me his arm and we walked inside.

After Marc chatted with some familiar faces, the host led us through the busy dining room and toward one of the private rooms. The last time we were here, we were in the Mucha room. This time, the door opened to the Lalique room. Inside, Aunt Evelyn and Girard waited for us along with Uncle Michael and Jack. All were dressed for the occasion: tailored suits and a sparkling silver off-the-shoulder gown on my aunt. I was soon surrounded by cheek kisses and embraces.

Once we all took our places at the table, the questions began.

"We are all dying to know how your studies are going." Uncle Michael handed me a Bellini.

I thanked him and took a dainty sip. The drink wasn't too sweet and it was refreshing. "I think Madam Fong likes me? She appreciates that I work hard, and underneath the general crabbiness, I think she respects me."

"I take it that the Mandarin lessons Marc's been giving you haven't stuck?" Jack asked with a chuckle.

"No. I'm fine living my life knowing only English and mangling it most days. I have him as a translator wherever I go anyway. It comes in handy." I gave my boyfriend a saucy grin. "You don't mind, do you?"

"Not at all." Marc kissed my cheek. "In addition to being a translator, I also cook. I know the way to her heart is through her stomach."

"It's the open secret that applies to everyone in the family." Aunt Evelyn nodded.

Girard added, "When we visited California last summer, I think I spent more time eating than I did talking to family."

"I was introduced during a wedding. Ten courses of food to keep the conversation flowing. What I want to know is if both of you got to taste Gloria's specialty dish?" Jack asked.

Marc and Girard both replied yes at the same time.

I sipped my aperitif. "It's because you're all handsome. Our family is shallow. No one wants to admit it."

"She's not incorrect." Aunt Evelyn laughed. "Now tell us how your matchmaking education is coming along."

"It's been nonstop since last year, and the lessons have been challenging. Like your lessons, except it's for matchmaking. I'm behind where Madam Fong expects a student of my age, but I'm catching up. She believes I have a natural aptitude. I honestly think it's why she took me on in the first place."

Girard smiled. "Despite your harsh assessment, it sounds like you're doing well."

"To Vanessa." Marc raised his glass. "We are all here together because of you. We are your success stories. To our soon-to-be-full-fledged matchmaker! We're proud of you."

I glanced around the table and at everyone's raised glasses.

When I left for Shanghai, I was certain it was what I was meant to do, but to have it confirmed by them, with joy in their eyes, was touching. I knew why Aunt Evelyn prided herself as clairvoyant.

"Thank you." I smiled. "This means so much to me. Oh, Aunt Evelyn, before I forget. Remember how you were confused as to why you have a red thread now? I asked Madam Fong. She believes I gave it to you when I matched you and Girard. No matchmaker has done it before, but my society thinks it's because I had two destinies and we were linked through our clairvoyance. I'm glad I was able to do this for both of you."

Aunt Evelyn sniffed and wiped her eyes. Girard mouthed his thanks to me before comforting her.

"I also have one more thing to say." I reached into my pocket and slipped the ring on my finger. I raised my hand and flashed a one-carat diamond engagement ring. "This was Marc's mother's ring. We haven't set a date yet, but it'll be after I finish my training with Madam Fong."

The room erupted.

The men pounded Marc's back. I received a flurry of kisses.

A little over a year ago, I found happiness in Paris. He followed me to Shanghai, and he told me he would go wherever I was. The future was ours to shape.

Acknowledgments

This book began as a dream.

All my life, I've yearned to visit Paris—for the art, and for the incredible cuisine. The Eiffel Tower called to me, yet it felt so far away. Growing up in the Philippines, my family had no interest in visiting Europe, preferring instead to visit Asia and North America. After I grew up and married, this trip remained a cherished desire placed on a high shelf: visible whenever I daydreamed, but just out of reach. I could never rationalize, nor justify, going—until the summer of 2019. I had been working on the manuscript for what would become *Vanessa Yu's Magical Paris Tea Shop* when I decided I *must* go—for book research—as I knew I could not do Paris justice without experiencing its charm firsthand.

The city of Paris is one of wonder, and yes, I fell in love! I'm already planning my return trip.

On June 11, 2019, my debut was published. We held a book launch party at Queen Books in Toronto (shout-out to Raevin), bringing together the family and friends who had supported me through years of struggle and uncertainty. I drank many glasses of wine in celebration, and capped the evening with a rooftop dinner with my family. After all, one can only have a debut launch once!

The next day, I went home, opened my iPad, and continued to work on my manuscript.

Now, after years of writing and editing (and rewriting and reediting), my words—my story—were in the hands of readers. I was terrified. I didn't know whether anyone would connect with Natalie and her community. My fears were assuaged when I began hearing from readers who understood Natalie's struggles and her need to make amends.

One of the major highlights for *Natalie Tan's Book of Luck & Fortune* was when Erin Jontow at John Wells Productions bought the TV rights, and when Michael Golamco signed on as the screenwriter. I feel so fortunate to have both Erin and Michael guiding my book toward its screen adaptation.

After an emotional debut year, I'm indebted to all the people who helped shape the story you're holding.

To my incredible agent, Jenny Bent, and her colleague Sarah Hornsley. Jenny, this book wouldn't exist without your enthusiastic encouragement to visit Paris. I'm so happy and thankful I did. It changed my life.

To my editor, Cindy Hwang. Thank you for believing in me and my stories. To the rest of the incredible Berkley team: Angela Kim, Fareeda Bullert, Tara O'Connor, and Dache Rogers. I am grateful for your work, guidance, and support. To my copy editor, Angelina Krahn, thank you for your eagle eyes. This book would not have come together without the tireless work of my production editor,

Lindsey Tulloch. A special thanks to Rita Frangie and Vikki Chu for another fantastic cover.

To Claire Pokorchak at PRH Canada. Thank you for arranging all the wonderful events during my debut year and beyond.

Thank you to Mary Pender and Orly Greenberg at UTA.

To my family: Robert (my ever-patient husband), Natalie (my encouraging daughter), and Chichi (my beautiful, cranky cat); Racquel (my sister); Rosemarie (my sis-in-law); my parents; my in-laws; and the rest of my extended family.

To my friends who exist outside of writing: Sneha Astles, Megan Hood, Andria Bancheri-Lewis, Jean and Dean Rainey, and Patti Earls-Ferguson.

To Claire Morrison and Kelly Grenon, for helping me take care of my mental health and my body.

I'm indebted to my village of writers and friends: Helen Hoang, Suzanne Park, Kellye Garrett, Sonia Hartl, Annette Christie, Andrea Contos, Farah Heron, Rachael Romero, Jenn Dugan, Karen Strong, Kess Costales, Victoria Chiu, Nafiza Azad, Tamara Mataya, Karma Brown, Tom Torre, and Samantha Tschida.

To the librarians, booksellers, bloggers, and readers, I can't thank you enough for your support: nothing fills my creativity well—and my writing—more than your encouragement and enthusiasm.

Vanessa Yu's Magical Paris Tea Shop

Roselle Lim

Discussion Questions

1. Do you believe in destiny? Why or why not?

2. Families are a big part of Vanessa's life: both her nuclear and her extended. How do you think this affects her life positively and negatively?

3. Vanessa and Evelyn have a complicated relationship. Do you believe they are in conflict because they are too alike or too different? Why?

4. Paris is an iconic tourist destination. If you had to take fortune-telling lessons yourself, where would your ideal locale be?

5. Vanessa has a fear of her fortune-telling gift. She never wanted it. If you were given this gift, would you accept it? Why or why not?

6. Vanessa and Evelyn share a love for French pastries. Do you have a favorite dessert or snack? Is there a significance to it?

7. Family secrets are a common theme in *Vanessa Yu's Magical Paris Tea Shop.* Why do you think Evelyn was so guarded about her personal life? What is she afraid of?

8. The blue butterfly and the wind are two important recurring symbols in the novel. What do they represent, and where do you see them?

9. Fortune-tellers do not have red threads. Vanessa is adamant about the unfairness of it all, while Evelyn is resigned to her fate. Why is there such a difference in their points of view?

Author photo by Shelley Smith

Roselle Lim is a Filipino Chinese writer living on the north shore of Lake Erie. She loves to write about food and magic. When she isn't writing, she is sewing, sketching, or pursuing the next craft project.

CONNECT ONLINE

RoselleLim.com

RoselleWriter